Massacre at Whip Station

DUSTY RICHARDS

MASSACRE AT WHIP STATION

THE O'MALLEYS OF TEXAS

PINNACLE BOOKS
Kensington Publishing Corp.
www.kensingtonbooks.com

PINNACLE BOOKS are published by

Kensington Publishing Corp.
119 West 40th Street
New York, NY 10018

All Kensington titles, imprints, and distributed lines are available at special quantity discounts for bulk purchases for sales promotions, premiums, fund-raising, educational, or institutional use. Special book excerpts or customized printings can also be created to fit specific needs. For details, write or phone the office of the Kensington sales manager: Kensington Publishing Corp., 119 West 40th Street, New York, NY 10018, attn: Sales Department; phone 1-800-221-2647.

PINNACLE BOOKS and the Pinnacle logo are Reg. U.S. Pat. & TM Off.

ISBN-13: 978-0-7860-4563-1
ISBN-10: 0-7860-4563-9

First printing: May 2020

10 9 8 7 6 5 4 3 2 1

Printed in the United States of America

Electronic edition:

ISBN-13: 978-0-7860-4564-8 (e-book)
ISBN-10: 0-7860-4564-7 (e-book)

CHAPTER 1

B. W. Beauregard Lafayette, stagecoach driver—
"Brother Whip" as those of his profession were
called—was a devout man.

His one constant companion was a rain-wrinkled,
sunbaked, dusty-spined, bullet-dinged Bible with the
words "God's Testimony" written in chipped red paint
across the cowhide cover. The book had ridden beside
B.W. on the stagecoach for the four years he had been
a Butterfield driver. When he wasn't eating or sleeping he was prone to turn its thin, thin pages. It bounced
beside him between the driver's box and the shotgun
seat to his right in good times and bad.

And they were bad right now.

Within the last few moments, the Good Book had
acquired a new blemish. It was right there on the side
of Deuteronomy, glistening in the afternoon sun.
Spotting the leather strip was a snake-like constella-
tion of splashed blood. It had been ripped from the
right thigh of the shotgun rider, Dick Ocean, by a
rifle shot. The bullet cracked as they passed through
Eagle Pass, which had lately been renamed Civil Gulch

by the local Californians. They had taken that step less than a year before, at the spot where a gunfight was about to erupt between Union Rebel hunters and the Confederate Yankee haters. Minutes after the men had assembled on the abutting cliff sides, even as the last of the locals were gathering on the plain to watch the fight, word reached them by a rider holding a newspaper that the War Between the States was done. Abe Lincoln had decreed, in so many words, that the men who were about to kill each other were to be loving brothers once more.

Men on both sides spit into the ground over one hundred feet below and began to leave. The assembled citizenry, with their picnic baskets and blankets, were determined to finish their outing. It was right there and then they selected the name Civil Gulch for the pass. There was a wooden sign at a post that bore the branded legend, LET ALL WHO PASS BE CIVIL. It had been shot at some, but was still legible. It would have been shot at more if more people could read. The War was over but the veterans who lived and migrated here had not made a true peace.

B.W. was Southern to the roots and had not embraced the reconciliation. Which wasn't to say he hated Northerners. Dick Ocean was a Caribe from Massachusetts, who he had ridden with for a while now, and who seemed a decent enough man. Ocean was certainly worthy of saving, which is why B.W. was racing ahead and the Bible was bouncing and a few of the six passengers—the preacher and reporter, it sounded like—were shouting with a combination of fear and discomfort.

The stagecoach had sped up after the shot. It had just cleared the high-walled rocks that bordered the gulch and was tearing across a well-rutted path in an open plain, stirring a ball of dust that was like some monster, cotton tumbleweed hitched to their rear box.

Seated on the right side of the driver's box, B.W. was snapping rein and whip with equal urgency.

"Why couldn't this have happened closer to Fort Yuma?" complained the injured man. "They got a doctor. Not a *girl*."

"'Cause the Lord Jesus has His way," B.W. replied.

"He must," Ocean bellowed to his right. "They was aiming at *you*!"

"Don't think so," B.W. replied. "Shot was too low."

"Where'd the other two shots hit?" Ocean asked.

"One kicked up dirt, the other splintered off the rear box."

"That don't make no sense," Ocean said through his teeth.

"No, it don't," B.W. replied.

"Had to be trying to hit you," Ocean resumed. "Horses too valuable."

"Mebbe," B.W. said. He didn't agree but he didn't want to argue with a wounded man. "If you're right, Dick, then thanks from me and the passengers."

The cannonballing stagecoach hopped unpleasantly over a flat rock and came down hard. The slender shotgun rider winced at the jolt. He was pressing on his leg with both of his long, slender palms, one atop the other. Though Ocean had slowed the leaking somewhat he could feel the throb of the vein pushing blood out. His carbine had dropped to the front box and it lay there still, bouncing around by his left box. He was grimacing through the pain, the burning sensation being preferable to bleeding out.

B.W. thumped and bumped in his seat as they raced ahead. The Whip Station was just about a mile away and the driver didn't want to stop until they reached it. He whipped the reins up and down to spur the horses, though the shots had stirred them up on their own. It was too loud and too dusty to determine if anyone was following them. He didn't hear any shooting, but then there really wasn't a target from behind. The rear box was stuffed with cargo and mail. More than passengers, it was the post office that paid the Butterfield overhead.

The stagecoach strained hard against the broad, sturdy leather straps that served to absorb some of the jolts. B.W. was glad when the steel-rimmed wheels bumped their way into the ruts cut over many years of travel. It was like a narrow flume in a logging camp where he'd once worked. The little gullies steadied the wheels, lessened the dips, and cut down the side-to-side sway of the carriage.

Ocean shook his head.

"Sounded like a revolver," the injured man said, wincing as blood crept along his ivory-colored trousers. He leaned into his leg, pressing harder, causing the pain to intensify.

"It was," B.W. told him. "Sound had no long-range guts to it. And no marksman behind it, which leaves me thinking that if they was soldiers they hadn't seen much action."

"*Banditos?*"

"Possible," B.W. said. "But they don't shoot from

faraway—they jump out and bushwhack you. Redskins prefer the long rifles, so not them."

"We ain't even got gold," Ocean said.

"No. And who in God's dry desert would care about the passengers we're carrying?"

It was a rhetorical question and neither man offered any additional thoughts.

With a good half a mile between the stagecoach and the gulch, B.W. slowed the horses and picked up the fallen carbine. He handed the reins to Ocean, who gripped them firmly in one hand. Then B.W. swiveled within the box, knelt on the seat, facing backward. He looked around the lumpy mounds of baggage that were also piled on top of the stagecoach.

"Crap and damnation!" he shouted.

"What is it?"

"An answer, I think." B.W. used the handrail to steady himself as he swung back around. Ocean handed him the well-worn leather reins. "There're two cowhands riding hard, side by side," the driver said.

"Uniforms?"

"None that I can tell," B.W. answered. He gave a hardy "*Gyahh!*" to the horses and whipped the reins to goad them on. "*Ha-yaaah—go! Go!*" he repeated, shouting as much to vent his own worry as to drive the horses.

Ocean released the pressure on his leg and took the carbine in his bloody hands. He did not have much mobility but he could pivot a little to keep the men from his side of the stagecoach.

"See to your leg," B.W. said. "No sense us both dying!"

"But you said—"

"Whatever happened back there, they'll like be coming after me for sure, if their aim is to stop us."

Ocean ignored his partner. He tried to turn and put a knee on the seat to shoot over the top of the luggage. But he cried out, the pain in his leg dropping him.

"Sit, damn your eyes!" B.W. shouted.

Ocean was forced to flop back and put his palms back on his sodden pant leg.

B.W. heard the hoofbeats approach—on his side, as he had expected. He stole a quick look at his Bible but did not think about dying, about God's golden grandfather clock ticking out what could be the last seconds of his life. He stayed focused on trying to stay ahead of the gunmen and watching the ruts for any rocks that might have been washed in. Better to slow if need be than to break a wheel.

The driver did pray, however. Silently. Not just for himself but also for his passengers, for Ocean, and for his family back in Louisiana. He used his own words, not those from God's Testimony. There were times for familiar prayer like at grace, and there were times for heartfelt sentiment, not recitation. This was one.

Suddenly, there was a sound louder than the clattering of the wheels, deeper than the *clunk-clunk-clunk* of the coach on the thoroughbrace. A sound sharper than the creak and groan of the straining tongue . . .

The West is a vista of unchanging wonders, from the rock formations to the majestic canyons, from the vast skies to the churning rivers. Since the earliest memories of the locals, the same birds and beasts and insects had flown and crept and buzzed around the eternal trees and caves and banks. Even among the humans, there were sights and sounds that endured the passing years.

From the time he could crawl, Slash O'Malley had played hide-and-seek with birds—first back home in the wild Oklahoma Territory, then in Texas, and now here in California. He used to scrape his knees, then, and didn't realize it, so fixed was he on following each bird he encountered. Nowadays he was tall enough to cut himself on cacti and still didn't pay it any mind.

Back then his quarry was usually roadrunners, darting one way and then the other, low-running and fast. They were a challenge and they made him laugh. Later, it was mostly quail. Today, like now, it was wild turkey. Slash had spotted this big male before, but the tom was always too alert. The big bird took off with a big head start each time. Now and then, while hunting, Slash thought back to his meeting at the river with the Pechanga medicine man who was skinwalking. That encounter had given him a brief, frightening insight into the way animals saw the world.

Slash preferred his own. It was safe and familiar. He enjoyed the challenge of being a man entering their abode, challenging them on grounds that were familiar to them. Especially today, like this afternoon, when the big gobbler got lazy from the heat.

Slash was a man now, and he had learned things about tracking and lurking and lying low. The nineteen-year-old was about a foot shy of lashing out and clipping the old boy's neck with his knife when he heard the distant shots. Gunfire was uncommon enough in this humid wilderness. Usually it was his pa or grandpa doing the shooting, or an Apache passing through. But the fact that it was so near and seemed to come from along the Butterfield Trail made it more surprising. Also, it didn't sound like Dick Ocean's carbine. That old girl let go with a coffee-pot *pop-pop*. What he had just heard was a series of tin-plate *bangs*.

The shots scared the turkey, which fled. Frowning, Slash glanced across the grass.

"You *will* be supper," the annoyed young man promised the turkey in the straw.

Rising and turning from his fast-moving prey, Slash sheathed his Bowie knife in a single, artful move. The twelve-inch blade and its beaded leather covering rested naturally, comfortably on his left hip. Both were a gift from Grandpa Joe on the boy's ninth birth-day and the two went on every morning, directly after his trousers. The Slash nickname followed, after young Lemuel caught and skinned his first hare that very day.

The rangy six-footer swung onto his black mustang, Young Thunder. Drawing his Remington six-shooter that rested on the other side of him, Slash galloped hard toward the rutted path. Leaning forward slightly, his head to the right of the horse's neck, he peered ahead, seeing the world as the mustang saw it. Everything was in motion up and down, the terrain rushing toward them, the wind blowing past. Within just a few moments it was no longer just the gunshots that inter-ested Slash but the twin dust clouds he saw roiling from behind a rise to the west. They came in steady, locomotive-like puffs, brownish white against the crisp early afternoon sky.

"Coach is moving fast," he said, tugging the reins gently to the right so he could intercept whatever trouble there was. That would be at the back end of what the local Indians called the *mpothsh mshidevk vidiik.*

The coming of the frightening dust.

Slash had learned that phrase from his twin sister Gert, who spent more time in primitive settlements than their parents would have liked. But then, both of the youngest O'Malleys had traits of which their parents disapproved. Like his, of getting involved in trouble that wasn't his to begin with.

Yet, it might *be necessary,* he thought.

What the Indians meant by that description was a natural phenomenon, a big rolling storm of wind and dust half as high as a mountain. But it came and went and things better built than a tepee were usually okay in their wake. When people stirred dust, it was almost always bad for someone.

Out here, anything that affected the Butterfield line affected the Whip Station, which the O'Malleys owned and would defend to the grave. It would be a real tragedy to lose the livelihood they had come for. Owning the new Whip Station was not the reason the family had left the Oklahoma Territory—the Cherokee civil war did that. But it was the reason they had come to California instead of staying in Texas, where they had family. For Grandpa Joe, opening new territories to the sea held a kind of spiritual appeal that being a cattle rancher did not represent.

The low hill quickly behind him, Slash tilted his new flat-brimmed Stetson to block the late afternoon sun. It had arrived on the previous stage, straight from Chicago, a birthday gift from his sister.

He saw the stagecoach, a silhouette drawn by black horses, careening ahead. There was no gunfire from the box. That was surprising. He saw the two men in pursuit, just behind the first cloud of dust. They were gaining on B.W. at a fast clip. Slash also saw the legs of the lead horse nearest him bend and wobble a little every few paces. The animals were tiring and at this rate they would not reach the station—either from exhaustion or from being taken.

The young man straightened in the saddle and fired three shots in the direction of the riders. The pursuers were out of range and so was he—but not for long. That was to get their attention. He got it. The men looked over and reared to a stop. Moments later the stagecoach slowed to its usual pace, safe from immediate danger.

Continuing his approach, Slash bent low again by the horse's ear.

"The varmints or B.W.?" he asked.

The idea of trying to outgun two men with just three bullets left held very little appeal. Instead, Slash veered toward the stagecoach, about three hundred yards away. The revolver was firmly in his right hand, pointed toward the men. They made no move to close in. Instead, they wheeled around and headed back the way they had come.

"They must not've wanted to face us," Slash said to the horse.

More likely, though, the pursuers didn't want to be delayed by him and then have to shoot it out closer to the station. The O'Malley reputation for strong justice was known to most around these parts.

The young rider turned so that he was parallel with

the stagecoach driver. The curtains inside the carriage were drawn and he had no idea who was inside. There was nothing but cargo in the rear box. He had guessed as much from how low the coach was riding. The extra lower paying passenger or two who could be tucked in there tended to be smaller and lighter.

Slash narrowed the distance between them, quickly coming up alongside B.W. Beauregard Lafayette. He noticed that Dick Ocean was listing toward the center of the box, the spot where the driver kept his Bible. That explained why the stage wasn't returning fire. Even from this low angle, Slash could see that the man was not carrying his carbine.

"Dick hurt bad?" Slash called up, rising in the saddle.

"Thigh," B.W. answered in his lightly accented Southern voice.

Ocean said something that Slash could not hear.

"Says he took the shot for me," B.W. remarked.

"He have a choice?" Slash joked.

B.W. made a long face and shook his head once.

"I'll ride ahead and let Ma know you're coming in wounded," Slash said, hunkering back down beside Young Thunder's neck. Before he rode off he asked, "Any idea who they were?"

"Not a noontime shadow of a clue," B.W. replied.

"Cargo? Passenger?" Slash asked.

"Passenger only possibility," B.W. replied, whipping the horses up. "Tell you more around some coffee."

Slash holstered his gun and threw B.W. a small salute. As he rode ahead of the team, he dragged a bare hand across the neck of the lead horse as he passed. Most people who did not spend much time in the saddle were unaware how much horses and dogs appreciated gestures like that after a hard run.

Pushing Young Thunder ahead of the coach team, Slash made for the large stacks of boulders that marked a natural passageway. The iron supports and wooden sign announced Whip Station just beyond.

The young man felt a deep sense of calm envelop him whenever he passed that threshold. That was especially true when the late afternoon sun was starting its final descent, as now. The winds changed. The day and its denizens—including the damned turkey— would be turning over the land to the creatures of the night. There was a sense of change everywhere he looked, listened, smelled.

Behind him, in the still-day-lit wilderness, Slash had to be constantly on guard. He had been out there a little over two hours, riding and then hunting. He stayed sharp by slicing cacti from horseback at a gallop, then turning and stabbing the severed pieces with his knife. In the open, there was danger from many quarters—human, animal, and element. But here, beyond the rock entrance, was safety and home. It was a feeling most Butterfield travelers experienced as well after their arduous journey from the last stop, in Vallicita. That timber and adobe structure—a long, flat shack with a well that tended to go dry every summer—was more than a day distant. It had been bought about a year earlier by a Southern transplant, a dandy named Brent Diamond, who showed up with his Colored lady and her boy. In terms of comfort, Whip Station was what B.W. once described as "a gift from God and St. Christopher to California."

However, as Slash rounded the innermost of the boulders, he saw something he was not expecting to see.

Outside the solid log structure, just beyond the inviting porch with its wooden benches, Grandpa Joe was talking to two men. They were familiar Mission Indians—one Yaqui, one Chumash—of the 1st California Cavalry Battalion.

Their presence was not likely sociable.

CHAPTER 2

Joe's hearing wasn't what it used to be, but he thought he had heard shots. The two Indians who were with him also turned in the direction of the flatlands beyond the station.

There were a lot of things out here that could sound like gunfire. Rocks hitting one another as they tumbled from a ridge. A whip cracking, then cracking again. A tree snapping, the branches cracking as it uprooted. With the echo and each sound stepping on the one before it, it was difficult to say.

The thing to pay attention to was whether the sounds happened again. They did not. There was no need for Joe to retreat to the station, to the door frame that was his usual spot to protect the women and seek cover, if needed.

Maybe Slash gave up and just plugged that bird he was talking about, Joe thought. That was the difference between man and wild turkey. We have more twists and turns in our kit.

Joseph James O'Malley was six-foot-three, seventy years old, with a ramrod straight posture and steel gray eyes. He was described by those who knew him as "that bull with the leather face and broom mustache." Joe didn't look anything like a bovine, save for his scowl, but maybe that was enough. A frontiersman didn't survive for very long without a strong, set, immediately threatening look.

"In that respect," his granddaughter Gert said when he turned his present age, "you *do* 'cow' other men."

Joe didn't like when people laughed at him, but there and then, at his party, it was good to laugh with family.

The "cowing" look worked on Red Men just as well as mountain lions, and it had helped Joe survive this man-killing land before it was even a little tamed.

For decades, the North Kansas–born frontiersman had been a scout. First for surveyors from the East, then for the military hunting Indians, and then for John Butterfield and his American Express Company. During that time he had endured desert and frostbite, war and savages, and gunslingers representing rival interests. In 1857, looking for an adventure westward, he went to work for the newly born Butterfield Overland Mail Line. Back then, when way stations were still in the talking stage, Joe staked a claim on this one for his son and daughter-in-law. But then he got to thinking about it.

There had been letters, a lot of them, between him and his young cousin Long O'Malley about joining their ranching operation in Texas. After a big cattle sale in Abilene, the O'Malley kin were building a family ranch—and probably a family empire—back in Texas. They were going to need good men and, looking ahead, their families as well.

While cattle was lucrative, and growing fast, ranching didn't seem right for Joe or for his son Jackson. Not after the younger O'Malley—a wrangler, then—fell from a horse and busted his leg. It set crooked and ended his career. Besides, though Texas was big open country, what Joe had seen of California while scouting was something more to his liking. It had mountains and water, sun and nourishing, cleansing gully washers of rain—and best of all, the smell of ocean coming from somewhere to the west.

The far west called to him. It called to Jackson. And it called to Jackson's devoted wife, Sarah.

Plus, here at the way station, Joe got to meet interesting people. Some of them were just passing through on the stage, everyone from actors to scientists. Some worked for Butterfield, like B.W. and Dick Ocean. Then there were others who were stationed out west by the federal government like Sisquoc and Malibu, who sometimes came just to visit but this time had come on the kind of mission Joe hated down to his knees.

The men made a striking contrast as they stood there. Joe wore the buckskins that made up the bulk of his wardrobe, save for the suit he wore whenever he went to the bank in San Diego or to church. The Indians were dressed in the dark blue jackets of the battalion but wore their own black trousers and hats. The tall, lean Sisquoc had on a brown beaver fur felt hat with an eagle feather in the band. Malibu, the Chumash, was a short, wide man who wore a white hat with a downturned ranch brim.

The three men were just outside the fence that ran along the front of the station. There were cowbells attached its entire len'th. Struck with a stick or the toe of a boot they'd frighten owls that hooted on the chimney or coyotes that crept toward the barn with ill intent. They also warned if a wind was building, the kind that could tear unfastened shutters from a window or carry uncooped chickens from the yard.

Farther toward the entrance of the compound, a few paces beyond the fence, was the sun-bleached trough and hitching post. In the back was the well, the barn with chickens and a milk cow, the stable, and Sarah's bountiful vegetable garden and apple trees. Jackson O'Malley was out back expanding the irrigation ditches for new plantings, digging down in a method of his own invention. Sarah and Gert were inside preparing to welcome the stage riders.

The attention of the three men was drawn to the south and the rock entrance as Slash galloped through. From inside the house, the two O'Malley collies—named Blood and Mud, after who liked to hunt and who liked to loll about—barked at the sound of pounding hooves. Joe's shotgun was never far from his reach. It was leaning against the trough and he went and picked it up now, his strong fingers wrapped tight around the barrel. His grandson didn't ride like that unless there was trouble, and the only trouble there could be right now likely involved the incoming stage.

Now Joe and the Indians were sure that what they heard were shots. The shotgun pointed down, Joe excused himself from his guests and walked toward the rider.

"Son?" he said. Joe's voice was a throaty rasp. It was a growl that came, his wife Dolley used to tease, from occasionally swallowing the cacti he chewed for moisture in the field.

"Stage is coming in bloody," Slash said breathlessly. He reined Young Thunder and dismounted in the same fluid move. "Ocean's leg, gunshot."

"Who by?" Joe asked.

"Two riders, white. That's all I saw."

"Were you followed?"

Slash shook his head.

"Did anyone fire from the coach, Mr. Slash?" Malibu asked.

"Not that I saw, sir," Slash replied.

Joe stepped aside as his grandson ran toward the station. He slowed at the door and quickly brushed the dust from the front of his trousers before entering. Hard riding caused a man to get dusty up front, and his mother appreciated a man who did not add to her work.

The older man's gray eyes shifted toward the Mission Indians. They were men born on one of Southern California's fifteen Franciscan missions, where their parents had lived and worked. In Joe's experience, few bore more than a passing allegiance to the tribes of their ancestors. Though there were those in the cavalry who worried that they'd revert to tribal alliances in the event of war, that had never been the case.

"That fracas have anything to do with the passenger you was talking about?" Joe asked.

It wasn't so much a question as a statement.

"It is possible," Malibu said, showing concern. "We were told there would be agents with him. The commander at Fort Mason does not trust Easterners. That is why he sent us to meet the stage here."

"Why here? Why not back at Vallicita?" Joe asked.

"General Williams's authority ends here," Malibu said. "General Guilford owns rest."

The onetime frontiersman set the shotgun back against the fence and peered out at the plain. The sinking sun threw a tawny orange on the plumes of dust B.W.'s team was now kicking up.

"Why don't you two go inside, have some coffee?" Joe said to the Indians. "Sarah made it, not Gert, so you know it's strong, the way you like it. I'll be along presently."

The two men left without comment. Joe had no idea who the other passengers were. Usually, they were Easterners who only knew about the West what they read in *Indian Jim* or the other one Gert read aloud and laughed her way through, *Maleska, the Indian Wife of the White Hunter.* Tired, rattled, cramped, and now gun-shot passengers might not take well to seeing Indians, even those who were in U.S. Cavalry uniforms.

The Indians went around the fence, to the back of the station where they were out of sight. 'Round this time the back door would be in shadow. The Indians could still look in through the back door without being clearly seen.

Joe turned and started toward the bouldered entrance. He walked with a side-to-side gait—just like a sailor, according to a sea captain who had stopped a few weeks before on his way to the Barbary Coast. The sway was a habit that many frontiersmen acquired crossing rocky terrain, where shifting posture was necessary to keep from falling. He smiled inside as he remembered Dolley stealing what she thought were hidden glances at his back as he walked. They never stopped admiring one another, right up until . . .

He winced at the sharp, sudden reminder of the emptiness between his strong arms. He took his mind somewhere else. Anywhere else. At the len'thening shadows to his left. The loss, four years removed, was still terrible to him. He knew, from the grief of his own mother and her father before her that the hole in the world would never be filled, would follow him around like his shadow in the dirt.

Joe raised his moist eyes, looked at distant, snowy mountaintops to the right, watched how the sinking sun caused them to glow like a fuse. Remembering Dolley was like a card sharp's sleight of hand. He cherished the vivid thoughts of his wife . . . but then they were pushed aside by a combination of will and necessity, by the immediacy of whatever it was he had to do. Even when Dolley was alive and young and he was away for months, he could not afford to let his mind roam like a lazy-circling eagle. That was how outlaws or mountain lions or a gopher hole got you. That was why he still moved like he was crossing a field of rocks. Because a man who lost his balance was food for buzzards.

Joe was hatless, his gray hair slicked back with perspiration. He raised his right hand like he was saluting low, shielding his eyes from the sun as he watched the stagecoach. The sun struck the front box full-on. Ocean was leaning toward B.W. like a swooning dame and the horses were even less a team than usual when they arrived. Brother Whip had driven them hard.

The rumble of the hooves and wheels came like the drum of approaching rain in the woods—faintly in the distance, then hammering the canopy of leaves, then suddenly all around you. There was not a great deal of room between the rocks and the fence. The coach always had to turn east, then sharp to the west to deposit passengers at the cowbell fence. As usual, as the team went into its turn, Joe matched the pace of the lead horse on the left and swung onto its back to help slow the animals as B.W. applied the brake. The stagecoach stopped with a jerk and a loud, complaining shifting of its cargo and passengers.

Slash came running out as Joe dismounted, both of them hastening to the shotgun side of the box, which was facing the front of the station. Sarah and Gert hurried out to see to the passengers—and to position themselves between them and the bloodied man.

"Hold off," B.W. said to the women as they approached. "Got an order."

"From who?" Joe asked as he stepped on the wheel hub to reach Ocean.

"Not *that* kind," an exasperated B.W. told the women. "Just let them that are inside handle this."

Sarah and Gert stepped two paces back from the coach to allow the door to swing open. As they did so, B.W. helped pass the injured Ocean to Joe and Slash. Jackson had come from the stable to see to the team. Seeing his wife just waiting, the middle O'Malley stood back and did the same. After Ocean had been eased down, Gert followed the men back into the house to arrange for treating the gunshot wound.

While Ocean had been seen to, Sarah watched the unmoving curtains inside the stagecoach. It was unusual for at least one of the two facing passengers on that side not to pull open the drape and have a look.

In the nearly two years that she had been the mistress of the Whip Station, Sarah had never known who was going to emerge from the coach. Butterfield did not share its passenger list with the stations and did not ask for or expect special treatment for anyone. All those who came to Whip Station got the same food and drink, used the same outhouse, washed from the same basin, enjoyed the same general courtesy as every other passenger. On occasion, someone driven a little loco by the cramped, humid, airless conditions of the coach needed extra care. They got a bed to lie down in—the one Ocean would be using—and were permitted a walk through the barn or stable if they needed privacy. There was nothing more the O'Malleys could do in a short hour.

About half the time, Sarah saw the same people coming and going. They were usually folks on business or visiting kin. They were usually fresher going back than coming in. Many learned, by hard experience, what to wear and how to amuse themselves for the return trip.

Families looking to settle down here still came mostly by wagon. When they happened by, and maybe didn't have enough—or any—silver to pay, the

O'Malleys took pains to accommodate them as well. They knew what it was like to be wandering.

Finally, there was the distinctive snap of the door handle releasing the sturdy catch. It swung out and the stairs were lowered from the dark inside.

The first passenger out was a tall, clean-shaven, rosy-cheeked, barrel-chested man wearing a tan, rumpled tweed suit. As he stepped heavily down the two creaking stairs, he pressed a blue Civil War fedora firmly on his head. He took a moment to adjust it to block the sinking sun. The hat did not look battle-worn, Sarah thought. It seemed new, something left over from the stores of the Union Quartermaster General. Something you wore to announce your affiliation, not your experience.

The man was about forty and sandy haired with a critical expression that seemed carved into his forehead and jowls. He stood for a very long moment facing the rock entranceway before looking around. He noticed Sarah and acknowledged her with a nod and a gentlemanly tip of the hat.

Eastern manners, she thought. A man from the South would have bowed.

A hand attached to a long arm stretched from the darkness of the coach. It handed the man a gun belt, which the big man put on. He made sure the shiny Colts drew easy. They, too, looked fresh and untested. Whatever experience this man had with them seemed to come from a gun range, not peacekeeping or combat. He was assembled to *look* intimidating.

Without taking his eyes from the horizon beyond

the boulders, the big man half turned toward the darkness within the stagecoach.

"Okay," he said to someone inside. "You, then His Honor."

Another man emerged, taller and not so round. He was the owner of the arm that had passed out the gun belt. He was somewhat younger, maybe seven or eight years, but dressed the same and carried a carbine similar to Ocean's. He had a big mustache and dark, hard eyes. He shook out a cramped leg before starting down the stairs.

There was a scar across the man's jawline, a knife—or bayonet?—wound, Sarah thought. He held the carbine in both hands, ready to put it to his shoulder for a quick discharge. This man had seen war.

Once the second man was out, a third figure emerged. He had to bend at the waist to pass through the door. Sarah did not know how he had been able to sit upright inside the stagecoach.

This passenger did not look the same as the other two. He was an Indian, not just half-a-head taller but the color of the sunset and dressed in a blanket adorned with symbols. He wore a multicolored glass pony bead neckpiece that covered the top half of his chest and several arm and wristbands of the same materials. A skirt made of buffalo hide covered him from just above the waist to above the knees. Leather bands encircled his lower legs. His moccasins were covered in snakeskin. Clutched in his left hand was a pow-wow headdress with feathers spraying from the top and center—not along the back, as she had seen in other noted Indians. He wore a large cow's-ear medicine bag strung from the right-side waistband of his skirt.

He did not look around, did not speak. He placed the headdress on with more the kind of pride that had been lacking in the other man when he donned his hat. Then the Indian waited for the man with the six-shooters to gesture where he was to go—which was to the station. The two white men stood on either side of the other as they departed. Only when they were gone did the remaining passengers emerge—all of them from one side of the coach, the rear bench.

"That added delay was an insulting and unnecessary show of federal hubris," said the first passenger to emerge.

This passenger was about fifty, with a full salt-and-pepper beard and mustache, spectacles, a white shirt, a floppy black bow tie, and old cigarette ash on his blue, four-pocket cotton vest. His trousers were black canvas and his boots were coated with dust—St. Louis dust, Sarah knew. She had seen that color and thick, clinging coat before. There were pencils and a notepad in two of his pockets, a tobacco pouch and cigarette paper in the third and fourth. The man greeted his hostess with a grunt and walked off to roll a smoke.

The next man out was younger, maybe thirty. He was dressed in a frock coat and cleric's neckpiece. He stepped down first and turned to help a lady down the stairs. She had a round, open face with large blue eyes and a small, straight mouth. A petite woman who looked to be in her twenties. She wore a pinstripe blouse and matching dress with a thick black belt. The lady graciously accepted—but clearly did not need—the preacher's helping hand. When he released her, she immediately put on a white muslin bonnet. Sarah recognized the woman's urgent attention. The hat wasn't to protect her from the sun but to conceal what she must have felt was the disarray beneath it.

Or, Sarah thought after observing the way the woman looked away, *to hide her face?*

These last two arrivals stood at the foot of the stairs, as though lost, and Sarah finally stepped forward.

"I'm Sarah O'Malley," she said with her lightly dusted German accent to the lady passenger.

The younger woman half-regarded Sarah but did not speak. She was most assuredly guarded. The man spoke up.

"I am the Reverend Merritt Michaels," he said in a pulpit-clear voice that was nonetheless dry with the dust of travel. "This is my sister, Miss Clarity Michaels."

"I am happy to make your acquaintance," Sarah said.

"Forgive my—*our*—hesitation," the gaunt man said with a wide, practiced smile. "It was a harrowing journey to my new parish even before . . . before the gunplay."

"I understand, of course, and will do my best to make your brief visit comfortable." Sarah smiled.

Still looking away, the lady tried to take a step and stumbled. Sarah caught her by the elbow.

"I'm very sorry," Clarity said, reddening with embarrassment from her near-fall.

"No need," Sarah assured her. "You have been through a great deal."

Clarity finally faced the woman fully. Her lips formed a half smile. "Yes, an arduous great deal," she agreed.

They continued forward, Clarity's arm hooked in that of her brother. He was self-consciously stiff-legged as they walked.

"Be assured that coach cramp is common," Sarah assured both Reverend and Clarity Michaels.

Sarah was referring to one of the most devilish aspects of coach travel. Unlike the threat of Indians and bad weather, of breakdowns and uneven terrain, immobility was a constant, certain reality. Riding as they did, packed in a too-small cabin with knees interlocked for hours on end, most passengers were unable to regain their legs quickly. In this case, with the three bigger men on one side, it would have been especially hard on those sitting across from them.

"I suspect that coach boorishness is frequent as well, I'm sure," Clarity said as they continued toward the station.

"I don't understand," Sarah said.

"My sister was trying to look out the window during the excitement," the reverend said. "That—that big, *rude* man, Mr. Kennedy, actually kept her from moving by locking his knees around hers."

"No doubt trying to protect Miss Michaels," Sarah suggested.

"I do not think so," the woman said, speaking more *and* more frankly than most ladies in Sarah's experience. "He wanted to prevent me from drawing the curtain."

"Again, for safety no doubt," Sarah remarked.

Clarity looked at Mrs. O'Malley, who was to her brother's right. "Did he look like a man who was concerned for the safety of a fellow passenger?" she asked.

Sarah had no opinion, nor would she have spoken it if she had. One of the jobs of station mistress was also to keep the peace, tempers often tending to be raw at this point in the journey.

"There's cool water and a warm welcome inside," Sarah told her, falling back on her standard welcome. "You'll soon feel yourself."

Once again, Clarity showed her a half smile, then turned away.

"That adventure just before we arrived," the reverend said. "Is that common, too?"

"Not at all," Sarah replied. "I am sure my father will be taking measures to make sure there is no—"

Reverend Michaels gasped, interrupting her, as they neared the door. Sisquoc and Malibu were standing just inside the back door, startling him with their dark faces and dour expressions. Mr. Kennedy went over to them, his back to the others.

"They are soldiers," Sarah assured Reverend and Clarity Michaels, though it was only the clergyman who had been startled.

"I thought—it might be whoever fired at us," he said.

"I am sure Mr. Kennedy is making sure they are not," Clarity said.

"I was asking if they knew anything about the attack," Kennedy said, returning to the table. "They say the fort had no specific information about trouble."

Sarah ushered the two toward the long table in the dining area of the station.

"Why don't you sit here while I get some water," she said.

"Thank you," Reverend Michaels replied. "I confess— I am not used to travel. It's made me a little excitable." To the Indians he said, "We are all God's creatures."

"Amen," said Gert.

"One thing you have to get used to out here, even

in San Francisco, is Indians," said the other man, the one who had rolled a cigarette and was smoking it at the table. "They will be in your church, most likely. In the back, along with Coloreds and Mexicans, but they will be there."

"As I said," Reverend Michaels replied, "I am not myself. All are welcome to God's embrace."

"May I ask why you decided to make this trip?" the other man asked.

It was Clarity who answered. "I shot a man."

CHAPTER 3

Upon entering the station, Slash and Joe O'Malley brought Ocean to a small room at the rear. Half underground, the room doubled as a bed for the coach driver, a nursing facility for the injured or faint, and a root cellar. They brought the man, bleeding and moaning, to a Civil War hospital cot set up in the center.

B.W. had paused to check the wheel, left rear, that had gone over the rock back at Civil Gulch. There was a hairline crack in one of the spokes and he went to the stable and asked Jackson to patch it with pitch.

"I should replace it," he said.

"Two hours at least," B.W. said. "And we got trouble chasing us." He shook his head. "Patch it."

"It'll take a sunny half day to completely dry," Jackson said.

"I know that, so I'll take 'er easy," B.W. said. "We got a schedule."

"Sure thing," Jackson said. He took a moment to study the man. "I ain't seen you this fidgety since those Spencer repeaters came out here and you were worried that the Indians would get them."

"Army's got greasy fingers and greedy pockets," he said. "I got reason to worry. We all do."

Jackson saw to the repair right away, hoping it would harden enough under the direct sunlight to keep it from splitting completely.

B.W. held his Bible tightly in his left hand and prayed for a warm wind to help the wood heal. Tucking his Bible under his armpit, he entered the room where the men had lain his injured shotgun rider down.

"Smells like a compost heap," the driver complained.

"Gert says the smell of herbs and vegetables have a curative quality," Slash informed him.

"Not 'smell,'" Gert corrected. "'Aroma.'"

The young woman entered behind them, wearing an apron and carrying a lantern. She hung the light from a hook over the cot, then went to get their first aid supplies. Some were from an abandoned Union outpost, others from an Apache settlement over the border in Arizona. She set them on the floor beside the cot.

"You learn that wisdom from the Injuns?" the driver asked with more than a hint of disapproval.

"Directly from," Gert said.

Joe left, his frowning and intense look suggesting how much he disliked his granddaughter fraternizing with the local Indian population. He went outside and got his gun from where he'd left it against the fence, brought it inside, and set it beside other carbines standing in a corner. In case of an Indian attack, everyone in the station knew where those guns were and could find them in the dark.

"Ever think they might want to *kill* us with such talk?" B.W. asked, unaware of what had passed between Joe and Gert. "Y'know, tell us something is good, like rattler venom, if you mix it with other ingredients."

"Don't be foolish, Brother Whip," snapped Gert.

"Don't be insulting," Joe warned her over his shoulder.

Gert acknowledged Joe's admonition. She continued more pleasantly, "What God provides to feed the insides also heals the outsides."

B.W. shrugged and stepped back as Slash used his knife to skillfully cut away the wounded man's trousers leg. Ocean was wincing, snorting hard as the fabric tore away from the dried blood, taking hair and some skin with it.

When Slash finished, Gert moved in.

"Fetch water and whiskey," Gert said to B.W., adding loudly for the sake of her grandfather, "if you please, sir."

"Liquid cures, coming up," B.W. said.

"Slash, please bring bandages, towels."

When the men were gone, Gert carried over a stool and sat beside Ocean. Like her strong voice, her long face with deep-set brown eyes and strong cheekbones—reminiscent of her grandfather—were set on her task.

"I appreciate . . . your help," Ocean said through his teeth. "You gotta do one thing more for me."

"What is that?"

Before he could ask, B.W. arrived with a ceramic basin filled with water. Gert set it on the floor and dipped a cloth in it.

"Why don't you just lie still," she told Ocean.

"I will, but I have to say what I was gonna tell you " he said. His pained eyes shifted to B.W. "Brother, don't leave without me."

"Dick, I'm not meaning to be heartless but you know we have a schedule."

"I know. You'll keep it better with me. Just give me time to get fixed, set a bit."

B.W. looked down sadly and Gert shooed him away.

"Mr. Ocean, I heard Slash tell Grandpa it was white men who shot at you," she said, wringing out the cloth.

"It . . . was."

"From concealment?"

Ocean nodded. "At first," he said. "Then . . . they . . . chased us."

Gert carefully dabbed around the wound. Caked blood came away but fresh blood immediately filled the opening and spilled down his skin.

"And they call the Red Men 'savages,'" she lamented quietly.

"Everyone out here . . . is a little . . . rough," he said.

Gert admired the man's evenhanded thoughts but did not embrace them. However, this was not the time or place to voice her views. She put the cloth in the basin and picked up a strip of leather. It was part of a bundle of tools that had once been used for amputations. She fed it under the thigh of the injured man.

"Hold!" Ocean blurted, straining and rising urgently on his elbows. "You're not—"

"No, no," she assured him. "I am not cutting. I have to tie the leg off to stop the bleeding."

"Not a tall O'Malley tale?"

She shook her head. Every time the shotgun was

here, and Joe or his granddaughter mentioned to passengers some of the things they'd seen, Ocean always felt they were dressing it up for the folks. Joe wouldn't, though only Gert ever bothered to say that the world out here was *different*—ancient, unknowable, and deeply contemptuous of human attempts to tame it.

Ocean nodded with understanding and lay back. The man had seen enough out here to know, however, that it was going to hurt. She took a leg bone of chicken from the bucket that was headed for the backyard compost and put it between his teeth. He gripped the sides of the cot and locked his teeth around the dry bone as Gert loosely bound the free ends of the strap together—then quickly pulled them tight.

B.W. was standing in the doorway holding a bottle of whiskey.

"Should I pour him a slug?" he asked, holding up the bottle.

"No," Gert told him. "What you can do is kneel beside me and set the bottle on the ground."

"Kneel?"

"By the bed here, if you don't mind."

B.W. looked confusedly from the woman to Ocean, then did as he was told.

"I want you to look overhead, at the garlic," Gert instructed Ocean.

As soon as he had done so, she removed a little leather kit from the apron. She set it between Ocean's slightly parted legs, opened the pouch, and selected a small paring knife.

B.W. looked at it and his face tightened. Gert

nudged him with her knee. He realized what he was doing, that Ocean might see him, and he relaxed.

Slash returned then and Gert instructed the men to hold Ocean still—B.W. leaning on his arms, her brother on his legs. When that was done, Gert opened the liquor bottle, poured some on the bullet hole, and immediately put the scalpel into the wound. The bullet was not visible, which meant she would have to dig for it.

"Bite hard," she cautioned Ocean.

He did and screamed through the bone as she circled the blade around the interior wall of the injury. The young woman probed gently but deeply for the bullet, pushed the blade beneath it, and popped it out. Blood splattered everywhere as the bullet jumped free, landing on the dirt floor. She immediately poured more whiskey on the wound, dropped the knife in the basin, and placed a towel on Ocean's thigh.

"Press down on this with your palm," she instructed B.W.

While the driver did as he was told, Gert unwrapped a len'th of bandage. Bending close to determine that the bleeding had slowed, she motioned B.W. aside. He raised his hands and stood.

"You too," she told Slash.

The young man released Ocean and stepped back. His sister turned several len'ths of white fabric around Ocean's leg, then removed the leather strap and retied it over the bandage to hold it in place.

"Don't move," she instructed her patient.

"Wasn't . . . planning on . . . dancing . . ." he wheezed.

Gert grinned and swished the knife in the bloody water before replacing it in the kit. She swished her own bloody fingers in the basin, wiped them on the towel, and rose.

"Everyone out," she said. "He needs to lie still. Let the plants help him recover."

"For how long?" B.W. asked.

"You can pick him up on the way back," she said.

"I was afraid you'd say that," B.W. said glumly. "After what happened, I can't go without a shotgun."

"You can get someone else to ride in the box," Slash suggested. "One of the two dudes?"

B.W. shook his head. "Those guards have to be inside with the Injun."

"You know that he's a Serrano shaman, don't you?" Gert said, openly disapproving of his ignorance.

"Is that what he is?" the driver asked.

Gert nodded. "His beads tell the story."

"Well, Miss O'Malley, shoot me for a cur but I can't read English *or* necklace," B.W. replied unapologetically.

"You seem almost proud of that," Gert said.

The driver shrugged. "A man shouldn't be ashamed of who he is."

"Both of you get out," Gert repeated, waving them toward the door. "This man needs to rest."

Taking the lantern, Gert recovered the bullet from the dirt floor and followed the men out.

Slash took B.W. aside just outside the root cellar.

"How'd ya feel about me riding with you?" he asked.

B.W. frowned. "Your pa would never permit it."

"The coach may still be in danger," Slash snickered. "I think I can work it."

"Son," B.W. said, "do your magic, then, with my gratitude. Me? I'm going to sleep."

Since his usual cot in the root cellar was presently occupied, B.W. lay down in a small closet-like space just beyond the root cellar. It had a cot typically kept there for passengers who felt faint from the journey. Joe offered his own bed, but B.W. had sweat almost as much as his horses during that race from Civil Gulch. He liked Joe too much to subject his bedding to what he smelt of.

That, he thought, *is a smell, not an aroma.*

Plus, in a bed, he'd have to remove his boots. His feet were too swollen now to risk getting them back on. As he dropped down, the cot didn't seem to care. And he ignored the loud complaints of his stomach. B.W. was hungry but he would do what he always did for meals. Eat jerky during the ride, along with fruit or vegetables a station could provide. Right now, rest was a priority.

He was asleep within moments.

Jackson had moved the horses to the stable for a change of teams and Slash went out to help him—and to discuss his idea. The two Mission Indians stood in the darkening expanse of backyard, smoking pipes. Joe went to check the baggage on the coach, making sure it had not come loose during the flight from the gunmen. The men knew the routine and how much time they had to perform it.

The Butterfield Overland Mail schedule allowed

twenty-five days to cover the 2,800-mile distance from St. Louis to San Francisco, traveling without any stops longer than were necessary to swap out the horses and see to the comfort—however briefly—of the passengers. Two coaches departed weekly. To allocate exactly the amount of space needed for postal cargo—the government offered highly lucrative contracts to carry their mail on time—passengers were required to purchase tickets that put them in narrow, thinly padded seats for the entire journey, whether terminal to terminal or intermediate stops.

It was a brutal journey with two meals each day, those breaks being the only rest stops. Riders slept in the coach, if at all. They could not do more than wash hands and face at the stations, and bribes were required to convince any Butterfield hands to retrieve luggage for a change of clothes or footwear or perfume. The stench in the carriage was often nauseating and the company did not warrant the mental or physical well-being of its customers. Departure points noted that the route took passengers through hostile territory where only God could guarantee their safety.

This California leg of the journey called for the stagecoach to remain at Whip Station for this one fast-passing hour and then head to Warren Ranch, which was due north. They would ride through the night and reach the spread by dawn. Even the events of the last mile could not hold them up. Not even the death of a horse, which was more severe to the company than the death of a passenger.

These passengers were presently seated at the long table in the main room of the station. Aware of the time, Sarah O'Malley had gently but in a timely manner got them settled. They were situated just as they had been during the ride, with the shaman and his guards on one side, the priest and his sister and the man with the overstuffed vest on the other. The latter had put out his cigarette before sitting, in deference to the lady.

The table had already been set, stew was on the fire—comprised primarily of slices of bacon steak, carrots, water, and flour—and Sarah was placing bread on every plate. She had found it was better to cut it rather than offend the ladies, and some men, by having dirty men's hands pull at the still-warm loaf.

There was no sense of camaraderie at the table. There never was. Sarah had long ago stopped trying to create conversation. By this point in the journey passengers were tired of one another if not downright hostile. One of the men was always around in case any fights broke out.

Only the lone male traveler spoke, and Sarah had no idea whether anyone at the table but himself was listening. It was the smoker. He pointed across the table before speaking.

"I have been puzzling over this gentleman," he said, indicating the Serrano sitting tall in the center. "As a journalist—Fletcher Small is my name—I try to understand all sides of a thing, whatever my personal opinions. My own opinions and prejudices cannot influence any report I file, you understand."

If anyone did understand, they did not say so. Each was involved in his or her own thoughts and business. Stew was ladled onto his plate and he sopped some of it with a chunk of bread. The man turned to his left, to the pastor. Sarah called over the collies who were milling about the table seeking scraps and sent them outside.

Fletcher Small continued.

"Reverend Michaels," he said, chewing the bread. "What is your opinion of these savages and their spiritual figures?"

The pastor picked up his knife and fork and cut a large slice of carrot into small pieces. "I have no opinion of faiths other than my own, Mr. Small."

"Then you acknowledge that magical beliefs are a faith?" the journalist pressed.

The reverend seemed uncomfortable with the question. "To me, no," he replied. "To this gentleman, the answer may be yes. You would have to inquire of him."

Michaels put a piece of carrot in his mouth and chewed it quietly. Bumping elbows, Fletcher Small tucked into his own stew with a fork.

"These are mighty good carrots," the reporter told his hostess. "Mighty good. Plump. Tasty."

"I was just thinking the same thing," Clarity said. She sounded eager to change the direction of the conversation.

Sarah acknowledged with a smile.

"I guess being a preacher means you have to be fair to everyone, even if you disagree," Small expanded on his previous thoughts.

"Especially when you're in their land," Gert responded.

Having finished in the root cellar, the young woman had come out to help her mother. She handed the flattened bullet to her grandfather, who had finished with the luggage and had just entered with water from the well. He placed the indoor bucket down, stepped near a window, and examined the lead in the fading light. He did not approve of his granddaughter's statement but there were guests present. He ignored it.

Small was intrigued. "An outspoken young lady," he said. "Do you believe that this is Indian land?"

Now her grandfather looked over. It was an expression that admonished caution. He disapproved of hearing her opinions under most circumstances, but disapproved more when they were spoken around guests.

Gert backed down but did not entirely retreat.

"I suspect President Johnson must believe that," she answered, "or he would not have asked to see this medicine man."

The two men on either side of the shaman turned to look at the young woman.

"Now I'm utterly enchanted and intrigued," Small said, sitting back. "What makes you say that Mrs.—?"

"Miss O'Malley," she said, busying herself with the apple pie on the cutting table. "The two gentlemen told me so."

Both turned around as one, frowning.

"Oh, not in words," Gert added quickly. "But those are Eastern city tweeds you're wearing. I know them from *Frank Leslie's Ladies' Gazette of Fashion and Fancy Needlework.* And you haven't had sun on your faces in months."

The barrel-chested man finished chewing a potato. "How do you know we weren't on business in New York or Philadelphia?"

"*You* might have been, but not the Serrano," Gert

said. "He is a high figure, according to his dress. He would only meet with a high figure. And he would not have sought one out. Mr. Johnson would have had to come to him, through an agent."

The Indian laughed once.

The man with the bulldog face nodded. "We ought to hire this little lady to work for us, Hathaway," he said. "You've quite an eye, Miss O'Malley."

"Yes," the reporter agreed. "What can you tell about any of the others around this table?"

Joe closed his hand tight around the bullet. "Gentlemen, my granddaughter is not a counting horse at a carnival," he said sternly.

"I'm sorry, sir," Small said. "I meant no impertinence."

Gert said, "We have your collected work ready for composting in the—"

"No more!" Joe said.

Gert pouted and cut the pie as if it were the rope that hung her abolitionist hero John Brown.

Joe regarded the reporter. "It was the girl's fault, Mr. Small, for hanging up her banner. It's been taken down now."

Small nodded gratefully and chuckled. "Lovely turns of phrase. You don't hear that much in Saint Louis. That's where I'm from," he went on. "I write the Trade and Business column for the *Daily Missouri Republican*. My publisher asked me to take this trip and write about the Butterfield line." He picked up his two-pronged fork and started spearing the fine-cut beef. "But personally, I am more interested in what Miss O'Malley called the 'high figure.'" He put the fork in his mouth and cleared off the meat, making an *mmmmm* sound as he fixed his eyes on the two men and the shaman. "This is very tasty, *Mrs.* O'Malley," he said.

"Thank you," the woman replied.

Small was still regarding the trio. "Why was this man in Washington meeting with the president?"

"You'll have to write to the president, ask him," answered the barrel-chested man. He touched his napkin to his mouth, folded it back on his lap, and resumed eating.

"You are surely with the Indian Bureau," Small said. "No other civilian would be authorized to escort this personage across the continent."

"I am," the man answered. He smiled broadly. "But before you go on, trust me, Mr. Small. We are the last to know what is going on with the Indians."

"I gather, from the laugh earlier, that this man speaks English?" Small nodded at the Indian.

"The man has a name, I'm sure," Gert said with annoyance.

"Girl, this is not your affair," Joe cautioned her with quiet authority.

The young woman presented her back to the group and retrieved plates for the pie.

Joe regarded the barrel-chested man. "I'm sorry, Mr.—?"

"Doug Kennedy," he said. "My partner is Jessup Hathaway. And there's no need to apologize." He regarded Small. "The lady is quite right. The man does have a name, sir. It is Tuchahu."

Sarah returned with a second plate of bread. A

brief silence settled on the table. Joe took advantage of it. Ordinarily, he did not intrude on the interactions of his guests. But he had seen Slash buttonhole B.W. outside the root cellar. From the boy's lightning-wide grin, he had an idea what that had been about.

"I have a question, Mr. Kennedy, and I'll ask it since it may involve the safety of the individuals sitting at this table," Joe said. He put the bullet down in front of the barrel-chested man. "Who would want to try and shoot the Shotgun or Brother Whip to a stage that carries no valuables? Is someone after the Serrano?"

"We have had no intelligence of such a scenario," Kennedy answered. "Our presence here is simply precautionary. An honor guard, if you will."

Joe looked at Hathaway. He didn't look like a guard or particularly honorable. His eyes shifted to the reporter.

"Mr. Small," Joe said. "Could there be someone who didn't like something you wrote?"

Small guffawed. "A great many people!" he answered. "The truth doesn't always sit well with the politicians, businessmen, and other persons I write about. But I wouldn't flatter myself into imagining that I'm worth an ambush."

Joe's gaze went to Reverend Michaels. "You preach something that folks didn't want to hear?"

"No sinner wants to hear of his sins," the parson said.

Sarah walked over with a pot and offered second helpings. "I think that is quite enough, Pa," she said softly. She nudged her father-in-law with her elbow in a way that he recognized. He backed away.

Peace returned to the O'Malley table. But only briefly. All the while, Small had been watching the two siblings.

"Hold on," Small said.

"Pardon?" Sarah answered.

"Oh, I'm sorry, Mrs. O'Malley. I didn't mean you." Small looked at the brother and sister seated beside him. "Maybe there's something else?" he said. His eyes shifted to the woman. "Is there? Something else?"

Clarity averted her eyes and her brother put a hand on hers. He looked over at Small.

"You are being a boor," the reverend said.

"The middle name of every good reporter," Small said. "No, Mr. O'Malley had a point. This affects every one of us. Is there something else?"

The reverend said, "Nothing that would affect anyone present. We have exculpated ourselves through prayer."

Kennedy barked out a laugh. "That's a mess of nothing. I hear it in Washington all the time."

"What'd you have to atone *for*?" Small asked.

Clarity's lips were pressed together but her brother replied, "My sister accidentally killed a bystander at a sharpshooting exhibition."

The table fell hard into a dead-of-night silence.

"You . . . are a marksman?" Gert asked her.

Joe ignored his granddaughter's latest intrusion—mostly because he was interested in the answer.

Clarity nodded.

"Who'd you murder?" Joe asked.

"Not 'murder,' 'kill,'" her brother clarified.

"'Murder,' 'kill,'" Small said. "One of the Commandments got shattered."

"By accident," Reverend Michaels said.

The table waited for an answer.

"My former fiancé," Clarity finally replied in a little voice.

Small sat back proudly, was about to ask for details when Jackson O'Malley limped through the back door.

"Pa, we got riders coming in from the east."

CHAPTER 4

When Whip Station first opened for business, Jackson O'Malley continued doing what he had done before the family came to California. He captured and broke horses for the United States Cavalry. He had them stabled out back, settled them from wild to tame in a corral that once stood where the expanding vegetable garden now sat. He and Slash both tended to the stage teams, the boy shouldering most of that responsibility.

Then, shortly after opening the station, he got bucked good and came down hard on his left leg. He heard the snap though he didn't feel it. The leg went numb.

While recuperating, Jackson became acquainted by something the late President Lincoln had said. He found the words in one of the newspapers stacked in the root cellar and bound for the fireplace or composting:

"With malice toward none . . ."

The young cowboy thought a lot about those words while he lay in bed, recovering. At first, lying where Dick Ocean now lay, Jackson was inconsolable. He was bitter each time he had to fling scented oil at his injury. It was summer and Jackson perspired. The padding between his leg and the wooden splint grew rank and drew flies. Gert's placement of the garlic and other herbs helped keep away the pests some—a trick she learned from the Indians. That was why he wasn't critical of her concord with the Red Men.

For weeks after the fall, Jackson hated the horse that threw him and he hated himself for being thrown. That fire inside him only intensified.

As a rule that bordered on religion, O'Malleys did not forgive. He heard stories about his cousins Harp and Long John and their fever for revenge. They were Texas Rangers, and during the Civil War their job was to protect the families of soldiers who were off fighting. It was an urgent need: the Indians, the Comanche in particular, looked to take advantage of the absence of the menfolk. That meant cutting down the savages without hesitation—or mercy. After the war, when the Rangers were disbanded, the two men and the Comanche continued to hold their red, red blood-grudges. Jackson heard that the O'Malleys were still fighting those old battles on their Texas ranch.

But horses weren't Comanche and Jackson wanted to be around them, still.

"*With malice toward none*," Mr. Lincoln said. "*With charity toward all.*"

Over time, Jackson realized that the horse had meant him no ill. He relived the fall in his mind and started to feel grateful when he realized how much worse it could have been. He might have been trampled and the leg would have had to come off. He might have snapped his spine and been paralyzed, like Ivan Pine who got shot in the small of the back at Gettysburg.

He began to consider, instead, what might come next. Jackson had spent his entire life around horses and cattle and he could not bear for that to change.

"What else would I do?" he had asked Sarah at the time. "O'Malleys don't run general stores."

With the help of Sarah and his father, he healed as best as he could and learned to embrace the words of Mr. Lincoln. As soon as he could walk, he made peace with Young Thunder and spent all his time with the incoming and outgoing stagecoaches. That freed Slash to take more and more of the hunting responsibilities from Joe. The boy quickly started making sounds like a man, and Jackson realized that the accident had been for a reason.

At first, Jackson had to hold on to the harnesses, the coaches, or use a crutch to walk. By the time summer turned to fall, he was free from all of those. He had never been much for gunplay but practiced his shooting and became proficient with his Colts. He kept one of them tucked in his belt, off to the left for a right-handed draw.

Typically, when anyone came in from the north, Jackson stood to meet them. This was different.

There were four riders bearing down hard on the station. They crossed the stream a quarter-mile distant that marked the boundary of the station. That was the area rented by Butterfield. The men were still on O'Malley land, uninvited, which stretched another hundred and three acres to the north. Jackson had once had it in mind to put a horse ranch there.

Given what had transpired at Civil Gulch, Jackson

did not want to face them alone. He also did not want to send up a shot to alert the house. If the intent of the visitors was hostile, they might return fire. Even with Slash beside him in the stable, those were not ideal odds.

His son had come out to talk to him about riding with B.W. when the stage left. They were in the middle of that conversation when they heard the hooves. Slash went up to the hayloft with a shotgun to lay down fire if necessary.

"Pa!" Jackson yelled as he ran. But that horse-fall had cost him some improperly healed ribs and breath and Joe's hearing wasn't what it once was. So he concentrated on running rather than shouting.

"*Pa!*" Jackson tried again when he was nearer.

This time the two Mission Indians heard him and turned. A moment later Joe O'Malley appeared just inside the door frame, looking out. That was his customary place. If there was a situation, Joe wanted to be able to duck behind the jamb for cover. Crouched in the shadows, he would be a difficult target for men on horseback with sun-accustomed eyesight.

The two Mission Indians moved into the station behind him, hovering in the near darkness, also watching. This matter of Tuchahu and his trip to see President Johnson affected them, too, as both Indians and as cavalrymen. General Rhodes Guilford, commander of the 1st California Cavalry Battalion, had ordered them to see to the safety of the holy man. He had not told them of any threats he was aware of; he did not have to. Indian members of the 1st had been placed at every stop in California to watch, listen, and act if necessary. A successful attack on the Serrano, even a scurrilous public affront, would cause grave and unpredictable repercussions among the local Indian population. Even historic enemies among the savages might be united in outrage.

The riders were charging forward four abreast. It took Joe just a moment to assess the situation. The fine dust trail floating well behind them, visible in the late, slanting sun, told him they had not come from the east, the direction of Civil Gulch. They had ridden from the northeast.

Privately, Joe had already worked out the timing. Two men, chasing the stage, had just enough time to retreat, gather up partners, and ride out. That would put them low in the foothills, a three-mile stretch of caves and abandoned mines.

The frontiersman raised a hand for his son to stop running. Jackson came loping to a halt. Joe half-turned to the Indians. Sisquoc had moved to the front door of the station to protect the occupants in the event of an attack.

"I'm going out," he said. "You cover me and the station."

Malibu acknowledged and Joe strode forward. He did not want to present a figure who seemed either alarmed or concerned by whoever was coming in.

"Where's Slash?" Joe asked as he was within talking range of his son.

"Hayloft with the rifle," Jackson replied.

Joe looked in that direction, saw his grandson in the shadows. He made a waving motion. The riders would take it to be a greeting. He was actually signaling the young man to do nothing if shots were fired by the newcomers.

Meanwhile, Jackson was squinting ahead, to the south. He thought he saw what looked like a dust devil stirring up rust-colored sand along the stagecoach trail. It was tough to say, given the creeping shadows and boulders in the way.

"Maybe someone coming toward the entrance," Jackson said. "Box us in."

"Could very well be," Joe said. "Folks seem to be organized. You keep watching."

Still looking ahead, the frontiersman knew at once what Malibu and Sisquoc would also recognize. The horses thundering in were cavalry. They were of uniform look preferred by the U.S. Army: dark colored for night riding, good expansive breathing, probably geldings. Each was about fifteen hands high and around a thousand pounds each, about five years old.

"Bought or stolen by Confederates for infiltration, most likely," Joe thought aloud.

"What was?" Jackson asked.

"The horses," Joe said. "Don't look like the boys're in blue."

"What's their beef with Butterfield?" Jackson wondered.

"I expect they'll inform us," Joe replied.

The senior O'Malley reached into his pocket and pulled out a chaw of tobacco. He pushed it in his mouth. Gert had brought the sun-dried brick from one of her recent Indian visits. It was a peace offering to her grandfather whose supply had run out. Joe had been saving this for when she couldn't see him use it. Now was that time. It helped him to think instead of doing what came naturally. Lives other than his might be at risk.

Renegade Rebel troops still roamed the Southwest. They had lost home and cause yet retained the desire for blood. Joe didn't blame them. He'd take to the warpath if someone took Whip Station. But he also could not support their methods, which included occasional raids on shipments by rail and coach, and also attacks on homesteaders, sodbusters, and even sodbusters just looking for work. Some of those were men from the ruined South. To his knowledge, though, none of the ranchers or sheepherders who occasionally came by reported actual visits from anyone who announced himself as a Confederate.

Joe angled the shotgun across his chest—pointing away from the men but not so it couldn't be swung around quickly. Jackson's left hand was hooked casually in his waistband.

The four men reined hard as they reached the two O'Malleys. Their sudden halt briefly covered the two men in dust, which was no doubt the visitors' intention. Careful, seasoned riders would have angled off. As the fine grains settled, Joe saw a quartet of young to middle-aged faces he did not recognize. All wore a patchwork of clothes ranging from deerskin to Eastern-cut trousers. These had likely come from a chest of wardrobe the Rebels once used to pass as whatever they needed to. One of them had Union-issued binoculars in a case attached to his saddle. The brown case was white-scuffed on one side. No doubt where a soldier had fallen on it, scraping it against the ground.

"O'Malley?" said one, his face a devilish orange in the setting sun.

"Mr. O'Malley," Joe replied over his chaw. "You'd've known who we are if you come in the front, like guests."

"We did!" shouted a voice from behind him.

Joe did not look away. Jackson was already facing in that direction. The elder O'Malley wore a look of genuine unconcern. His gun was loaded with scattershot that could take most of them down from where he was standing. He did not want to lose that advantage.

"Two men crawling on the rocks, by the sign," Jackson told his father.

"You ain't guests, belly-walkers!" Joe shouted over his shoulder.

None of the men rose to the insult.

"Which one of you is the snake who shot Dick Ocean?" Joe provoked. He wanted to know the burning point of their fuse.

The leader did not prolong what was ultimately time-wasting palaver. But he wasn't exactly cool.

"Tell the Mission Injuns to come out," the leader snapped with sudden impatience or irritation—it didn't matter to Joe which. "And get the man down from the hayloft, too. The one who made this visit necessary. Everyone else stay where they are."

It was obvious that one of the men had been watching the station for some time. Sisquoc and Malibu had arrived a good hour before the stage to tell Joe about the special visitor.

Joe spit at the foot of the man's horse.

"No one comes to my home and tells me what to do," he said. "Especially when I don't know his name or his purpose."

The leader leaned forward.

"Our purpose is to see the three parties I just named standing with you two," said the man with his first show of impatience.

"What if we don't oblige you?" Jackson demanded.

The mounted man replied, "Then people will die on both sides. If that's what you want, we are ready."

"Spoken like a true Rebel," Joe said.

The man seemed unclear whether that was an insult or a compliment, which is what Joe had intended. The ensuing silence was broken only by the daily wind that rose from the west at dusk, carrying the faintest hint of salty sea breeze.

Joe decided to stay in the present game, which was truce instead of war. He motioned for Slash to come down and, without turning, called for the two Mission Indians to come out. Joe then moved the shotgun so it was under his arm, pointing in the direction, though not directly at, the man who had spoken. The move wasn't made in a threatening way. Joe was just letting the man know that he would be one of those casualties. The other three men pointed their own weapons at Joe and Jackson.

Slash and the Indians emerged in the twilight, dragging long shadows behind them. Jackson saw one of the men on the rocks nod to his boss, letting him know that the man from the hayloft was on his way.

All the while Joe was looking for additional clues as to the identities of the men. Something that might allow him to scare them off or at least talk them down from whatever they were planning. The man beside the apparent leader had a leather cartridge box on his belt. Joe could not read the stamp except for the

GA in the center. Georgia. Definitely a Reb. The third man had a tin-tip scabbard and sabre that also looked like those he had seen on former Rebels. The last man wore a US belt buckle, not CSA. It might have been taken from a captured or dead Yankee. Confederates were sometimes like Injuns that way. They liked souvenirs.

So they were Rebels. Unless they were friends or kin of the man Clarity Michaels shot, or had some gripe with the Indian Bureau, Joe couldn't imagine what they'd want with anyone here.

By this time the three O'Malleys and the two Mission Indians had lined up shoulder to shoulder. Like his father, Slash stood with his back to the four men, his eyes on both of the men side-lit by the setting sun on the top stones of the entranceway. They were shifting side to side a little, the rocks having been baking in the sun all day and still not cooled. Slash knew the feeling. He also knew that rattlers sometimes moved to the top of the rocks to catch the last of the sun's heat. He watched hopefully for any sudden movement by the men.

Just then, the group heard a brief conversation, a short commotion, and then a moan from inside the station.

"Sarah?" Jackson yelled, turning toward the doorway.

Joe's fingers tightened around his shotgun.

"I'm all right—we are all right," the woman shouted back.

"What was it?" Joe demanded. His eyes were fixed on the leader, daring him to interfere.

"B.W. got hit on the head."

Joe gazed hard at the leader of the horsemen. The man looked down with equal resolve.

"No one touched the ladies and no one will, as long as they stay cooperative," the leader said. "All you folks have to do is nothing."

"Who's in my station, striking my visitors?" Joe demanded. "Either you talk or I'm going in."

"The Whip got uppity and had to be dealt with," someone declared from the door of the station.

CHAPTER 5

The O'Malleys and their Indian companions turned toward the voice.

The man who spoke drew an oath from the lips of Joe O'Malley and a scowl from Slash. It was the barrel-chested Kennedy, who adjusted his Union hat to block the orange sun and walked confidently forward. The Indian shaman was behind him and Hathaway was behind him. Hathaway was the only one who was armed. He had a gun pointed at the back of the Serrano.

The Indian did not seem to understand what was expected of him. He walked along, looking at the riders and at the O'Malley party—stoic but there was hesitancy in his steps. There was noise at the entrance-way as the men on the rock climbed down. Slash resolved to cut the head off the next rattlesnake he saw for its failure to do its job. The men emerged from behind the boulders on horseback. They were leading three other mounts, saddled and riderless.

"You committed violence in front of our women," Joe said as Kennedy approached. "You will answer for that."

"Now, O'Malley, there is no need for anyone else to get struck," Kennedy said pleasantly. "No one has died and no one need die."

"Except Dick Ocean, nearly," Jackson remarked.

"An accident, I assure you," Kennedy said. "Too little rain, too much dust. The target was a horse."

Joe turned back to the man in front of him. "That how you lost the war?" he goaded.

The leader snarlingly raised his gun and Joe beat him to it. The shotgun was leveled at the man's chest and he froze. His companions raised or cocked their weapons but the leader shouted at them to hold.

"I second that, to *everyone!*" Kennedy barked. He reached Joe's side. The burly man wore a relaxed, satisfied expression that gave the frontiersman a fever. The man from the Indian bureau regarded Joe. "Please lower the gun so no one makes a stupid mistake."

Joe obliged. He glared at Kennedy and turned toward him, the shotgun swiveling with him.

"You weren't a Reb," Joe said, spitting around his chaw.

"No," Kennedy replied, twitching a little as the glob landed by his boot.

"So what's your game when you're not scaring women?" Joe pressed.

"I'm afraid that cannot be shared at present," the man remarked. He looked at Joe's shotgun. "And you can lower that, Mr. O'Malley. You understand, I hope, that our intentions here are not violent."

"I hear the words, but I see yer guns."

"Have it your way," Kennedy said. "But don't do anything hasty."

Joe remained just as he was and the riders who had been at the front of the station rode to Kennedy's side.

"Three extra mounts," Joe said. "It appears you intend to kidnap a guest from my station."

Kennedy frowned. "A harsh word to apply when speaking of a Red Man," he said.

"One who just visited with our president." He added, "Your president."

Kennedy just smiled his beefy smile and mounted one of the horses. Still smiling, he drew his pistol and pointed it at Joe's head.

"I have had enough of you, Mr. Joe O'Malley," Kennedy said. "Point your shotgun at the ground, sir, and shut your mouth or your son will be wearing your guts."

Once again, Joe did not oblige.

"I'll give you courage if not brains," Kennedy said. He kept his gun level with Joe's forehead while Hathaway drew his own handgun and urged the Serrano to mount another of the steeds.

The shaman declined, crossing his forearms diagonally across his chest, and shutting his eyes.

"Eagle spirit ain't gonna help you," Hathaway said, jerking his knee hard into the small of the shaman's back. The Serrano buckled a little, then stood erect, his hands still pressed gently to his breast, wings in repose. Hathaway swatted the man's headdress from his graying hair. "Fly if you want, but get up there!"

"Leave him be!" Gert shouted from the door. "He's a man of peace!"

"Go back inside!" Jackson yelled.

The abductors ignored her. Hathaway continued his assault on the Indian.

"Red Man, we are already behind schedule," he said. "You can ride the horse or run alongside it, leashed to the saddle, don't matter to me. Make your call."

The shaman didn't move and, huffing impatiently, Hathaway walked to the lead rider and took the braided rawhide ranch rope from its hook on the saddle. He walked back to the shaman and, shaking the rope out, began to loop it around the point where the man's forearms crossed. Hathaway took a step back and pulled the knot tight. He went to lash the other end to the saddle horn.

There was a loud pop from the station and the rope blew apart in the middle. The shaman didn't move but Hathaway was startled as his end went slack. A second pop chewed off the segment that dangled from the fist of the Indian agent. The rope was chewed off leaving just an inch behind. This time, Hathaway felt the buzz of the bullet as it whizzed past.

"Next one takes your thumb!" a woman shouted from the house.

Kennedy turned in his saddle. "The lady sharpshooter."

Hathaway's fist opened at once and the tiny remaining piece of rope dropped to the dust.

"A woman?" the leader of the Rebel group said with disbelief. He wheeled his horse from the line, turned it toward the station, and spurred the animal forward. At the same time he drew his six-shooter and peered into the darkness beyond the doorway.

A shot from inside punched through the shoulder of the man's gun arm. The wounded man listed to one side and turned his horse from its charge. A fourth shot split the reins of the man who was next in line. This man took a fistful of mane in his hands to steady the steed. Before any of the others could act, Slash had drawn his knife, spun, and put a cut in the saddle cinch of the next rider. The horse was startled and reared, the rider fighting to steady him causing the compromised saddle to slide off—him with it.

All of that happened within moments. The fourth rider, as yet untouched, swung his horse toward the back of the station and rode off. The man holding the mane moved to the side of the injured leader and took the reins. Without waiting for instructions, he followed his companion back the way they'd come. The Rebel with the slipping-and-sliding saddle re-mounted and did the same, although with less speed.

Joe took advantage of the confusion to rally Jackson and the shaman, hustling them toward the station. Slash followed behind. He had left his gun in the loft and, anyway, cared less about justice than about catching up to his father and grandfather and protecting their retreat.

Kennedy and Hathaway did not try to stop the O'Malleys. Hathaway mounted and, covered by the two men who had been at the front of the station, all four of the would-be kidnappers rode off—without the man they had come for or the horse to which he was about to be tied.

The door to the station slammed shut just as the two retreating riders turned. They peppered the door and windows with gunshot, then rode off hard before the O'Malleys could return fire.

* * *

From inside the station, Joe heard the hoofbeats and peered cautiously through a shattered pane of glass. He resented, down to his heels, having to be cautious in his own home and promised himself these men would be made to atone.

The varmints were not quite out of range but, detestable as they were, and though his desire for revenge was strong, he would not shoot them in the back.

He spit the tobacco out the window, then asked everyone if they were okay.

There was a round of affirmatives, as well as sighs— most of them from the preacher. The two Mission Indians went to see to B.W., who was sitting on the floor where he'd been knocked flat from behind. They hefted him to a chair. Sarah surveyed her shattered window and the nicked furniture. Gert began picking up shards of glass so the dogs wouldn't step on them. The dogs had retreated to B.W.'s little bedroom, where they barked at the gunfire.

Clarity stood just behind the front door. She held her carbine with restless intensity. She had not moved toward the window. Had she gone there, she would have used the gun. It wouldn't be shooting a man in the back if you hit him in the arm or leg or buttocks.

Jackson walked over to her.

"I want to thank you for what you did," he said. He nodded toward the Serrano. "I'm guessing he's grateful, too."

The shaman said nothing. He was no longer summoning the eagle spirit. He was looking out a window.

"I'll get your headdress as soon as it's safe," Gert promised.

The man acknowledged her kindness with a nod.

Sarah walked over to Clarity and their eyes met. "You have my deep thanks as well," the woman said. She came a little closer. "You didn't kill your fiancé by accident," she added.

Clarity did not look away but did not immediately reply. The subject was dropped when Joe spoke.

"When the sun's down, I'm going to track those cusses," he said, opening the door a crack and craning out so he could see to the west.

"Pa," Jackson said, "those boys were organized."

"Not when they left."

"She surprised them," Jackson said, jerking a thumb at Clarity. "She surprised all of us. But they wouldn't've left without expecting pursuit and covering their flank."

"You're right," Joe said. "They're army trained, they'll use military tactics. Straight line reverse course, anticipating at least one of us to follow their trail. That's not what I'll do. Besides," he said, "we got the next hour to consider. Stage is gonna leave with the Serrano on board. Has to. They're expecting him on t'other end. So these boys'll regroup and come at the stage hard next time."

"The stage—and you," Jackson said.

"They won't see, hear, or smell me," Joe assured his son.

Sarah did not bother to protest, nor did Gert. B.W. was another matter. Malibu had brought over the lantern and held it at the spot where the driver had been pistol-whipped.

"Joe, you were lucky to get outta that fix," the driver said.

"Luckier than you," Malibu remarked. "Big bump."

"I was trying to help," B.W. said, frowning at the Indian. Sarah handed him a damp cloth to press against his head. He winced with one eye as he dabbed at the injury, turning the open eye to Joe. "They could just as well have shot me."

"I don't think Kennedy ever shot anyone," Slash suggested.

"He shot off his mouth enough," B.W. said, starting as he carelessly shook his head and sent pain shooting through his skull. He blinked away the pain. "Hey, Slash—your leg's bleeding."

Sarah shot a look at her son. There was blood on the front of his trousers, just above the knee.

"It's nothing, a little poke," he said. "Someone left a knife in the hayloft."

"A knife?" Sarah said.

Joe changed the subject. "Whip, you're okay to go, yeah?"

"I got a choice?"

"Not actually," Joe said.

"How is he going to drive?" Gert asked.

"I don't need my head for that," B.W. said.

"You won't say that when it's bumping up and down," Sarah warned him.

B.W. shrugged. "Gotta do it, woman. That's all there is."

Joe took a pouch from a wooden wall peg and slung it over his shoulder. The rattle announced that it was full of shot. He took a colt and a box of ammunition from a drawer in the kitchen. He shoved a flint into his shirt pocket. The gun went in his belt, the cartridges in his pocket. He went to the door with his shotgun, looked at the sun, then turned to his son and grandson.

"Slash, what do you think about riding with B.W.?" Joe said.

The young man grinned. Joe was puzzled.

"He already asked my permission to sit in the box," Jackson said.

Joe smiled proudly. "Good man. That means— Jackson, you stay put. And Malibu, can I count on you and Sisquoc staying here?"

The Mission Indian nodded once.

Sarah crossed her arms. "Pa, what are you doing?"

"Going hunting for rats."

"And how do you expect to stop an ambush on the stage?" she asked.

"He's Joe O'Malley!" B.W. cheered.

"And Joe O'Malley is outnumbered," Sarah protested.

"Maybe I can discourage 'em before they get to the stage," he suggested.

"'Discourage,'" Jackson said. "You mean pick them off?"

"Just the horses," Joe replied.

"It's a sound plan, which is why I'd like to come with you, Mr. O'Malley."

Everyone in the station turned toward the door. The speaker was Clarity Michaels.

Reverend Michaels strode toward her. "That is reckless and unwarranted," he said firmly. "We are leaving *together* on the stage."

"Where I'd be useless, not to mention helpless," his sister replied in kind. "You heard what that man

Kennedy said. They hit Mr. Ocean when they were aiming at a horse. That could happen again." The woman exhaled, decided. "Mr. O'Malley was right, what he said a minute ago. Those men will be more careful and better prepared the next time they attack the stage. I wish to be outside, not inside, when that happens." She turned to Joe. "We'll be following them, correct?"

The older man studied her. "I'll be doing that. Didn't say you could come."

"Do I need your permission to ride hereabout?" she asked.

Gert grinned. Sarah made a face at her daughter. Gert turned away but the grin remained.

Joe rethought his own position. "That *was* some impressive shooting." He looked her up and down with a plainsman's eye. "You ride as good as you shoot?"

"The question, Mr. O'Malley, is can I shoot while I ride? The answer is yes."

He smiled a little. "You got riding clothes?"

She tried not to smile. "If you will be kind enough to get my trunk, I can be ready before the sun is down," she answered.

Joe looked at Slash.

"I'll get it," the young man volunteered. "Which—"

"Black with a brown leather band," Clarity said quickly.

"Back box," B.W. added. He shook his head, then turned back to Joe. "And I still think you're loco for going, let alone with Miss Michaels."

"The showman P. T. Barnum had a tiger, in a cage. To onlookers, it was just a large cat."

The people in the station looked at Fletcher Small.

The man had not moved from his seat at the table since the riders had arrived. He had been listening, an ear turned to the front door, writing busily in a notebook. The journalist stood now.

"No one asked, but I agree with the lady," he said to the room, but he looked directly at the woman. "I have never met or even read about a woman who could shoot like Clarity. There's a story in it. But that story doesn't unfold inside a stagecoach—a cage."

"I'm not interested in notoriety," the woman said.

Small shrugged. "A newspaperman reports news, not preferences."

"I'll trouble you to watch your manners with our guests," Jackson said. "The woman wishes her privacy."

"As well she should, or else why make the hard journey all the way out to the continental wilderness," Small said. "Yet a story such as this could make the subject money, if they were of a mind. And money helps buy privacy."

"That's enough, sir," Jackson cautioned.

Small nodded agreeably and returned to the table where he began rolling a cigarette. The reverend gently took his sister's arm and drew her aside.

"See what you've done?" Merritt Michaels said softly.

"I've prevented a kidnapping," she replied. "Maybe saved men's lives."

"That is *not* what I mean," the pastor told her. "It was my understanding, sister Clarity, that we did not wish to draw attention to our actions—*or* our whereabouts."

"Murray, Kentucky, is a long way off."

"*We* made the journey," her brother pointed out. He pointed toward the door and the yard beyond. "Until now, we did not know who those people wanted."

"The Roches are not made of such solid stuff," she replied. She nodded slightly toward the reporter. "And this one? How will any story he writes reach so far?"

"Newspapers circulate their reports widely now, by wire," the clergyman said. "One never knows where they will land, especially if it is as special as he says."

"Mr. Small does not and will not know our final destination," Clarity said as her trunk arrived on Slash's back. "Now please—I must change clothes."

The reverend gripped her upper am. "I urge you not to do this."

Clarity glared at him and he released her. She withdrew from her brother's side and followed Slash and the trunk to the small room where B.W. had been. The young man shut the door, depriving Clarity of ventilation but giving her privacy. He returned to the room where his father was using blacksmith's tongs to pull broken bits of glass from the window frame. He was glad they had built heavy shutters for all the windows. They were meant to protect the interior from sandstorms, which could be long-lived and violent. If necessary, they would surely slow a bullet.

Slash went to get a drink from the indoor bucket. He had just filled his tin cup when, quicker than he had ever known a woman to dress, he saw Clarity step from the room. She was garbed in an ankle-len'th brown riding skirt and a white blouse.

"That's a sidesaddle outfit," Jackson noted.

"Would you prefer I ride that way?" Clarity asked.

Small laughed without looking up from his notebook, where he was taking this all down. Reverend Michaels stalked over, standing between the reporter and his sister.

"Do you not even care that you could be putting a woman's life in danger?" he demanded.

"Sounds like she can take care of herself," the reporter answered.

"That isn't the point. We are trying to start a new life."

Small looked up through the swirling smoke of his cigarette. "Seems to me, preacher, that you are looking to continue your old life—just somewhere else. This lady, she is the one bent on doing something new."

"You hardly know her!" the parson charged.

"That appears, then, to make two of us."

Reverend Michaels stormed away, toward his sister, then turned and went to the kitchen where Sarah busied herself with cleaning the supper dishes. She was purposefully trying not to engage in this matter any further.

B.W. stood, winced with both eyes this time, and grunted disapprovingly.

"I'm not taking sides here," he said, "but you folks act like this is a church picnic. It's not! Ask Dick Ocean!"

"We know this is no picnic," Joe said softly. "We know a great deal, in fact, about what this isn't. What we have to find out is what this *is*."

B.W. struggled to follow that. While he did so, Joe looked out again and made sure that darkness had fully settled upon the compound. Satisfied, he asked Jackson to ready a pair of horses.

"Young Thunder for the lady, one of those that came with the stage for me," he added.

"Why?" B.W. asked. "They'll be tired."

"That's what I want," Joe replied. "We won't be riding hard and I don't want 'em putting up a fuss and making noise. Nighttime brings out the worst in this territory. And when Thunder is rested, if we're still out there, he'll give the lady the speed to overtake anyone who might need overtaking."

That was true, B.W. had to agree. Just one screeching owl or darting hare could turn a fresh, alert horse into a frightened foal.

Jackson left and Joe motioned for Clarity to stay where she was. It was dark inside the house and everyone had known not to turn on the lanterns or feed the ebbing fire in the kitchen. Joe eased into the near-blackness outside and shut the shot-peppered door behind him. With seasoned eyes, he turned an arc slowly from the entrance to the stable. He knew every contour of those structures and he looked for any sign of change that might indicate a concealed man or gun. He didn't think there had been time for anyone to dismount and double back—but he did not want to bet his life or that of Clarity's on the enemy being panicked or unprepared.

The ears listened, not quite as sharp as they once were but still aware of every kind of animal that came out at dusk. He could distinguish where their dens or warrens or burrows were, and what kinds of sounds they made with their mouths, or with their feet or tails on sand or brush. He could tell animal sounds from

Indians imitating animal sounds. There was always the chance that roaming Apaches might come by, take it upon themselves to raid the stables. It had never happened here, but then young bucks were always looking for new ways to prove their courage.

The funny thing was, Joe didn't dislike Apaches. He had lived like them long enough to respect their ability to survive. Keeping a tribe alive meant more than hunting and making war on rival tribes. The Indian way also included taking and keeping white women. Part of surviving is making your enemy watch out not just for their own lives but the lives of their families. Taking a white wife or mother, little son or daughter, forced settlers to bring war to the Indian camp. They rarely arrived, the Indians lying outside the camp in ambush, expecting just such a move.

That was the reason Joe didn't like Gert socializing with the Pechanga, Apaches, Serrano, Mojave, and other tribes, why she was confused by his disapproval. Joe and the Indians were alike, it seemed to her.

The station and its surroundings were devoid of human activity, other than Jackson in the stable. Joe stepped out a little farther. He made a point of dragging his boots on the dirt, hoping to get a reaction, a movement, a sound from anyone who might be watching. *No one bit my foxtail,* as his own father used to say about the British and the cap he wore during the War for Independence.

A cooling wind blew from the east, adding smell to the senses he could use. Joe was not just alert, there was a familiar burn low in his belly. He often wondered if animals felt that fire, too, when they were prepared for action, even if an attack didn't come.

Or was that only a human thing? Did animals just simply run to or from danger using only the muscles and instincts God gave them?

He wondered what it would be like to not think and worry. Since he'd been in from the frontier, running this place with his son and daughter-in-law, it seemed like that was mostly what he did.

Standing there for several minutes, Joe sensed nothing out of the ordinary. Just the usual scent of something dead blowing from the coyote hunting grounds to the west. A little bit of wet fur, probably a mountain lion, came from the stream behind the station. Joe liked it that the cats came to drink. They left the barn alone and scared away other predators.

Joe stood there and waited for his son to bring the horses. If there was someone watching—including someone hidden out on the rise to the north—they might hear them and likely figure out what was up. Especially because Jackson wasn't bringing the team of four the stage would need.

"You really think someone is out there, Pa?" Jackson asked.

"No," Joe said.

"I'm guessing they didn't know this terrain well enough to risk coming around at night," Jackson added.

"I was thinking that myself," Joe replied. "They never expected to have to ride it in the dark. That's also gotta be worrying them about hightailing after the stage, which gives us an advantage."

Jackson regarded his father's eyes, which caught the rising full moon.

"Pa, you sure about this?" Jackson asked. "This is a matter for Butterfield, for the Bureau of Indian Affairs."

"I agree with that, son," Joe said. "But like it or not we're the agent of one and the other's corrupted. We got no choice."

"Our contract says nothing about armed enforcement of Butterfield rights."

"I guess I shoulda read it," Joe confessed.

Jackson couldn't help but smile and sigh. That was Joe.

"But I know the Butterfield people," the older O'Malley went on. "They don't like anything that disrupts service. If a station can't protect the stage and its passengers and cargo, move them along in a timely fashion, Butterfield may not blame the station exactly, but they might move the route somewhere safer. Closer to Fort Yuma, Fort Mason—longer route but not as risky. That passage wouldn't include Whip Station."

Jackson had to concede the point.

"As for the Indian Bureau," Joe said, "we always knew they can't be trusted farther than a snake can spit. I'm more worried about whatever these boys have planned. That's something we have to find out."

Again, though Jackson did not want his father riding out on this hunt, he could not disagree with the man's reasoning.

Joe went back inside and swapped out his shotgun for a carbine. It was less gun, easier to handle. He told Clarity they were ready to go, then went back outside. He slid the gun in the holster Jackson had fixed to the saddle. Then he mounted the lead horse, White Paint.

"We gotta move B.W. out as close to his regular time as possible. Soon's I'm gone, help see to that." The older man turned toward the house. He was about to call Clarity when the woman walked briskly to Young Thunder, put herself in the saddle, and settled in. She took a moment to make sure both her Colts were easy draws.

Both men were impressed by her speed and her easy handling of the revolvers.

"You ready?" Joe asked.

In response, the woman nudged the horse in the ribs and rode up beside him.

Smiling to himself, Joe said, "Stay close 'cause I know where the gopher holes are."

Clarify nodded and the two cantered to the entrance.

"Take care of yourself, Pa!" Jackson called after him.

Joe raised a hand in acknowledgment as they passed through the main entrance and set off at a slow gallop.

CHAPTER 6

Douglas James Kennedy, renegade bureaucrat, was not a happy man.

He stood by the entrance of the old copper mine, glowering at the rising moon. In his hand he held a Colt with an ivory handle, one of two that had been presented to him by the Bureau of Indian Affairs for this difficult journey. He looked at the BIA engraved in the grip and felt impatient disgust.

It wasn't just a matter of a carefully planned operation becoming unraveled. It was also the fact that a woman had done the unraveling. That was not something he intended to report to his superior. It was bad enough that Hathaway and the other men in the party had seen who did the shooting. The only reason it would not cost him extra to make sure they forgot it was that they would be mortified as well.

But for him to find out—

Kennedy did not want the intimidating, cigar-smoking swagger of the man at the top compounded by laughter. That reputation would stay with him for the rest of his life.

The quick, disorganized departure from the station had been bad enough, Kennedy thought.

After being driven from the station, the men had ridden to their refuge in the foothills. It lay half a mile beyond Civil Gulch, in a turn off from the stagecoach trail. The rugged path, too narrow for more than one horse in spots, ended in a copper mine that had been played out shortly before the War. The mine was an ideal hiding place and Confederate soldiers, these men included, had used it as a staging area for raids and as a sanctuary from Apaches. The Serrano and Pechanga Indians were much less hostile. Their presence in the region, crisscrossing the trail, gave it the appearance of being uninhabited. That helped keep cavalry patrols from coming around. No one wanted to stir up peaceful Red Men.

The entrance wasn't wide but it was long with a shallow incline. It ended with a rock wall, the result of a cave-in. The collapse left natural chimneys that carried the smoke from fires into a nighttime wind that caused it to quickly disperse. A branch of the mine had been excavated in a futile search for more copper, which the South needed for bayonets. It was an ideal place to stable horses. A ledge waist-high in the wall, protected from any seeping rainwater, was used to store ammunition and black powder. The men rarely used the explosive, which would attract attention. They had used it only once, to create a path higher into the foothills in the event they needed to escape quickly.

Like in our original plan, Kennedy thought.

It was ironic that one of the plans they had discarded for today was to use the powder to block Civil Gulch. Kennedy had been afraid the noise would attract the O'Malleys, who might have rescued the trapped stage. Their superior agreed. He did not want the men coming out, armed for war. Shooting a horse, stopping the coach for a time, would be enough.

"Especially if there is a lady on board," the luminary had said around his cigar. "No one will risk injury to a woman."

The irony was how *wrong* that thinking had been.

In that original plan, the one that failed, the mine was where six of the men—most of the complement of nine former soldiers—had intended to lead any pursuers while Kennedy and Hathaway, along with the shaman, headed through the path they had created. Up through the foothills and then north, to where the rest of their money was waiting to pay the former soldiers. North, to where the second part of the plan awaited hatching.

"But for a woman," Kennedy muttered.

"What was that?" Hathaway asked. The taller man was standing beside and a little behind Kennedy, looking down at the field mice that darted under the scrub off to the side.

"Huh?" Kennedy said as though starting from a nap. "Oh, nothing. Nothing."

The other men were spread out through the dark mine, licking their wounds. Hathaway had his back against a timber that seemed sturdier, despite its burden, than any of the men present.

"I say we go back and burn 'em out," said Hathaway. "Or blast 'em to hell."

Kennedy turned toward him. "And if we kill the medicine man?"

"One fewer Injun," said a man from the darkness.

Kennedy took a few steps toward the man who had spoken. "Maybe we oughta hang you, Marcus," he said. "One fewer beef-head."

The man was on his feet in an instant, breathing heavily. The two were almost equal in height and stood chest to chest like puffed quail.

"Take care, friend," the former Confederate warned. "Your status don't mean beans out here."

"Maybe not, '*friend*,' but my money does have status, Private Stone," said the other. "If you hope to earn the rest of yours, you will sit down and shut your overheated mouth."

"Better overheated than what you did back there," Stone said, nonetheless turning away. "'G'wan, keep your guns. We don't need to shoot one another. No killing. Let's be gentlemen about all this.'"

"Let him vent," Hathaway said into Kennedy's ear. "No good us fighting one another."

"I suppose not," Kennedy agreed. And, in truth, Stone wasn't wrong.

Ordinarily, a unit would not have allowed the station men to retain their weapons. Kennedy didn't think the O'Malley men would start shooting with women present. Ordinarily, the raiders would have had men on the roof of the structure as a precaution. Ordinarily, they would not have been so civil. The way it was during the War, Crane's Cavalry—named for Captain Tod Crane, the man with the shoulder wound—would either come in shooting or leave shooting, with only the most necessary talk in between. But with two men on the inside, Kennedy and

Hathaway, none of them had expected resistance. The men from Washington, who had been listening to the dinner conversation where Joe O'Malley was confused as a junior Congressman, had miscalculated. They had finalized their plans at the previous station stop in Vallicita, where Brent Diamond assured them they would be fine if they corralled the men. They sealed the deal by swapping firearms—in Alabama, a symbol of trust and a long relationship.

"They won't risk their women," he was assured.

They did not expect a mousey *girl* with a preacher for a brother to get involved.

And now that stain of miscalculation was on Crane and his elect band. They were right to be bitter. The money was important but so was removing that blot. Kennedy suspected it would be removed either with his cooperation or without it.

Kennedy continued looking out the mouth of the mine. The air here wasn't quite as damp and tart as it was inside. Each breath still carried a taste of copper, groundwater releasing whatever particles still remained in the stone walls. Those slivers were stirred by walking and lodged in the nostrils, giving every breath a metallic taste. There was also a smell of burned flesh and doctoring in the stable area. Gus Peterson, the group's medic, was finishing up with Crane. The bullet had gone clear through the man's shoulder. The entrance and exit had been cauterized and Tod had nearly passed out from the pain. He fought to stay awake, not just as an act of bravado but to finish the mission he had started. It was now a matter of bandaging the wound. One of his men, Dan Ridgewood, had the man's head in his lap and was pouring water between his lips from a tarnished CSA canteen. Another, Mute Pete, stood nearby looking down. Pete had been Crane's aide during the War. The giant of a man wasn't mute. He just preferred to talk with his fists.

Kennedy envied the obvious care the former sergeant showed to his captain.

"We gotta go after the stage," Stone said from the dark.

Hathaway turned. "You really think they'll try and leave?"

"I know these drivers," Stone answered. "This one is going to try and make up every minute of lost time."

"The way I hit him?" Hathaway said dubiously.

"Hell, he could take that trail in his sleep," Stone replied. "I drunk with him once at Vallicita. He's like a bull in a ring. Jab, jab, jab, he keeps going. He will also honor every ticket that was purchased for the ride. That includes getting the Indian to San Francisco."

"His Shotgun ain't going anywhere," said Silas Welch, the rider with the GA-stamped ammunition box. He was chewing on beef jerky and washing it down with river water from his canteen.

"No, he ain't," agreed Stone. "But he won't ride alone and he won't take the gimp. That means either Joe O'Malley or that kid, Slash, will sit in the box."

"Or the two Mission Injuns?" a man named Madison suggested.

"Not the Indians," Kennedy finally spoke. "They'd need orders from whichever fort they came from before taking on that duty. And from what I saw back there, I don't think this Joe O'Malley would leave the station in the hands of just one man, two women, and an injured Shotgun."

Hathaway paced around a circle of moonlight on the floor of the mine. "What are the O'Malleys doing right now, you suppose?" he asked.

Kennedy looked back at him. "That's what I'm wondering. He didn't strike me as the kind of man who liked sitting still."

"You think he'll come looking for us alone?" Hathaway said.

"I don't know," Kennedy replied.

"Why not?" Stone said. "This is his land. He probably knows every stone and gully."

"It'll be tough to follow a trail at night, even if he does know the terrain," Madison pointed out.

Kennedy turned to Silas Welch. The lean, tall, bearded man was the one who had brought the horses to the station.

"Silas, maybe you better pick a lookout spot and keep watch over things," Kennedy said. "Marcus will relieve you in a few hours."

"'Watch over' meaning what?" he asked.

Kennedy shook his head. "What was so confusing about that instruction? Watch over means go out there and see if anyone comes looking for us. It's pretty simple."

Silas rose. "Simple? If I have a shot, do I take it?"

"To what end?"

"He sniffs us out, goes back for the two Indians," Welch said. "You want that?"

"I do not," Kennedy said. "I also don't want this to become a matter for a U.S. Marshal."

"Mr. Kennedy," Madison said, "he finds us, and he's

not alone, he can pin us here while another of the O'Malleys gets help from the Gutenbrunner place to the north."

He was referring to an inn southeast of the Oak Grove Station. The German immigrant was a sympathizer to anyone who could pay for lodgings or storage—which included weapons or people. It was said that more bodies were buried on his property than in Gettysburg. Rebels were frequent, long-term guests. They were allowed to stay in exchange for hunting and providing protection from troops or Indians.

Kennedy nodded. "That's true. That's possible. But we're here for something larger than horses or a mine and you're being very well paid to advance that cause."

"Which you still haven't told us about," said Welch. "Maybe them two purposes, yours and ours, merge, like great rivers."

Kennedy stepped closer to the man he still could not see. "You know something, Silas? You have accidentally stumbled upon the truth. Our purposes *do* merge. You have undying hatred of Washington, and we share some of your views. So why don't you just trust me, do as you're told, and see if it all doesn't work out in the end?"

Silas Welch snatched a rifle from where it leaned against the wall. His back was to the others. Where he stood, it was lit by the dull glow of the doctor's lamp as he retrieved a box of shells from the ammunition niche. There was also a collection of Apache weapons in the cleft, snuck from their settlement the previous day. Welch turned and lay the gun across his shoulder, looking to Kennedy like a thin, rusted tin soldier.

"I'll do my job," Welch promised him. He stopped

briefly as he passed the man from Washington. "I don't wanna see your cause or ours suffer another setback."

Stepping from the mine, the rangy Southerner went across the rocks that had been excavated from the mine years earlier. Though there was a path, dirt and dry brush made sounds when you stepped on them. After four years out west, fighting for the losing side in a great cause, Welch knew that if he could hear something, chances were good that an enemy could hear it better. The country had a way of magnifying sounds through endless, hidden echoes.

The men in the cave heard his scraping footsteps—and then silence.

"You shouldn't talk like that to Silas, to any of these men."

The voice belonged to Gus Peterson, the medic who had been with the original unit. He said it loud enough for all to hear. "They're proud men, Douglas. They fought a proud war."

Hathaway wandered into the back of the mine. He had no desire to be caught in this verbal crossfire . . . again.

"Seven months ago, that mattered," Kennedy replied. He also spoke loud enough for the benefit of others. "They're being paid now to put aside that fight and win this one."

"Nevertheless, sir, you need Silas. You need every man here."

"We all need each other," Kennedy said moderately. "You folks weren't exactly swimming in prosperity from the occasional holdup and bounty."

"We accepted our lot—"

"And my money," Kennedy said thickly. "*And*, today,

you failed to deliver that for which you have already been paid a substantial sum. You want to talk to me about prairie honor and cruel history, I will be happy to do so in a saloon in San Francisco. Not before." He looked around the dark chamber. "We recover from this setback and we move forward aggressively."

Gus Peterson sighed and took the empty canteen from Ridgewood. He ambled to one of the barrels that held their water. He filled the container and went back to where his patient lay. Ridgewood was wiping perspiration from his grit-covered forehead.

Kennedy resumed staring out across the lowlands, then up at the stars as they struggled to be seen above the moonlight. His ears drew his eyes back down to the plain. He wondered about the meaning of the cries he heard in the distance from coyotes and owls. Were they hunting? Mating? Dying?

Were they Indians?

Though he had been with the Indian Bureau for three years, Kennedy was no closer to understanding the Red Man than when he started. They wanted peace but they made war. They wanted goods but they attacked the wagons that brought them. They wanted their way of life but they fell to pestilence and weather and hunger.

They made no natural sense—and each tribe had its own form of madness, whether it was torturing for amusement or proving how brave they were by dying. It was no wonder that Washington struggled with moving them around or killing them off outright.

And concerns like Butterfield were caught in the middle. Eastern interests were reluctant to invest in the West as long as there was no peace. Coming out here, Kennedy had seen what he had only heard about, the Butterfield terminals each bearing a poster with this legend:

☞ You Will Be Traveling Through
<u>INDIAN</u> <u>COUNTRY</u>
And the Safety of Your Person Cannot Be
Vouchsafed by Anyone but
<u>GOD</u>.

For all the confidence in his voice, in his manner, the Easterner did not feel at ease out here. That bothered Kennedy a great deal. He knew Boston, New York, Philadelphia, Washington, not territories. He knew restaurants, not jerky. He knew metal or glass washbasins, not barrels and creeks. He knew hotels, not bedrolls. He had expected to be on his way north now, camped in the higher elevations miles from here—not hiding in a rank hole-in-a-hillside with unshaven, unwashed Confederates.

But President Andrew Johnson, the ranking hypocrite among a district of liars and self-absorbed men, wanted this thing taken care of. He was busy trying to rebuild the South, trying to fight back the radical Reconstructionists in Congress who wanted the former Confederacy turned into a military fiefdom. The president did not have time to concern himself with the pacification of the western Indian. He wanted them dead. That was why he had the Serrano Tuchahu brought to Washington. To make promises to the revered and influential leader. Have the shaman's photograph taken with the white chief and distributed to newspapers and posted on billboards.

Johnson wanted to send him home with assurances of peace and plenty.

Then make sure he did not reach his home. That would cause the Serrano and other western tribes to go to war with the settlers. Then, with the support of the press, the electorate, and finally Congress, the president would send the cavalry after the savages in force, with merciless resolve. After all, he had all those generals, North and South, who—like these Confederates—still wanted to go to war against *someone*.

They would solve the western Indian problem. It would also hopefully subdue the Indians in the South and the new Indians the federal government would acquire if they purchased the northwest lands above Canada from Russia.

Kennedy did not think large like that. He and Hathaway were just college-trained administrators who enjoyed the fine life and, like everyone else in the Bureau, skimmed funds that were supposed to go for food and clothes for the Indians to food and clothes for themselves and their wives and mistresses.

What did savages need blankets for, anyway? They had their animal skins. Tuchahu was not wearing anything from among the many garments and decorations that had been gifted to him in Washington. All of that was done for the press, for the pitying, soft shell old widows whose fortunes lined political war chests and endowed the charities of politicians' wives. It was for students whose anger could turn to rock-throwing protests unless it was deflected.

It had nothing to do with the way things really were.

Governance never did. And the men who practiced it . . .

Douglas James Kennedy was out here for his own well-being, not that of the Indians or the President of the United States. And certainly not for the corpse of the Confederacy and the maggots who still crawled on it. He did business with them because he had to. These pockets of once-feared cavalry were now guns-for-hire. Even the doctor, the most rational of the bunch, was still haunted by the ghosts of his fallen cause. He and General Guilford spent hours, Kennedy had heard, toasting their departed comrades on both sides.

Suddenly, Jessup Hathaway came hastening from the back of the mine to Kennedy's side. He leaned close to his partner's ear.

"I think there's gonna be trouble," the taller man whispered.

"Why?"

"I thought I heard a kind of shifting noise when Silas was back with the ammunition. I was right."

"Shifting?" Kennedy said. "What do you mean?"

"While you and the doc were talking, I went back and checked," Hathaway said. "Silas took one of the small sacks of black powder."

CHAPTER 7

Joe O'Malley did not attempt to follow the riders' tracks. That wasn't just because it was dark, there was also no need.

Still at a slow gallop, with Clarity riding ably at his side, he took the stagecoach trail back toward Civil Gulch. The Confederates had most likely holed up in the foothills northeast of the pass, where there were hidden mines and dangerously unstable mine shafts. Taking the Butterfield Trail would bring them to where the stage was attacked. That would also likely put Joe and Clarity close to the hideout in a much shorter span of time.

Joe knew that it also opened them to an ambush, the same as the coach. For that reason he intended to take a cut before the pass that took them north of the place, which is why he had told Clarity to ride close beside and follow what he did. At night, with the moon still behind the cliff, and the way sound traveled among the old boulders here, anyone trying to shoot would be firing wild. The most they would do is scare the horses, and Joe warned the woman to hold tight to the reins in case that happened.

"Do we return fire?" Clarity asked.

"We can't be sure they will have a horse to frighten back," Joe said. "You'll only rile Young Thunder additional."

"They would have walked here?" she asked.

"Maybe," he said. "Or they may have put their horse some ways away, so it wouldn't whinny and give them away."

"Oh," Clarity replied. She thought for a moment. "Do you know this area?"

"You mean for hiding spots?" Joe asked.

"That's right."

"No, ma'am," Joe said. "Slash is out here most days and even he doesn't know it all. The *Avii Hanupach*, what the Mojave call this region, is scatter shot with caves and old mines. If they don't light a fire, they can hide out in the open foothills."

As they approached Civil Gulch, Joe looked up the steep rock on both sides. His keen eyes were looking for any hint of a silhouette blocking the stars on top. Atop a horse in motion, it would be possible to see them blink on and off.

There was nothing. He listened for an animal that didn't quite sound like an animal. A signal to others who might be lurking on the other side. Again, there was nothing.

And then, suddenly, just before they reached the turnoff to the north, the night erupted in thunder and fury.

* * *

Jackson and B.W. were working by the light of a lantern hanging from the top railing of the stagecoach, efficiently hitching a fresh team. When they heard the blast, both men froze.

"The Gulch," B.W. said softly. He reached for his Bible, which he'd placed in the box.

"Yeah."

The sound had arrived shortly after the detonation. Jackson had already looked over when he saw a flash. It was too low on the horizon for lightning, he knew that much. The man resumed his labors with greater urgency.

Slash ran from the station followed by the two Mission Indians.

"What was that?" the young man asked.

"Sounded like powder," Jackson said.

"Would your pa have gone that route?" B.W. asked the O'Malleys.

"Very likely," the man replied. "He'd stick to clear road as much as possible, especially with a woman." Jackson thought for a moment. "Let's get you and my son on the road."

"But what about Granddad?" Slash demanded as the O'Malley women and the Indians emerged from the station.

"If he's ambushed, they may be ready for us to ride in," Jackson snapped. "Or they may be headed here. They got explosives—and we got passengers to look out for."

Sarah had heard all she needed to hear. She ushered Gert and the coach passengers back inside while the Indians went to watch the entrance.

Slash seemed torn, but only for a moment. He

huffed his displeasure, not with his father but with the situation, but he did not disagree. Growing up O'Malley, you learned that nothing comes before duty and honor . . . not even the safety of your loved ones.

"I'm going to the stable," the young man said, a hint of defiance in his voice. "I'll look out till you're ready to ride."

"Don't go to the hayloft."

"Why not?"

"If the riders are coming back they'll figure you're up there, likely try to burn you out," his father said. "Situate yourself behind the oak where you can pick off any fire-bringers."

Slash raised an arm in acknowledgment as he ran ahead.

"Lord," B.W. said, glancing at the Good Book as they redoubled their efforts. "What in God's great plan are these Rebels up to?"

"Pretty clear they've gone beyond robbing," Jackson said. "The pair from Washington must have set them on some sinister new path."

"They were so polite coming from Saint Louis," he said, pronouncing it '*Louie.*' "Treated the Injun okay, too."

"Because they need him for something," Jackson surmised.

There were two faint pops from the area of the explosion. Both men started.

"Gunfire," B.W. said.

The sounds merged and echoed across the flatlands, scrambling any hope of identifying the weapon.

"I'll bet it was the lady," B.W. said hopefully. "She took two ambushers out."

Jackson was not so sure and, like Slash, he fought the strong instinct to ride out. It would take time to reach the Gulch and him leaving here would leave his wife and daughter a gun down. He continued working.

Suddenly, there was a third loud sound.

This one was not like the last two. It was, in fact, like nothing Jackson had ever heard out here.

The blast deafened Clarity and caused Young Thunder to bolt and throw her to the ground. It proved to be a happy misfortune since the mare was struck side-on by a landslide that broke her rib cage. Bucked clear and landing on her bunched riding skirt, Clarity was able to roll from the brunt of the rock fall.

Because he was on the other side of Clarity, Joe was able to wheel his panicked horse away from the avalanche, which was the direction the animal already wanted to go. Joe's six-shooter was already in hand as he spun the horse back toward the cliff, seeking a target before the rising dust cloud obscured his view. He had already seen Clarity get herself out of the way and knew she was safe.

A pair of shots whizzed down at Joe, pinging off the medium-sized boulders that had been dislodged by the detonation. He suspected the gunman was firing blind since his own visibility was severely impaired. Still, he might strike Clarity. Joe dismounted, swatting his horse toward the other side of the gulch. Then he ran to Clarity and lay across her, shielding her as he continued to crane his head up in search of a target.

B.W. would have said that what happened next was

God's work, not Joe's. There was a prolonged series of sharp snaps, like something breaking underwater—no doubt a trick of Joe's own muffled hearing, a condition caused by the loud explosion. The reverberating gunshots dislodged already-weakened earth and rock from the gulch wall. It came down with an earthen drumroll, with occasional cracks of rock-striking-rock as it fell. The sound wasn't as loud as before, and not loud enough to drown out the cry of the man who fell with it—presumably the rogue who caused the upheaval in the first place.

That scream was brief and cut off suddenly as the slide settled atop what had already come down.

Joe pulled his kerchief over his mouth and nose while the dust thickened.

"Hold your breath!" he shouted to Clarity.

A moment later he holstered his gun and swept the woman up in his arms. He ran with her to the opposite side of the gulch, bending low to prevent less of a target from any additional stones that might bounce down.

Apart from trickling pebbles there was nothing more. Civil Gulch was once again worthy of its name.

The dust continued to billow. Joe didn't stop moving until he had relocated himself and Clarity just west of the unscathed side of the pass. Joe set Clarity on her feet and gazed into the pass. Clarity tried to get past him. He stopped her with a stiff arm.

"The horse!" she managed to say, coughing out dust.

"Buried," Joe told her.

When the earth fall stopped there was nothing but thick silence. No more rocks fell or even grated ominously. Any animal that had been chattering or baying was mute. Everything had hidden or fled.

Drawing his gun, Joe took a few steps forward. He stopped behind a rock that was nearly as tall as he was. Clarity followed. The cascade had cleared the way for a full moon to illuminate on the tableau. Each dust mote seemed to glitter. The tawny haze had begun to dissipate though the musky smell of black powder lingered. There was still enough road for a stagecoach to pass, but just barely. The arm of the man who had fired at them stuck out from amidst the rubble, a rifle still defiantly gripped in his cold, dead hand. By fitting coincidence, their shadow caused a moonlit cross to fall across several rocks.

Young Thunder was missing beneath the rubble. The loss of this prized animal was going to break Slash's heart. Joe was glad he had gone with B.W. Safer for everyone to have him on the road, unaware.

Because the moonlight fell flush on Joe's face, the frontiersman backed away in case the dead man had accomplices. If so, they may not have met his fate.

There were no voices, no horses other than White Paint making a sound.

"I think we're safe for now," Joe said. "Their trail must lead northeast, where the mines are. He must've intended to block our way and pick us off."

"What do we do now?" she asked. "We can't both ride your horse for very long."

"We won't need to," Joe said. "I'm guessing the Rebels'll bring one right to us when their boy doesn't return. Gives us time to set up to meet them."

"We're going to just shoot them?" she asked. It was a question, not a judgment.

"Not if we can help it, though I trust 'em to do something stupid," Joe said.

"If we put them down, there will be less of them to pursue the stage."

Joe regarded her in the shadow of the boulder. Her face was without expression. "I like your logic but not your heart," he said. "Out here, a man is the law. He must be just."

"What does 'just' look like, then?"

"If we can, we'll just persuade 'em to dismount. Horseless, they won't be much of a threat against the stage."

"And while we're negotiating this surrender, their companions will set out after the stage."

"They may. They may already be on the road. That's something we can find out. Our aim right now is to cut down the odds."

Clarity pursed her lips thoughtfully, then asked, "Isn't that a little uncertain, as plans go?"

Joe continued to look at her. "I prefer little plans, little steps. What woulda been the point of having a big plan before the cliff came down? Out here, we do a fast dance, making up steps as we go. And right now, what we have to do is be ready when they get here."

Clarity nodded and stood, waving Joe away when he moved to assist her.

"I'm sorry," she said. "I'm just angry and frustrated." She drew her guns and used the heels of her palms to knock dirt from the holsters. "What exactly is the little plan?"

"Bait," Joe said. "We have to get to a place where they can see me clearly but not you. An open place, where they'll see just one horse."

"Did the man with the explosives climb the rock or start from up there?"

"There's a slope behind and he likely came up that, like the bushwhackers who attacked the coach," Joe said. "Foot of it is a short distance from the foothills. If that's where they are he might not've come on horseback. One less noisemaker for him to worry about. Horses get spooked at night."

"Then we go east."

Joe nodded. "East of the gulch this road curves around and forks. Part of it leads straight on to Arizona, the way your stage came in. The other leg intersects that slope I was talking about and goes up into the foothills, the way the ambusher probably didn't want us to go. We'll head up that trail a piece and reconnoiter."

Clarity was on her feet now, brushing herself off. It wasn't vanity but practicality. She didn't want dust getting into her eyes when she was lining up a shot.

"Do you think anyone from the station will come to investigate?" she asked.

"I don't think so," Joe replied. He moved away from the boulder to retrieve his horse. "They know I'll crack heads if they do."

The animal was reluctant to move and Joe didn't force it. He faced White Paint, spoke soothingly while caressing its neck, then backed the horse from the rock pile. The animal came willingly. Joe had always believed that there was a sacred bond between three animals: humans, horses, and dogs. When one was weak, the other gave it stren'th. When all were strong, there was nothing quite like it for survival and fellowship—even among humans. That kinship had never failed him. Not the way some human relationships had. His beloved wife Dolley used to say he was closer to their collies than to her when he was home. She was right, though he used to reassure her it didn't mean he loved them more.

"They're content just to be petted," he once told her. "Even when I ain't bathed."

"Just remember, Joe O'Malley," she had replied, "the dogs or horses licking your greasy fingers don't mean love *or* that you took a bath."

His late wife was not a romantic in that sense. Dolley was anvil-hard practical. She was the daughter of a Massachusetts sea captain who lost everything in a wreck. She was just nine at the time and had to go to work with her mother and older sister. They ended up cooking for some slob who tried to marry off the girls, then moved west to open a bean stand on the Mississippi. Grew their own till a flood wiped them out. They went farther west and both her mother and sister succumbed to disease before they reached Colorado. Dolley was just twelve, and survived working as a maid for a rancher.

Years later, that was where she met Joe.

Even when the sickness was eating her insides, she insisted on doing whatever she could because Sarah was young and pregnant and neither Joe nor Jackson had a mortal, foggy notion how to do things around the cabin where they lived at the time.

Except to patch leaks, fix the stove, or muck the outhouse, Joe and Jackson and also Slash still didn't know much about what went on inside the four walls of the station. Out here, however, they bowed to no masters.

Joe mounted carefully and, with equal tenderness toward the horse, he helped pull Clarity up behind him. There wasn't time to circle around the cliff. That meant riding through what remained of the gulch trail—past the dead horse, which would take some coaxing. The last thing they needed was for their remaining animal to panic.

The experienced frontiersman leaned forward, holding his left hand a few inches from the horse's eye to block the dusty rubble. If his palm got too close, that would upset the horse as well. But that is not the animal's only sense, and it smelled death. Joe was forced to put the horse into a side pass gait, angled away from the landslide, moving as though it were being blown sideways by a strong wind. When they made it through after a slow, cautious passage, Joe let the horse go in a slow gallop. Clarity held on tight to his waist. It was only after they reached the end of the gulch that he noticed where she'd been holding him. Each of her hands had been near his gun belt and one of the colts.

They continued to ride toward the northeast, turning north at the fork. The ground rose as it headed into the foothills. Joe did not stop until they had a clear view of the long, jagged expanse beyond. When they were well clear of the partly toppled cliff, Joe dismounted. He let Clarity have the saddle as he walked slowly ahead, watching for anyone coming at them from the area of the mines and caves.

He left the well-worn path and continued on for several minutes. Then he tied the horse behind a lone cottonwood. It would likely stand still there, unseen, grazing and motionless, unless there was shooting.

Clarity slid from the saddle as Joe drew the carbine from the holster. He gave it to the woman.

"I'm thinking you should stay to the west of the tree, where you won't be seen if anyone spots White Paint," Joe said. He looked around. "Just thinking about cover for you—"

"Won't need it," she said. "I'll lie flat, belly down."

Like that, it was decided.

"If they don't see anyone out here," Joe went on, "they're likely to go up to the slope to the top, not down through the gulch. I'm thinking I'll stay near you with the tree between. If they see one they won't see the other."

"And they can't come between us, a risk if you went back to the trail."

Joe did not know how Clarity knew he had been considering that. She was a woman of many talents. But like he'd learned long ago, you do something long enough you develop a sense for it, an instinct, like an animal. And other animals that are like you think and feel the same way.

Joe went on, "I'll call out to anyone who comes by and if they start shooting—"

"You're not going to make it there," Clarity said.

"Why not?" he asked.

"Listen."

It took Joe's older ears a few moments to catch up

to what the woman had heard. Hoofbeats, coming fast. At least two riders, maybe more.

"There!" Clarity said suddenly, pointing ahead in the moonlight.

Coming from the eastern leg of the road were three men, black ghosts against a pale plain.

They weren't the men Joe had been expecting.

They were the ones he had been fearing.

CHAPTER 8

Reverend Michaels had been sitting with the sleeping Dick Ocean, prayerfully reading from the O'Malley family Bible, when he heard the detonation. He leaped from the bedside so suddenly that Ocean woke from his liquor-aided rest.

"I'm hit!" he cried, rising from a dream.

The preacher remembered himself and turned to the wounded man. He rested a soft, practiced, comforting hand on the man's bare shoulder.

"You're safe," he consoled the shotgun rider. "You're fine."

Ocean eased swiftly back into sleep. Michaels, however, was not fine and returned to his newly agitated state. He hurried on quiet feet to the main room.

Michaels was a fussy man under normal circumstances. Back in Kentucky, he worried about his appearance whenever he walked among his parishioners. He carefully inspected utensils for cleanliness, drinking water for bugs and particles, his fingernails for dirt.

During the ride on the stagecoach, many of those

concerns were not discarded. They were simply transferred, like a detailed letter from home, to something else. In this case, it was vengeful Roche family members or friends. He worried that they were already pursuing Clarity on the next stage or on horseback with a posse.

Now he fretted about what might have happened to her in the field. Hearing the explosion, he went out to the main room where he found Jackson and B.W. just returning to the station.

"Do you think my sister is all right?" he asked with a catch in his voice.

The parson's question was as heartfelt as it was impossible to answer.

"She's with my pa," Jackson replied. "I'm still trying to—"

"And he's with her," B.W. interrupted. "Together out there it's like it says in Proverbs, 'Iron sharpeneth iron.'"

Michaels was not at the moment consoled even by the Word itself.

"But even they might not be able to protect one another from— What *was* that?" Michaels asked.

"I was about to say I don't know," Jackson went on.

"Powder, most likely," B.W. replied. "Like for blasting mines, which they used to have a lot of out here."

"And the gunshots?" the preacher said. "Those *were* shots, yes?"

"Sounded like 'em," Jackson replied. "And just as likely they came from Pa or Clarity. If something happened to them in that blast, no one woulda been firing at them."

"I suppose that's true," Michaels said without calming.

Jackson walked over to him not to coddle but to rouse.

"Look, shooting all around the target don't help us," Jackson said. "Our job, right now, is to put you folks on the stage, get it rolling, and keep the station secure. My boy is watching the north end and I'll hear anyone riding from the south. Now, the horses are hitched and it's time to get the rest of you moving."

"Right now, we're frogs in a small pond," B.W. added. "Gotta break it up, mebbe divide the enemy."

"I see," Michaels said. "Of course."

"I'll pick up Slash on the way out," B.W. told Jackson. "Have him watch the road ahead till the last instant."

"I'll need just a minute to finish packing your supplies," Sarah said to the Whip.

The woman had pulled a canvas bag from its pegboard in the kitchen. She was filling it with clothes, tobacco, and jerky. She also took his water skin from where it hung near the back door. Gert had already filled it with well water. The mistress of Whip Station hefted it, looking for punctures it might have suffered during the gunfight. There were none.

Jackson turned back to the front door. "Malibu?"

The Indian came over.

"Would you relieve Slash out back when the stage pulls out?" he asked. "We'll need eyes there."

"Yes," Malibu replied.

Sisquoc had already gone out front to keep watch at the entrance. The two veteran plainsmen had joined the cavalry in 1858, when they were in their late twenties and wanting a more secure life for their widowed mothers and new wives. All four women lived together in a hut the Indians owned outside of Fort Mason.

It was unlikely that any living thing could approach the station without being seen or heard.

When the Indian had gone, Fletcher Small rose once more from the table, slapping his hands on the surface to signify that he was finished here and ready to depart. He had been eating bread from Clarity's plate, watching the preparations with keen attention, making notes—especially of what was said.

"This is more of a story than I could have dreamed of," he enthused. No one had been waiting for his assessment and no one stopped what they were doing to acknowledge it. That did not deter him from continuing. "It's like something out of *Beadle's Dime Novels*—but real. *Real.*"

"You have published with them?" Gert asked.

"Three times," he answered proudly.

"Under your name?"

"One must not mix flame and kindling," he replied. "My journalistic name must be pure." He shook his head. "Even so, the truth is not always entirely credible. I wonder if anyone will even believe it."

"*I* wonder if you'll live to write it," Gert said as she began clearing the table. That was more than just housekeeping; it was tactical. In an attack, turned on its side, the heavy oak table afforded protection from gunfire and arrows. Metal plates, cups, forks, and knives could cause you to slip in the dark.

The preacher turned at her pronouncement.

"Do you really think we're in jeopardy? Should we be staying here?"

"Anyone who comes west is in danger," Small observed.

"You are in no more danger here than back east," Gert said, "where there are fires and riots and industrial smoke in your lungs."

"I've covered riots," Small noted. He added provocatively, "Cowards and anarchists mostly."

"Let's pay attention to what we're doing," Jackson cautioned.

Gert leaned near the reporter who snickered as he walked by. "And they say the Indians are uneducated," she said very quietly.

"I've never uttered a sentiment like that," he replied without looking at her. "Not in a story, anyway."

Jackson and B.W. went out to the well to fill the rest of the water pouches. The stagecoach carried one for every two people. Though they refilled at every stop, passengers often carried their own in case of mishap. Butterfield was not required to provide more than two cups of water for each person between stops while in transit.

After swapping places with Malibu, Slash returned to the station to begin arming himself for the journey. He worked silently, like the kind of man his mother was not accustomed to seeing in her boy. In addition to a full deerskin, he would need extra ammunition for his carbine and Remington revolver. He wore the gun on his left side for a cross-handed draw. In addition to the sheathed Bowie knife on his right hip, he strapped a long-blade Green River knife to the inside of his left thigh. His grandfather had carried the knife for years and there were times that called for two-fisted knife fighting. That was the kind of blade Slash liked best, especially against a bear or a renegade Indian.

"You want my rabbit skin?" Gert asked her brother.

Sarah was standing nearby. "Why would he want that musty old thing?"

"For luck." Gert grinned.

"I think I'll be okay," her brother replied.

B.W. put the water pouches on the hooks inside the coach and outside the driver's box. The cool night wind was picking up and he left the windows down. The passengers could argue among one another whether stuffy heat or invasive dust was more troublesome. They usually reached a compromise: windows open, curtains drawn.

The driver returned to the station, stood before the two men from the East.

"Reverend, Mr. Small—if the two of you would board?"

The men did not hesitate, the preacher propelled by nervous energy, the reporter with the eagerness of a reader wanting to see how a tale ended up. As they left, B.W. went over to the shaman. The Serrano had settled his big form in a rocking chair, which he seemed to enjoy.

"We'll be leaving now, Your Eminence," B.W. said with deference. It was the first time he had addressed the man and wasn't sure what else to call him or how to say it.

Tuchahu nodded once. He used his moccasins to

halt the movement of the chair. Then, with his hands firmly gripping the arm rests—as though the chair had a spirit of its own, one whose hands he was shaking—he pushed off the seat and stood. He looked at Sarah and smiled.

"Thank . . . you," he said in a gravelly voice.

"I'm glad you liked it." She smiled back. "It is *my* Mr. O'Malley's favorite chair as well."

Retrieving his headdress from the small wooden table beside the seat, the Indian bowed slightly to all of his hosts and then preceded B.W. out the door.

The two joined the others by the stagecoach. B.W. opened the door.

"I cannot say I will mind the added leg room," Small remarked as he climbed in.

"Or the night air," the priest said, foreshadowing a debate as he followed him in.

The shaman was the last to enter, sitting across from the two men, in the center. He was facing the front of the coach.

B.W. shut the door behind him and exhaled. Slash approached from the station, looking every inch a picture-book knight with wood and metal projections from weapons along his sides and under his armpits.

"You ever had a situation like this?" Slash asked as they climbed into the driver's box.

"Never like this," he answered. "Run from Injuns a couple times. Once they wanted our horses but Dick chased 'em off. Second occasion they was just having fun, I think—young braves, probably out to prove themselves. Both times, the Red Man's blood was shed."

"Day or night?" Slash asked.

"The youngsters came at night," B.W. replied as he climbed aboard. "Their appaloosas actually ran one into t'other in the darkness. Just glad o' one thing."

"What's that?"

"We got a split spoke," he said. "Less weight on it, the better."

Slash looked toward the rear of the stagecoach. He had considered riding in the back, covering their rear. He dismissed the idea because he would be a penned bull there, among the luggage and letters—one shot and they'd know where to shoot back.

Slash adjusted his knives so they weren't sticking straight down. He made sure his guns and rifles were in ready reach.

"We have a battle plan when we move out?" the young man asked.

"Prayer is good," B.W. replied.

"I'm saving all I got for my grandpa," Slash said, looking out at the black eastern sky. There appeared to be a haze across it, most likely dust, not mist. "I'm still worried about whatever happened out there."

"Gonna need your full attention here," B.W. reminded him.

"It's yours," Slash assured him.

B.W. nodded and took up the reins. He saw Jackson and his wife watching from the door and he threw them a grateful salute. Maybe they, too, were sending prayers eastward.

Then, with a chucking sound deep in his full, grizzled cheek, the Whip urged the team toward the entrance.

* * *

Nearly two miles away, though washed by the same caressing wind, Joe O'Malley and Clarity Michaels were lying on their bellies. Joe had moved the horse behind a boulder and joined the woman who was watching the riders over the carbine. He was to her right and had his right hand full of Colt, lying flat beside his head.

"They're not white men," Joe said in a voice barely a whisper. "Looks like they got blankets, not saddles— and they're riding forward, holding reins or manes. Can't be sure."

"Hostiles?" Clarity asked in the same barely audible tone.

"Likely Apache this time of day, so likely yes," Joe responded.

"Will they see us?"

"Apaches? They can probably see us, smell us, and hear what we're saying. It's not just from living in the wild for generations. All their animal spirits help them."

"I thought you didn't believe that?"

"Doesn't matter," he said. "They do. Now don't do anything unless I say. Don't even move if they come running at us. That'll be to see what we're made of."

Clarity reflected for a moment, then asked, "What *are* we made of?"

"Faith and patience," he replied. "They run us over, they fall. They know it and now you do. Tumble like that can kill a man."

"Won't benefit me much, either," she noted.

Despite the urgency in the moment, Joe smiled. He liked this woman very much. Cool in the face of peril the way his Dolley used to be.

"I was wrong to oppose your being out here," he admitted.

"If that's the last thing I hear, I'm grateful," she answered.

"It won't be if you hush now," he said as the Indians neared.

Joe and Clarity fell silent as they could not only see the horses and riders but could feel their approach. The ground rumbled under their bellies, and Joe had an odd memory just then of Dolley once telling little Jackson that thunder came when God spanked the clouds for being dark and brooding. If that was true, who would she have said sent the rumbling of the Apaches?

He smiled again—with likely hostile Indians not twenty, thirty yards distant.

Suddenly, Joe heard a shout in Apache and the three riders pulled hard to a stop. Maybe they smelled the two or heard them, but it was the moonlight must have given away their location. Joe lay a reassuring, cautioning hand on Clarity's arm.

"They spotted us," Joe said. "I'm gonna stand."

"I'm going to cover you," she replied firmly.

Joe was feeling his age a little when he got to his feet after lying flat. He had wrenched around more than he realized back at the gulch. His body, however, had kept track of every twist and start.

He holstered his revolver slowly, exaggerating the action so the Indians could see. Then he held up both hands as he stood. Joe did not know these men, whose faces were in shadow. He had not expected to. If they came here at all, it was to hunt or harass the stagecoach. Maybe Slash knew them or had seen them, but Joe did not have much to do with any Apaches. Not since his days as a scout and hunter.

These men were dressed in deerskin, no war paint, which was a good sign.

Only one of them carried a bow and quiver. The others had rifles. All carried small pouches that would contain necessities like flint for a fire and dried strips of rabbit or elk, perhaps nuts. They might have been headed for a powwow with another tribe or on a hunting expedition for nocturnal beasts.

"*Da'anzho,*" Joe said, using one of the few words he knew in Western Apache—"Hello."

After a moment, the Indian in the center moved his feisty animal forward several steps. The other Indians stayed where they were. The brave ignored the woman.

"Hello," the Apache said in deep-throated English. He gestured past Joe, toward the gulch. "You?"

"Not me," Joe replied. "A Rebel. He tried to kill us."

"Maybe same who attack settlement?"

"I'm sorry?" Joe said.

"We hunt—men in masks come, take weapons, leave," the Indian said. "We search."

"Could be the same men," Joe said. "I don't know why they'd be looking to rob you, though. Maybe same as Apache who go to settlers' homes, take food and livestock."

"This *our* land, those belong to *us*," the Apache replied.

"Maybe these Rebels don't agree with that thinking," Joe suggested.

"Rebel war over," the Apache replied with a horizontal sweep of one arm.

"That's another story," Joe said. "War not over for some Rebels. They tried to kidnap shaman."

"Kid-nap?"

"Take. Steal," Joe said, closing his fist.

"Who shaman?"

"Serrano. Name Tuchahu."

"Serrano," the Apache snorted. He thumped his chest. "All medicine . . . no man."

It wasn't bad for an Indian attempt at humor.

Joe shrugged. "Rebels attacked stage to take Tuchahu. Two Indian agents help them. My job— protect."

"We see your camp, we know your job," the Indian said with a trace of annoyance. Within this man's living memory, there had been no stagecoach, no stations. "I see boy." He made a cutting gesture in both directions, diagonally. "Yours?"

"Grandson," Joe explained. "Slash is his name."

"Slash," the Indian repeated. He pointed. "You?"

"My name is Joe."

The Indian touched his chest again. "My name Baishan. Mean knife."

"You are knife, my grandson's name means 'cutting with knife.'" Joe linked his hands before his chest. "Maybe you and Slash meet."

"I win."

Joe shook his head. "Not to fight. As friends."

The Indian swept that idea away with a sideward movement of his hand across his chest. Turning on the back of the horse, he faced his companions. By showing Joe his back, he was signaling that he trusted the man. He still ignored the woman—and her leveled carbine.

The Indian conferred quietly with the two Apaches. Joe did not catch any of it. After a moment, Baishan turned back.

"Where Rebels?" the Apache asked.

"I don't know," Joe said. "We lost a horse. We lost time. We came here to find trail."

The Apache dismounted, rolled his shoulders to establish his ownership of the ground where he was about to tread. Joe knew that gesture well enough from the days when he insisted on taking a trail that passed through Indian hunting grounds.

The Indian walked toward him. But only a step. He made a point of planting both feet.

"It's you," Joe said.

"What?"

"Lower your gun," Joe advised Clarity. "We are making peace."

"That seems like surrender to me."

"Lower that carbine or I will *take* it," Joe said harshly.

Reluctantly, Clarity obliged.

"Now set it on the ground in front of you, stock first," Joe advised.

Clarity did that, too. "Can I get up?" she asked angrily. "I don't like groveling."

"What you like or dislike was not a condition for you coming along," Joe pointed out. While he spoke, he walked slowly toward her. He extended his left hand toward the woman. "Take it."

Clarity reached up and he helped her stand. She brushed herself off.

"Now take a step back," Joe said.

The woman huffed but did as Joe instructed. When

she had done so, Baishan resumed coming forward. The Apache picked up the woman's carbine and considered it for a moment. Joe knew that if the Indian kept the gun, it would mean a fight. Clarity had surrendered the gun. If Joe did the same, it would mean he was a woman.

The moon was behind the Indian. He held the rifle close and examined it in the moonlight with sharp, knowing eyes. He turned to pass it to the Apache to his right, the one wearing a quiver. Both had a hand on it.

"No!" Joe barked.

The Indian did not stop what he was doing and Joe moved toward him. In an instant, the third Indian trained a rifle on him. Joe looked at the gun pointed at his chest. With frontier-trained reflexes, and without hesitation, Joe jumped forward and grabbed the barrel hard, pulling it toward his right side. The Indian was surprised and so was his horse, which whinnied and shied. The Apache released the gun to tend to his horse.

Joe filled both hands with rifle and pointed it at the Indian who had been set to receive Clarity's carbine. The mounted Apache froze.

Baishan shouted something in his own tongue, cowing his companion, then strode angrily toward Joe. The frontiersman leaped back and turned the rifle not toward Baishan but at the head of Baishan's horse.

The Apache stopped.

"Yeah," Joe sneered. "You'd've walked your own puffed red chest straight into this barrel, show me how brave you are. But trade your horse for my gun? You'd be shamed among your pals."

Clarity watched the three Indians with growing concern. Her hands were at her sides. She wondered if the Apaches saw—or cared—that they were just inches from her six-shooters. If they intended for her to be the next pawn in this game, she didn't care what Joe said or did. She'd shoot these savages—the braves on the end in one salvo, then two bullets into Baishan's heart.

Baishan and the other Apache still had one hand each on Clarity's carbine. After a stretch that seemed to last longer than the trip from St. Louis, but was only seconds, the leader wrenched the carbine from his companion and thrust it toward Joe, barrel up. Joe immediately turned his own weapon from the horse, also pointed toward the night sky. If he aimed down after the Indian aimed up, that, too, would seem like submission. They traded weapons and the confrontation was over.

"We hear shots," the Apache continued as if nothing had transpired.

Joe jerked a thumb toward the gulch. "The one who fired—he cannot speak," Joe said, dragging a thumb down through his heart, indicating he was dead.

"He speak," Baishan insisted, adding, "show."

CHAPTER 9

"What does he mean, 'He speak'?" Clarity asked. "Is he going to try and talk to the spirit of the dead man?"

Joe and the woman had moved behind the cotton-wood where White Paint had been tethered. The man took his time unknotting the reins. He had a concern he wanted to think through.

"No," Joe advised her as he tugged at the leather. "At least, I don't think so. I believe he means to look for clues. Indians see things that white men don't. Even white men like me."

"What does it mean if they help you?" Clarity asked.

He smiled crookedly. "You're smart," Joe said. "That's just what was concerning me. You don't want to be in an Indian's debt. I also don't want to help him massacre the Rebs and leave the road clear for him to go after the Serrano for his own bragging reasons."

They mounted, Joe first. He returned the carbine to its saddle holster. The Apaches waited for him to start out, then followed behind several paces. That, too, was a show of superiority. Joe was a scout, like a dog. He was not a warrior. That particular distinction wasn't important to Joe, who'd known many great scouts in his time. That included the great William Clark, partner of Meriwether Lewis, who he met in St. Louis about twenty-seven, twenty-eight years ago. Joe let the insult pass.

"Do you think that's why this man is suddenly being cooperative?" Clarity asked, leaning close to Joe's ear so the Indians wouldn't hear. "To capture the shaman?"

"That, or rescue him," Joe said. "You help another tribe like that, especially saving a big medicine, they are in your debt."

"Only one of them is carrying a bow and arrow," Clarity said. "Why?"

"These make noise," he said, patting his sidearm.

"Of course," Clarity said. She thought for a moment. "All of what just happened between you two. That was—like a totem, yes? Whoever's head places the highest is the most important?"

"That's a pretty comparison," Joe said. "Baishan—he feels he won the fight back there. So his head is higher."

Clarity was openly surprised. "How does he figure that?"

"In his mind, he traded a gun for a horse," Joe answered. "That's a very good deal to him."

"Even though he ended up back where he started."

"Not quite," Joe said. "He learned something about the situation, about my ways, about the Rebels. He learned enough to make him want to find out more. The Apache still consider these to be their lands, and anything that happens out here affects his people."

"Can we afford to spend this time indulging him

instead of chasing the Rebels or preparing for them to come after us?"

"They come for us, the Rebels, these are the boys you want nearby," Joe said. "As for the rest, I'm a tracker but these fellas—this land flows through their veins. They see and hear and smell things we might miss. Plus, their ancestors lived here and—you asked about spirits. Many Indians believe they can communicate with them. Maybe. Considering how little we got, it can't hurt."

"You're more trusting than I am," Clarity replied.

"Of what? These men or their skills?"

"Both," she answered.

"Is that just Injuns or men in general?"

She thought for a moment. "Both," she replied.

"That include your brother?"

"No," she said without hesitation. "He's different. It's a habit of his. Merritt has looked out for me since we were kids."

"I'm guessing he's not the one who taught you to shoot like you do."

"Learning how to shoot was a necessity of living in Murray, Kentucky," she said.

"Hunting?"

"Partly that," she said. "A flash flood at the family farm took our parents and all our possessions. Save one."

"What was that?" Joe asked.

"My name."

"I was wondering about that," Joe said. "Uncommon."

"It was a gift from my mother," she said. "A wish, a blessing. A quality she hoped would always be with me."

"Sounds like it worked."

"Very much so," Clarity said. "I feel, in a way, that my mother is always with me, saying it softly in my ear."

"But you were saying—?"

"Yes," she said. "Merritt worked for the church, sweeping and cleaning at first, and I provided the food. It was a hard life but we were happy. My brother was ordained—and then the War came."

"Kentucky was neutral," Joe said. "You?"

"We did not support the secessionists and Murray was in a Confederate stronghold, maybe the strongest still in the Union," she said. "I discovered that the man I was engaged to marry, a gunsmith, Billy Roche, was providing weapons to the Yankees. At the end of the struggle he wanted me to flee west with him. I refused."

"Might I ask why?"

"I decided that being a spinster in my home was better than being with a man I didn't really love away from my home," she said. "But Billy—he liked the idea of having a wife who knew guns and could help him set up a new business somewhere out Pacific way. He tried to force me."

"So there was this accident," Joe said.

"There was," Clarity replied. "With one of his new guns. And the joke is, of course, I ended up going west."

"At least it's with a man you care about, and who cares about you."

"Yes," she said. "Though that is not the same thing, of course."

The party reached the gulch and the landslide that had spilled just beyond it. The Indians dismounted and left their horses at the eastern edge of the rocks.

There was only a sliver of moonlight coming from over the blown-off top of the cliff.

The Indians chattered among themselves, pointing, apparently discussing the damage caused by the powder.

"Where Rebel?" the leader finally asked.

In response, Joe drew and fired from the hip. The Indians started at the suddenness of his movement as the shot pinged off a rock just over halfway across.

"He's over there," Joe said, holstering his weapon before the Indians could swing their own guns around.

The Apaches relaxed and Clarity grinned with understanding. Joe O'Malley had just demonstrated to the Indians that this lead dog had teeth. Teeth that *could* have bitten them.

The two Apaches who had been riding on either side of the leader moved forward in the dark. Their leather moccasins were like a second skin, feeling their way over the rounded or jagged surfaces of exploded rock. As they moved they also listened to what was happening above them, making sure their passage or hidden cracks were not disturbing rocks that had not yet fallen.

When they reached the spot that bore Joe's fresh bullet scar, the Apaches saw the arm and gun jutting from the rubble. The rocks around the dead man were too large to move.

The two Indians spoke—to each other, Joe assumed, not a ghost. When they were finished, one of them walked to the part of the path that was still clear. The other drew his knife. While the first Apache gathered dry brush and pulled a flint from the medicine pouch he carried, the other squatted and casually cut off the dead man's arm.

Clarity watched with fascination.

"You have to admire their efficiency," she remarked.

"What they are is heartless savages who'd just as soon do that to a live man," Joe responded. "Or woman," he added.

"Your granddaughter does not seem to feel at risk. She seemed to have an affinity for the shaman."

"She has her own way of looking at Injuns," Joe admitted. "She fawns on them like they're all wiser and holier than your brother, say. We don't share those opinions."

The two fell silent as they watched the proceedings. The severed arm did not bleed very much. The skin was bluish white, a combination of death and lit by the moon. Joe imagined that most of the man's blood was on the underside of the rocks. The Apache brought the limb to the fire that the other Indian had started. He looked it over. He sniffed it, tasted a fingertip as if he were sucking ants from a reed, then shook the arm into the flames. There were faint, short-lived sparkles in the air above the fire.

The Apache was done with the arm and dropped it to the ground. While the other brave doused the fire, his companion spoke to the leader. Then Baishan regarded Joe.

"Red metal," the Apache announced.

"Copper," Joe said. "From one of the abandoned mines, as I figgered."

"How many mines are there?" Clarity asked.

"At least a half dozen scattered through the foothills," Joe informed her.

"One path," Baishan said. "All."

It took a moment for Clarity to understand his meaning. "He's saying the Rebels can only leave by a single path, regardless of where they are?"

"If their intent is to meet up with the stage, yeah," Joe answered. "To escape, which I don't think they'll do, there are plenty of ways to go."

"Right," she said. "They want the shaman."

"No," Joe said. "They must really *need* the shaman. Otherwise, after you plucked their feathers, they would've gathered their things and ridden east. They wouldn't have bothered bringing a hill down on us."

Joe approached the Indians, who were all standing by the horses now, talking among themselves. The moon had inched above the ravaged cliff and cast a ghostly light on the trio.

"We are going west," Joe said, pointing. "Get a new horse." He grabbed his own wrist. "The Rebels must be stopped."

Baishan regarded the frontiersman. "Serrano on coach?"

Joe stiffened a little. He didn't like the question or the way it sounded—more like a statement than a query. The belittling way the Apache had spoken of the shaman and his people earlier did not match his sudden interest.

Joe made a point of hooking his thumbs in his gun belt, not far from the revolvers. It wasn't threatening. Yet.

"Why does Baishan ask?"

The Apache ignored Joe's move and dragged a finger across his closed lips.

"He's done talking," Joe told Clarity.

The Indian had already turned his back on Joe and moved without haste toward his horse. That was not a challenge to shoot him in the back. It meant he was finished with Joe. The frontiersman continued to stand in a casual but ready posture though he did not expect the other two Indians to attack.

He was correct. The three mounted swiftly and rode off the way they had come. The drumming of their hooves was swallowed by the wall of tumbled rock.

"I do not understand what just happened," Clarity said.

"One of two things," her companion informed her. "Either they are going after the Rebels or they are going after the shaman."

"Why?"

"I couldn't say," Joe told her. "No white man knows why Apaches do what they do. But we better get you another horse and go after the stage. That's the only thing I care about."

"What if we meet them on the road, with the same intention."

Joe answered, "We defend what's ours. And for now, the passengers are ours."

Joe went over to White Paint and mounted, offered her his hand. A moment later they were galloping back toward the station.

A quiet had settled over the copper mine after the detonation and subsequent gunfire. Marcus, the man who was scheduled to relieve Silas, had waited a minute, listening, before he approached Kennedy and Hathaway. Both of the Easterners were at the mouth of the mine, listening.

"I should go out," Marcus said. "Find out what happened."

"No," Kennedy said. "Either Silas took care of this his own way or Silas got taken care of."

Dr. Peterson had picked up a plate of cold beans, took a mouthful. He set the dish down and ambled over to the three men.

"We won't have been the only ones who heard that," he pointed out. "There are the folks at the Whip Station or possibly Apaches. Maybe a night patrol from Fort Yuma or Fort Mason."

"Are you suggesting we go out and risk meeting any of them?" Kennedy asked.

"No, sir. I'm saying we should maybe set out after the reason we came here," Peterson said. "To secure the medicine man."

"That ain't gonna tell us what happened to Silas," Marcus snapped at the medic. He turned back to Kennedy. "I fought shoulder to shoulder with him fer four years. I'm going out."

"You fought with everyone here, other than us," Kennedy barked. "If those gunshots weren't from Silas, I can't afford to have you dead."

"Or to lead an enemy back here," Hathaway said.

Marcus made a sound to show that he didn't like that option. But he also didn't have a more suitable response. He huffed unhappily, turned, and stalked back to the rear of the mine.

"Marcus," Peterson said, "we could probably do

with someone watching the foothills from higher ground."

The former Confederate considered that, then turned back toward the front of the cave. "You got any objections, Kennedy?"

"Not to that," the leader replied.

Marcus took one of the rifles and shouldered past Kennedy and Hathaway, making sure to bump into them both. The two men let it pass. When you ally yourself with bitter, vengeful soldiers, it's not just one enemy they're angry at. It's anyone who tells them "no."

The Rebel climbed the small rocks that had been dumped outside the mine years before and made his way to a ledge some thirty feet above. He sat there like a statue, indistinguishable in his tattered gray jacket from the surrounding rock.

Kennedy turned to the other men and suggested they arm themselves in case something had gone wrong and someone somehow figured out where Silas had come from.

Hathaway and Kennedy resumed listening. The former leaned close.

"Y'know, I don't disagree with the doc," Hathaway said. "What *about* the mission? The stage'll be heading back out if it hasn't left already."

"I know," Kennedy replied. "But it will also make a stop in the morning. Might be better to try and catch it in the light of dawn than to set out in the dark."

Tod Crane, the injured man, propped himself on an elbow. His friend, Dan Ridgewood, gently tried to urge him back.

"I'll be okay," Crane said. "I'm ready to ride now!"

"No, you're not," Peterson told him.

"Doc, I'm done surrendering!"

"A lovely sentiment," Peterson said dryly.

"Doc's right," Kennedy told him. "But if you take ill on the trail, then someone has to stay with you."

"When, then?" Crane demanded.

The doctor looked at the wounded man. "Tomorrow afternoon at the earliest, and not at a gallop that'll pop the wound wide open."

"Sidesaddle, too?" Crane said. He lay back, once again urged by Ridgewood.

Kennedy sighed. They were children, all of them.

"I swear," Kennedy quietly told his companion. "When this is over I will resign before I work with Southern guns again."

"Don't worry," Hathaway whispered. "When this is done there will be no need for us to come back. And your stool at Ebbitt's place will still be there."

Kennedy smiled lightly. Hathaway was referring to Bill Ebbitt's bar on the edge of Chinatown. Kennedy had been a patron since 1856, when he was thirty years old and relocated from Philadelphia to Washington. He took a room at Ebbitt's new boardinghouse and was the bar's first customer.

"That alone is reason to right now," Kennedy said. "Sooner this is done, sooner I get back."

There was a distant clopping that drew the attention of both men to the east. They squinted into the moonlit expanse and saw the movement of three horses pushing westward, hard.

"Now what?" Kennedy wondered aloud.

A rain of pebbles announced Marcus scrabbling back down the rocks. "Injuns," he said in a low, breathless voice.

"Yeah," Hathaway said, squinting ahead. "They're not headed this way. But they are in a hurry."

"Get the horses," Kennedy decided, addressing no one in particular. No one moved. Anger rising, he turned and shouted into the mine. "*Get the horses!*"

"What is it?" Peterson asked, rising with his plate.

"Apache, most likely, and in a hurry," Kennedy said.

"Maybe they got to Silas," Marcus said.

"He'll have to take care of himself, if he's alive," Kennedy said, moving toward the stable area. "Those renegades may be trying to pick off our quarry!"

CHAPTER 10

Taking the well-worn stage path but riding the flat ground between the deep wheel ridges, Joe and Clarity galloped into the entrance of the station. For all the times Joe had come this way over the years, this was the first in which he felt a sense of dread purpose. He was glad that, just now, Slash wasn't present. The death of Young Thunder would have set him on a course of vengeance.

Not that Joe felt much differently. As he rode, he considered the many ways these Rebels had crossed the lines of honor and consideration. By their actions they had endangered the very civilization the O'Malleys and others were attempting to establish out here.

Which got Joe O'Malley wondering if that was in fact their purpose. He couldn't think of any other.

They were met halfway to the station by his son and by Sisquoc, who slid from one of the boulders and followed the horse in.

"Thank God you're okay," Jackson said as his father reined. The younger O'Malley looked behind his father. "Thunder?"

"Kilt," Joe replied, his voice somber.

As he helped Clarity down, Joe explained what had happened.

"I'm glad Slash isn't here," Jackson said.

"I was thinking that," Joe replied. "Daylight, it'll probably be safe enough here to ride out and get the saddle. How long since the stage left?"

"About a quarter-hour," Jackson answered.

"We have to catch it," Joe said, grabbing his water pouch and carbine from the saddle.

"Why?"

Joe offered Clarity a drink, then took one himself. "Apaches seem as interested in the medicine man as the Rebels."

While Jackson led White Paint to the stable, Sisquoc remarked, "Apache are not friends of the Serrano."

"I know," Joe said as he headed for the station to see his daughter-in-law and granddaughter and refill the skin. "I don't mind if the Rebs and Apache kill each other, but I don't want Slash to have to kill one of our Indian neighbors and I don't want Butterfield unhappy."

"What do you plan to do?" the Mission Indian asked, walking beside Joe as Clarity followed.

"Not sure," Joe admitted.

Sisquoc turned and hurried back to the front entrance. He didn't trust Apaches and would not have been surprised had they doubled back to make sure Joe O'Malley didn't get involved with their pursuit of the stage.

Sarah and Gert met Joe and Clarity at the door. Both were relieved to see Joe and he hugged them tightly in turn. The frontiersman left the door open when he entered. Though a closed door offered protection, it also afforded an opportunity for someone to sneak up on them.

"Pa, I'm so glad—" Sarah blurted, then wept as she hugged him tight. "We didn't know if you were hurt—what we should do!"

"You did the right thing," Joe assured her, touching her damp cheek as he wriggled free. He embraced Gert briefly in his strong arms, then looked at her in the moonlight. "We'll have to talk about Apache ways when I get back."

"I want to hear it all." She smiled.

"Jackson'll say what I told him, but now we have to hurry." He gave Gert the deerskin. "We need supplies for four days, two sacks."

The women moved quickly toward the kitchen while Joe gathered ammunition. He stuffed the cartridges into pockets, to be transferred to their saddlebags when they left. While he did that, Clarity went to the washing basin to splash the dust from her eyes. The woman had learned, lying on her belly, waiting an hour or more for a morning deer, never to let dirt or eyelashes cost her a clean shot. The "little scoundrels," as she called them, could lie in wait on the forehead, temples, or eyelids. Today, by the time she had faced the Apaches, Clarity was already trying to blink out sharp, painful grains.

Sarah was nearby, knotting the ropes atop the two grips. She stole a look at the woman. Clarity did not know it, but the wide, oak bowl was one of the oldest possessions in the O'Malley household. Probably older than the person using it. Her father-in-law had carved it over forty years ago. He carried it with him wherever he went, Dolley had told her.

"*A little touch of civilization and home,*" her mother-in-law had said. "*It reminded him of his new wife and the other new wives he was helping to welcome west.*"

Clarity left to visit the privy. Looking out the back window, Sarah took a moment to remember her mother-in-law. Just outside was another of the grand old O'Malley homesteading items—the washboard and wooden tub with its long maiden-stick plunger. She couldn't see it in the dark but she could hear the old boards of the tub creaking slightly in the wind. Joe had made that, too, made it so well it had served three generations. Only the clothesline strung between the house and the maple tree was new. Sarah could still see Jackson's mother putting the rain-wrinkled or dirt-stiffened garments into the basin, plunging them clean with her strong grip and tireless arm, or scrubbing them on the board to remove burrs or soap or blood or even the guts of a snake that splattered because it had to be shot.

A tear formed. Then another followed it down her right cheek. God, how she missed Dolley, remembering how the woman had protected her from the dangers around them. Home was sanctuary. And Joe—bless him—had never given up the sacred task of protecting it for everyone who crossed the mountains and rivers to be here.

"You almost ready?" Joe asked. He came over, rattling with shells in his pockets as he walked. He stopped to settle them lest Apaches or Rebels hear him, too.

"Done," she said. "I still don't like this, Pa."

"You never do when I go afar."

"This is different," she said. "This is an army of Confederates who aren't protecting anything like the Indians or Mexicans. They're out for revenge."

"That makes them over-eager and sloppy," Joe said. "We seen that twice now."

"The Indians won't be," she said as she handed him the two lumpy canvas bags. "Slash won't even suspect that they're coming, will he?"

"Not as such, but there're Indians other than Apache out there and he'll be watching," Joe assured her. "B.W. also. He'll be alert. Always is, for Injuns."

"The Confederates surprised B.W. *and* Mr. Ocean," she pointed out. "And that was in daylight."

"That was an ambush from on high, set up ahead of their coming," Joe pointed out. "Can't happen here. It's mostly open trail they'll be on tonight."

"But after that, at the next station—?"

"We'll pass 'em there, too, and ride ahead."

"Then you'll be in danger," Sarah said quietly.

Joe frowned a little. "What's got you in this state? I've been out there in dangerous situations many a time."

"I know." She smiled, more tears falling. "I know. I just hope—well, I hope you come back so you can make me that second washbasin we need, the one you're always threatening to carve me. We're a growing business, you know."

Joe smiled and took her hand in his. "You spoilt my surprise," he said.

Sarah looked up at his dark face. "Surprise?"

"In the hayloft . . . almost done."

She grinned. "The knife in the hayloft—the one that cut Slash?"

"I didn't think anybody'd be going up there," Joe said in a boyish, bashful tone. He kissed her forehead. "I expect us all to be around for many more years, Sarah, but nothing is guaranteed, you know that. One thing they got out there, though, is B.W.'s mighty belief in God looking over them. I have to believe the shot that got Dick also got the attention of the Almighty. I pray that He or Dolley or both is watching all of us, even those who don't practice their faith quite so strong."

Sarah smiled bravely as she took the lantern from the hook over the table and left—to see to Dick Ocean, she said. Joe could hear him snoring all the way out here. He suspected his daughter-in-law also wanted to say a silent prayer. Sarah liked to talk to God in private, just like Dolley did.

Not like my granddaughter, he thought as she cleaned up bits of glass they'd missed before. He had seen her once when she went out at dawn, behind the stable, and lit fungus on fire. Then she sat beside it, whispering to heathen spirits over the fumes. Pechanga magic. He heard that in some colonies, years ago, that kind of thing got women hanged or burned alive. Those rituals hadn't done the Indians any good and he just couldn't understand why she bothered. Or how she had the time. When he was young, when Jackson was a boy, they didn't have time for hocus-pocus and woolgathering.

Joe set the grips on the table. Before leaving, he helped himself to some of the nearly burned coffee hanging over the fire. He actually liked it that way.

Thinking back to his youth, it reminded him of the plains when he was first starting out. He never did get the knack for cooking it right, or else he got distracted by noises that could have been animals, could have been Indians. More often than not he left it boiling for too long. This taste and those days were inseparable, even separated by more than half a century.

While downing the last of the hot, black cup Joe heard the clops of the horses. He took a moment to splash the sleep from his wizened eyes, then fetched the canvas bags and went out. His days usually ran from sunup to sundown, and this day had not only been long, it had been particularly tiring. It had been a while since he had taken a night ride, let alone two. They required a certain kind of alertness and he was eager for the coffee to fire him up.

Clarity strode around the station as if she'd just had a long, rejuvenating nap. They met by the horses. Joe didn't know if it was her relative youth or her bird-of-prey nature, but she seemed ready for whatever lay to the north.

"Thank you, son," he said to Jackson.

He couldn't see the boy's face but he could hear his breathing, his feet shifting on the dirt. He was restless, wishing he could go. Joe touched him on the shoulder and squeezed.

"Pa—"

"I know," Joe said. "But even if it was otherwise, you're needed here."

Joe told Clarity to take the Appaloosa and mounted the calico. He handed the woman one of the grub sacks, which she looped around the back housing of the saddle, out of the way.

Sarah and Gert came to the front door but stayed just inside the darkness. Joe could hear them and wheeled the horse so it was facing them.

"Love you both," he said before giving the horse a soft "*gyah*" and turning it toward the entrance to follow the stagecoach path. He threw a wave at the Mission Indian as he rode out. Clarity lingered a moment to thank them all before following Joe into the night. The sound of the horses was quickly lost to distance and the whistle of the wind.

"I like her," Gert said as Jackson joined them.

"I'm betting she'll have a better chance of taming San Francisco than her brother will," her father suggested.

"Taming it or running it?" Gert asked.

Sarah sighed. "It's too confusing a thought for me," she said. "I'm not even sure who'll break who, her or your granddad."

"I'm betting on Pa," Jackson said as he headed back to the stables to feed and water the horse Joe had ridden in.

"I'm just happy it's even a question," Gert said with a smile.

Two miles to the northeast, another departure was taking place.

Leaving behind just two men, Tod Crane and Dr. Peterson, the remaining members of the Kennedy party rode from the copper mine into the silver night. Dr. Peterson and his patient would remain in the mine until the latter was deemed well enough to travel. Peterson would decide that when he saw how Crane sat a horse.

Peterson was crouched in the middle of the shaft, about ten feet from the entrance. He watched the men grow smaller and smaller until they turned north and weren't visible at all.

That was fine with Peterson. He found most of them insufferable, especially the two from the East. And, besides, he had something he needed to do. He just couldn't do it while they were here.

The injured man was propped against a flat section of rock wall, his legs spread before him. His chest was bare, save for the shoulder-girdling bandage. There was no light other than the moon, which shone into the mouth of the mine and made both men look like ghosts. The departure of the men had let the night breeze flow unimpaired, which felt good on Crane's sweaty skin and Peterson's grizzled, thoughtful face.

He was thinking now. Not about what happened or what was happening but what would happen.

Peterson was not a Rebel at heart but by default. He was not a friend of any federal government, that of Abe Lincoln or Jeff Davis. He believed that people and communities should determine their own fate, and what was good for Boston wasn't necessarily good for Cincinnati or St. Louis or Dallas. The entire war had been the bloody result of pride over intelligence, of moral certainty over life itself. As a doctor, he had yet to hear an opinion that was worth more than the breath it rode out on.

What the hell is wrong with everyone?

They started one war after another, convinced that one way of life was better than another. And all that was accomplished was violently, painfully, needlessly ending so many of those lives.

The Maryland-born Peterson had supported the Confederacy for two reasons. First, he did not believe bankers and manufacturers and politicians from the North should impose their views on farmers and politicians in the South. That was wrong. Second, it was a matter of where he had been living. Peterson had married a Georgia girl and she was adamant and that was that.

Now forty-nine, the doctor had lost everything that had mattered to him. It was consumed in the fiery sack of Atlanta. His practice went up in converging seas of blood and flame. He was a Confederate in the eyes of the invading army and was forced to work in a Union hospital. That made him a traitor in the eyes of his family and patients. When it was all over, he was truly a man without a country. There was nothing left for him but to go west with mercenaries who had their own mission: to prolong the struggle and avenge themselves on the Yankees.

None of it sat well with the man whose only desire had ever been to heal the sick or injured. He certainly did not have the bullying nature of Tod Crane, Silas Welch, Marcus Stone, or the others in the makeshift unit.

But then, Gus Peterson had a plan. A plan that was different from those of these other men. A plan that would take everyone by surprise, especially Kennedy and Hathaway.

Those two particularly annoyed him. They were bureaucrats, the kind who had ground down and looted the people of the South. The fact that these two had transferred their wicked policies from Confederates to Indians did not make him feel any better about working with them. The only thing that made his association with them bearable was the help they were inadvertently providing.

"Sure seems bigger and airier without all them horses," Crane muttered.

The man was trying hard to muster his stren'th, to stay sharp and alert.

Peterson half-turned toward the other. "Seems roomier without all your friends, too," he said. "Quieter, anyway. You really ought to rest."

"I rested enough," Crane protested.

Peterson shook his head. "Lord help you, you're as stubborn as the rest."

Crane made a disapproving sound. "Why you always such a naysayer with everyone?"

Peterson rose, arched his back, and walked to where Crane was sprawled. "I keep hoping someone'll listen to me," he said. "Stop fighting a lost war."

"Wars and causes ain't always the same thing. Anyway," he said, wincing as he shifted his shoulders, "I didn't surrender to nobody."

"That's true, but the Confederacy is as dead as a beaver hat," Peterson said. "Plantations are not coming back. Slaves are gone for good. So many gentlemen are dead— I know, I watched 'em die. Some of them with proud little feathers still in their hatbands. I fear civility may also be dead."

"I agree with you there," Crane said. "Look at our new taskmasters."

"That's right," Peterson said. "Look at those louts. So

what's left to *be* a cause? Anger at the North? Violence against Negroes that will bring violence against us?"

"Honor," Crane said.

"Ah," Peterson remarked. "One of the four horsemen that brought this hell on us all." The doctor shook his head. "I had honor, purpose, dignity, and good intentions when my wife took my children and went to live with her folks in Florida. If I'd spent those four years with her, accepting what was and starting a new life, instead of trying to save lives, I wouldn't—as you put it, and you're right—be such a naysayer."

Crane made a disapproving sound. "I can't agree with you, Doc. Ideas and values are worth fighting for, regardless of your numbers."

"Or whether you're alive to benefit?"

"That's right," Crane said.

"There's a word for that," Peterson said. "It's 'martyr.' Debating, discussing, yes. Dying? Losing an arm or both eyes or a loved one? That's a price too steep for something that can't be touched or held or smiled at."

"Not to some," Crane replied.

Peterson sighed. "Well, maybe you're right. But out here, all I see is a pack of animals destroying, not building or even rebuilding. Silas Welch is out there, somewhere. You don't bury a dead body, my friend, and all you get are maggots and disease."

Crane had forgotten about his companion. He deflated somewhat. He had also forgotten the food Ridgewood had left for him and began eating. He inhaled painfully, adjusted the way he was sitting so he was straight against the rock wall. Then he exhaled.

"I guess nothing's easy, ever," Crane said. "But if you can't live with yourself nothing's even possible.

I like what I'm doing out here. I like the country. I like my saddle mates. If I can't have what I left, this is the next best thing to me. This life."

"I can't argue with you about the place," Peterson agreed. "I just wish we didn't have to kill people to live in it."

"We tried that, with the Butterfield horse," Crane reminded him. "Didn't work out. Shoulda shot the driver, then Silas'd still be alive."

"I don't mean just that," Peterson told him. "I'm talking about the whole idea of stealing, waylaying the innocent."

Crane used his left hand, his uninjured side, to spoon beans into his mouth. He chomped as he answered. "It's what's being done to us. That makes it fair."

Peterson wasn't sure what to do with Crane's simple, occasionally idiotic views, but he knew that it wasn't helping the man's health to spout them. And whether he liked Crane or not, it was his job to keep the man alive.

Now that the rest of the party had ridden off, there was something else he had to do.

"Do you think you can fend for yourself till morning?" the doctor asked.

"I wasn't planning on sightseeing, if that's what you mean."

"That's what I mean," Peterson said.

Crane ate more beans. "You give me some guns for protection against varmints or savages, I'll be fine. Why you asking?"

"I was thinking of taking a ride," he said. "See what happened to Silas, maybe watch tonight to see if anyone sets out after our boys."

"Sounds a little ambitious for you, Doc," Crane said suspiciously.

"Maybe I want to see if there's any merit to your notions of teamwork."

"You are a puzzle," Crane said. "But sure."

Peterson went to one of the two horses left in the stable and put on a saddle. He gave Crane the man's own revolver and shotgun, left him with shells, and also made sure he had water and bread.

"You going for a week?" Crane asked, looking at one of three loaves they'd taken from migrant Mexicans—along with the beans on his plate.

"Who knows what could happen out there," Peterson said. "Want to make sure you're taken care of."

"I'll come and get you if you're not back this time tomorrow."

"I will be, but you stay put just the same."

"Yeah, I'll just sit here counting mine weevils," he said—his voice growing weaker from the exertion, if not his bravado.

With that, the doctor finished his preparations, grabbed a half-full canteen and his medical kit, and walked the horse to the opening of the mine. The bright moon silhouetted his departure.

It did not, however, shed any light on his purpose.

CHAPTER 11

At this moment, in this place, Clarity Michaels was loving everything about her life.

Riding a few paces behind Joe, along a flat and narrow path between dark ruts, the woman felt as if she was both free and a captive. She was as unfettered as the wind that brushed by her, yet her soul was held tight—as a newly hatched sparrow to its nest—by the moonlit plain and rocks and trees and distant hills. There were fresh and exotic scents that made her lungs feel twice as large, that filled her soul with new life, her mind with new thoughts.

This was what Gert had to be seeking, Clarity thought. *This freedom, these new horizons.*

No wonder Joe did not understand. Roaming the land, the mountains, embraced by boundless sky with no artificial structure in view, he had been a part of the earth and heavens from his youth. He couldn't possibly grasp what it was like to be a prisoner to a spot, to chores that forced you to look down without respite. Gert's new way gave her the old and the new and that scared her very traditional grandfather.

That, plus making peace with a people who had always

been regarded as an enemy. Clarity smirked. *Be careful who you judge,* she warned herself. *You'd as soon shoot a Roche as break bread with one.*

There was a time, when she was still an adolescent, shooting stew ingredients for herself and her brother, when there was nothing she wanted more than to become an officer of the law. She dreamed of being a sheriff or even better a marshal, traveling from township to township fixing problems and making things safe for people. Things had never been safe for her. There had always been bears and big cats, there had been sick men with little ideas, and there had been bullying girls who liked to laugh at orphans or those who had fair-skinned kin working at church. There was occasional kindness—the church organist, Mrs. Senter, brought her cakes and preserves—but even under the blanket of the church, things were difficult. Her brother worked long hours, and when he was at the seminary, at St. Mary's College, she did not see him for months on end.

By then, Clarity had moved in with a friend, Birgit Hartvigsen, who was teased because of her Scandinavian accent. Her mother and father raised sheep—not many, but well. The family did not starve. One of the reasons the family loved having Clarity around was that, when Mr. Hartvigsen was asleep or away, she shot the wolves, foxes, and other predators that threatened their livelihood.

Clarity did not like shooting animals, who were only trying to survive. But she recognized the need. When she shot Billy Roche—that was different. She told the sheriff it was an accident, and she *had* just fallen over a chair, but that was because he pulled her to get her out the door. It felt good to stop him. It was everything she had imagined a peace officer might feel.

This evening—was it *just* this evening?—Clarity had not delayed a heartbeat to shoot at the Rebels. Not to kill, unless they made it necessary, but she felt no hesitation whatsoever. She would not have hesitated with the Apaches, either. Not if they tried to harm Joe O'Malley.

What Clarity Michaels did not know, what she was puzzling about at this moment, was whether she *yearned* to do it again.

She was, without any doubt, thrilled and challenged to be part of this new adventure. The danger was not daunting. Closed in a coach over which she had no control—that was Clarity's definition of purgatory. Her senses hungry, her heart more ravenously open than ever, she was more excited to be riding with Joe O'Malley than she had been with the prospect of simply relocating to the West. That had been a vague notion filled half with promise, half with questions. This mission was like a map with a legend: she knew where they were going, why, and who might need shooting.

They were passing near a mass of boulders that resembled the entrance to Whip Station when Joe raised a hand, signaling for her to slow. At the same time his horse began to whinny and fight. The frontiersman set him right and stopped. The rocks were ten feet or so to their right.

"Don't come forward," Joe said.

"What is it?" Clarity asked, her own mount skittish.

"Smell it?" Joe asked.

She sniffed. There was something faintly musky in the air.

"Bear," he said before she could guess. "In those rocks."

Clarity had never seen a bear, except stuffed and gaunt in a traveling carnival.

"Can we circle around?" she asked.

"No. This entire area is its grounds. We move, it charges."

"Is there only one?" Clarity asked.

"Not likely," Joe informed her. "It's in the opening there—cubs inside, most likely. See its eyes?"

Clarity looked at the uneven gash that marked the opening of its lair. She saw two tiny lights inside, reflecting the moon.

"The stagecoach had to come this way—it doesn't seem to have bothered them," she said.

"Woulda looked and growled like a big bear pulled by horses," he said. "Bears are brave but not fool-hardy."

"Do we have to kill it?" Clarity asked.

"That's not what worries me," Joe said. "Question is, can we cut it down before it reaches us? We're just as dead if it dies with those claws mauling us or our horses—which will panic when it comes charging, making us easier to catch."

"I could hit those eyes."

"It can still smell, blind." Joe added, "And you *might* miss."

There was a guttural sound from the rocks.

"It's getting impatient," Joe said. "We're gonna have to ride in opposite directions."

"Do you have matches?"

"Rebs and Apaches will see that for sure, know where it's coming from," Joe told her. "We got a chance if we run toward the rocks, to either side. It can't charge if it has to turn. Bear's poorly built that way."

"I go south side?"

"You do. On—"

Joe was about to start the count when a monster of a grizzly surged from the rift in the rocks, roaring displeasure and menace.

"Go!" Joe cried as the horses attempted to bolt toward the open field. There, the bear would have the advantage of having built up speed.

Fighting their own mounts, Joe and Clarity spun in the direction of the charging animal, causing it to roar and swat, anticipating a close passage. But the riders went wide, passing the bear with enough distance between them and the knife-long claws.

As the two riders passed, the bear lunged for Joe, barely missing the horse's flanks, and then it lumbered after him, covering the earth in massive strides. Joe was in the open plain but opted to continue his circuit around the rocks.

"Go straight back!" he yelled to Clarity. "When you're in the clear, turn north!"

The woman waved that she'd heard as she passed the boulders and galloped ahead, toward the east.

Joe circled around the other side, the bear turning to keep up. He could hear the thump of its massive weight with every step. But Joe, having built up speed, was able to hit the westward side of the rocks several strides from the bear. The animal had to turn again to give chase, by which time Joe was hurrying westward into the lowlands.

The animal stopped, rose on its hind legs, and bellowed into the night. Then it dropped onto its paws, snorted, and moved slowly back to its den.

Joe reined and looked back. He could barely see the animal as it disappeared into the darkness whence it had come. He could not see or hear Clarity. He peered into the pale-lit expanse and finally saw her, sitting upright, the horse still.

Suddenly, she raised her arm toward the north. Her rifle was in it, pointing.

There must be something she wanted Joe to see.

He looked in that direction and saw smoke to the northwest. That was on the opposite side of the coach trail, his side. The Apaches and Rebels would have been coming from the southeast.

Joe raised his arm and swept it down and ahead. It could be more Indians or it could be a military patrol. In either case, it was not anything they needed to be concerned with.

He rode ahead and Clarity followed suit.

Major Colonel Alexander Howard did not understand why, with so much territory to control, General Guilford ordered him to come to this out-of-the-way, largely uninhabited region, during each of his weekly patrols. Howard understood even less why his superior officer sent a rider with special instructions for this trip: Howard was to leave the San Diego barracks and make camp below Temecula Point and await a civilian rider. Then he was to send a courier to Fort Yuma to deliver the unread message personally to General Guilford. After that, he was to remain encamped until ordered otherwise by the general.

Those were his instructions in their entirety.

The forty-four-year-old officer pulled at the closely cropped beard that filled out his lean face. It wasn't that the officer minded an easy detail. He spent four years fighting against General Lee and his formidable commanders—most memorably the tenacious Stonewall Jackson in the Northern Virginia Campaign. He was a man whose accidental shooting by his own soldier was both celebrated and mourned by fighting men of the North. Afterward, there were endless skirmishes with the Redskins, whose ruthlessness exceeded anything he had seen in the War. With seven years of that clinging to him like the smoke of endless campfires, Major Colonel Howard was happy to have a relatively easy task. But it puzzled him and his men. They didn't mind, either, though they all would have preferred being close to a town where there was a saloon and women instead of the wilderness where there were buzzing insects, snakes and scorpions, and baking sun.

But now, as they camped on a rise beside a low mesa, with a valley cut low and long to the west, Howard didn't know which was worse: action or inaction. Boredom was a pernicious foe. It made you hear Indians where there were night birds. It made you smell coyotes that were just lightning-struck trees, rotting. It caused you to twitch, thinking the lights that shot through the sky were not falling stars but shells fired by some distant army.

Thinking of the stars made him wish he had gotten the chance to ride in one of those observation balloons during the War. He had been on mountains in his native West Virginia. He had looked down at the ground and up at the sky. But he always wondered what would happen if he cut loose one of those big gas bags and rode it higher and higher . . .

"Halt!"

The cry of the sentry on the eastern perimeter caused Howard to stride briskly to that side. He went wide around the six tents that had been pitched to house the dozen-man detachment. Since Howard did not know how long they would be here, or what weather they would encounter, a supply cart with tents had seemed a sensible part of the patrol.

The officer arrived just as a rider was loping into the light of the campfire burning by that picket. There was another campfire to the south, where the horses were tethered to pikes. Between the two blazes, flickering light covered a significant area inside and outside the encampment.

The new arrival stopped where he was and awaited further instructions. Major Howard looked him over quickly. The rider was dressed in a twill jacket and blue trousers—Union, it appeared—that looked as depressed as the man who wore them.

"Identify yourself!" the young sentry ordered.

"Dr. Gus Peterson with a message for General Guilford."

"Let him pass," Howard said.

"Yes, sir," the sentry said. "Enter," he told the rider.

With a lackluster nudge of the heels, Peterson urged the horse to enter the camp. Heads had poked from tents, some with mess, some with cards, to see who had arrived and whether or not they would be needed.

"As you were," Howard ordered. Almost as one, the heads withdrew.

The cavalry soldier was not by nature a nosy man. Soldiers who showed too much interest in an officer's activities often found themselves dangerously riding point or sent to the fort for some tedious assignment like filing or sweeping. Since most recruits had signed up for adventure with pay, a uniform, and the women that were drawn to that uniform, it was best to see and hear nothing. Like the navy, promotion in the cavalry came about one of two ways. That was through family connections or merit. Most recruits came from poor backgrounds, so good soldiering was their best chance at rising in rank. The alternative to a military career was a return to the very lives they were trying to leave behind.

Though he had arrived without incident, Peterson was sorry half his brief journey was over. It felt good to be alone, not listening to idiotic or pointless talk. It also lifted his spirits to be out of the mine, though they had not been raised enough for it to show on his lined face or sloped shoulders. It had been a long journey from peace through war, and he was tired to the very marrow of his bones. Being out here had given him a chance to air out his soul, to clean the filth from what he knew to be a good and important mission.

Accompanied by the major, the doctor tied his

horse to one of the southern pikes and removed his medicine bag. Howard then showed him into his tent at the northern end, away from the sound and smell of the horses. Peterson entered before the major.

"Coffee?" the officer asked. "Whiskey?"

"I'll take coffee, black, if you don't mind," Peterson said.

The major called for a private to fetch the pot from the fire. There were no amenities in the tent other than a bedroll, and Peterson half-sat, half-dropped on the cool dirt. He positioned himself cross-legged with some effort, below a hanging lantern. When his coffee arrived, brought by a sun-burned bugler, Peterson accepted it gratefully. Then he set it on the ground and opened his bag and withdrew paper and pencil. He put the paper on a knee and began writing.

"Do you know anything about this business?" Peterson asked.

"I do not, sir," the major replied.

The doctor nodded. "I will write out the message. It is important that the general receive this as soon as possible."

"Those were my instructions," Howard said. "May I ask, though, why you didn't take it yourself? The fort is east, you came from the east—"

"This place is much, much closer," Peterson said. "And it is imperative that I return before sunup."

Peterson wrote down the events of the day and the plans he had heard.

"You have patients?" Howard asked. The major was standing several steps in front of Peterson, making a point of not looking down as he wrote.

"How did you—?" Peterson began, then noticed his own medical bag covered with the dirt of the road and the red dust of the mine. In the old days, when he was still a respected member of a community, he always kept the leather polished. "Yes," he answered as he wrote. "I do."

"May I ask, out of concern for my men, is there some illness about that I should be aware of?"

Peterson snorted. "Not a fever that you have to worry about. It's more in the nature of a mental derangement."

"Lunacy?"

"More like bureaucracy, which is the same thing," Peterson said with a crooked smile.

"I don't understand," the major admitted.

"Oh, people in Washington have one way of doing things," Peterson said. "We out here have a different way."

The medic was being purposely evasive, almost like an Indian, Howard thought. He guessed that the doctor was referring to some kind of ore strike, something that made men crazy. Something that might bring an influx of settlers to the region and cause more strife with the Indians.

That had to be it, Howard thought. And it might well be on Apache or Pechanga land, which would cause additional troubles.

But why would that be kept secret, especially from a commander in the field?

Howard had an explanation for that, too. General Guilford knew that upon hearing about a precious metal strike, troopers might desert. The major was a patriot but not everyone in his command felt the same deep love for the United States of America. Some, he suspected, may even have been Confederate sympathizers. They would desert in a moment for the chance to pan for gold or dig for silver, hard money that would allow them to go home wealthy. Especially if their family fortunes had suffered during the War. So enriched, they could even buy their way out of a court-martial.

"May I ask another question?" the major said, surprised by his own boldness.

"No such thing as a stupid question," the doctor replied.

"I have been coming out here for weeks. Are you the gentleman who was due each time?"

"I am," he said. "And not so much 'due' as 'hoped for.'"

"Are you in the military, sir?"

"Not now, not ever," Peterson replied. "I mean no insult, Major—it just was not the path I took."

"Then, at the risk of imposing on your patience, what is your connection to the general?"

Peterson snickered. "Our paths crossed when I heard of the illness of his wife at Fort Yuma."

"The grippe epidemic," the major said.

"Not quite that, but yes," Peterson said. "About, oh, a third of the complement had influenza. The general and I—we had a lot of time to talk."

The medic was finished writing, put his pencil in the bag, and folded the paper in quarters.

The major went to an unlit candle in a holder near his bedroll. "Would you care to wax a seal?"

"Not necessary," Peterson said. His expression was pained as he rose creakily. "Anyone who reads it will not understand what it's about. You can look, if you want."

The major hesitated. As a military man he prized honor and information equally. Since he had been invited, he unfolded the document.

> *Objective missed, party back on road, night pursuit.*
>
> *Whip Station and Indians now involved. Man killed, another injured. Will inform upon their return.*
>
> Gus

"Your assessment was quite accurate," the major said with a wry smile. He refolded the paper and called for a rider. "Whatever your business with the general, I wish you great success. He is a great leader and a good man. If you are in league with him, then I wish you Godspeed and a safe journey—to wherever you are headed."

"Most gracious," Peterson said in earnest. He regarded Howard for a moment.

"Does everyone feel the way you do, about the general?" the doctor asked.

"He is the reason many of us remain out here when we could transfer out," Howard replied.

The medic smiled. "I feel the same way."

A different young man arrived, armed with a canteen, a sidearm, and an eager expression. Peterson knew, from having been with the Union Army, that couriers were a breed apart from ordinary soldiers.

They thrived on what one of them told him were the three R's: the ride, the responsibility, and the risk. To that, Peterson had added one more: rest. These soldiers grabbed it when they could, since they often rode great distances to deliver both message and response.

Those qualities were present in this young man's eager brown eyes and sharply snapped salute. Major Howard handed him the message, which he tucked in his vest pocket.

"Hand-deliver to General Guilford at Fort Yuma. No one else."

Howard looked to Peterson for confirmation of that last part. The medic nodded once.

The courier saluted again and eased quickly through the flaps of the tent. Peterson finished his coffee.

"I'll hand it off when I leave," the doctor said, indicating the cup.

"Would you like a plate of supper before you go?"

Peterson shook his head. "Thank you, Major. But my services are needed elsewhere."

The men made their way to where Peterson had left his horse. It was grazing contentedly and protested, slightly, the doctor untying the reins. Peterson regarded the major before mounting.

"I suspect this will be your last time out here waiting for me, Major," Peterson said.

Howard regarded the man's face in the light, half campfire on one side, half white moonlight on the other.

"Will it, I wonder, be the last time I see you, Doctor?" the major asked directly.

Peterson climbed into the saddle. "Do you know, Major Howard, why men think so much about the past?"

"A variety of reasons, I suspect."

"There's just one," Peterson said. "It's easier to remember things than to predict them."

With that, the medic walked his horse into the night and was soon gone, save for the sounds of the hooves and then even they were gone.

Major Howard stood in reflection for several minutes after his departure. He wasn't thinking about the message. Not exactly. He was thinking about whatever might come because of that message.

A good officer might not be nosy, but he develops instincts. Like leaves in a stream, those instincts circle a man's inborn sense of duty. If he doesn't have one, he doesn't belong in uniform. Together, that partnership helps a man rise from green private. They grow strong together until instinct and duty are inseparable.

Right now, the major had a standing order. All right. He and his company were to stay put until ordered either back to the barracks or on a mission. That did not, however, preclude a night patrol. Something was afoot and he would rather have his best men on horseback than sitting here, indistinguishable from the scenery.

"Lieutenant Levey!" he called out.

Everyone in camp came alert. They knew the major's tone. A tall, beefy man came running through the maze of men and tents and saluted.

"Sir!"

"You're in command here," Howard told the young, rosy-cheeked man.

"Yes, sir."

"I want Sergeant Wayne along with Cooper, Horton, Gonzalez, Locke, Zachary, Flint, and Two Hats ready to ride out in five minutes," Howard said. "Patrol, provisions for two days."

"Sir!" Levey said, snapping out a salute and hustling away.

Howard returned to his tent where his aide was already gathering what the major would need. The officer got the leather portfolio containing the regimental maps. He only needed one and he took it, folding it into his pocket.

The Indians were quiet, and he would have heard from other officers if there was any threat of an uprising. Except for infrequent war parties, even the Apaches stayed on their reservation. They had seen the influx of uniformed men after the War and did not seem keen to face battle-hardened soldiers. Unlike most white men, the Indians had patience.

The Mexicans were also content to stay where they were. They had fought their internal Reform War and now able-bodied patriots were busy fighting the opportunistic French. Seems Europe wasn't happy having lost their foothold on the continent, save for Canada. And they weren't any kind of threat.

So Howard had to wonder what might be a flashpoint.

The only thing he could think of was gold or silver. And the only way that would involve the U.S. Cavalry was to secure a claim for some big outfit, well-connected in Washington. There was talk that railroads and surveyors had been out here. Maybe they found something? Except for that, the biggest concerns out here were the shipping companies, whose interests were only on the coastline. General Guilford would not have pulled Major Howard inland to tend to their interests.

That left Butterfield. His coaches carried the mail and that was the kind of thing that got you leverage with presidents. Did one of their scouts find something? Or were they thinking of expanding service and needed protection?

Howard did not have enough information to do more than guess. But whatever it was, he was likely to get more information riding north, observing, than sitting here.

The eight men were mounted and riding out within the allotted time. Whatever was going on, Howard felt strong in his saddle, in front of his men.

He was ready and eager to see if his instincts were as righteous as his sense of duty.

CHAPTER 12

Slash O'Malley never told his grandfather about
skin-walking. It was an Indian practice. On principle
alone, Joe would have rejected it. But just now, in this
place, the old Pechanga Chicon would have been a
very helpful passenger.

The young man had tried the Indian mystic art a
little over a year before, when his father had sent him
to collect Gert from the Pechanga camp four or so
miles due south. It was late winter and darkness came
early—too early for Gert to come back alone, and
Jackson O'Malley did not want his daughter remaining among them.

"She is young and easily impressed," Jackson had
said.

The man's tone, his worried expression, said more
than his words. He did not want to be the grandfather
of a Pechanga child.

So Slash went, holding no deep personal opinion
on the matter but not wanting to see his father or
mother upset. Or Joe heading into the settlement
with a shotgun. Out here, mongrel children, however

born of love and loved themselves, made outcasts of the parents from all races.

He found his sister at the wide river, deep and surging with melted snows. She was standing alone among a spread of daisies grown tall and colorful in their damp soil. The passage of birds had further enriched the earth with their droppings as they passed overhead.

"Pa's mad at you for overstaying your visit," Slash had said to her.

"I wasn't in any danger," his sister had replied, her shoulders back with indignation. "Just the opposite."

He had looked around. "What are you even doing here? Just standing around when there are chores?"

"I'm watching."

"What?"

"A transformation."

Slash was puzzled and she had taken his hand, coaxing him toward an area, near the river where an aged medicine man sat unseen in the shadow of a tall, ancient oak. Able to see deeper into the shadow now, Slash was no longer sure where the tree ended or the man began, its bark as rippled as the skin on the old man's bones. His eyes were closed and his hands hovered before him as if resting on the air itself.

But that was not the most unusual thing about the tableau. The wizened man was huddled in a cloak of feathers that rested on his shoulders and were tied, by leather strips, about his wrists. His gray hair was tied back. Two talons hung from the deerskin ribbon that bound it. His thin, pale lips were shut and there was a slight upward tilt of his long, beak-like nose.

The siblings had approached quietly. Slash felt that

even if they had tromped in, the elderly man would not have heard them.

"This is Chicon," she had said quietly. "He is on the wind."

"'On the wind,'" Slash had repeated with confusion.

"Flying," Gert had clarified.

Slash thought the statement, and his sister, were silly. Until she handed him a pelt that was lying nearby.

"Rabbit," Slash had said.

"Sit beside him, put it on your head."

Slash protested the game but Gert insisted and it was easier to do it than to argue. She was a woman with a mind like the western winds: they decided when to stop, one did not order it.

He draped the skin on his head, sat where he had been told—close enough to smell pungent tobacco clinging to the shaman's clothes—and closed his eyes as Gert also instructed.

"Breathe deeply," she had told him. "Like when you were a baby."

It turned out to be a trick on Gert's part. He tried to remember what it was like to breathe as a baby. He started remembering things from that time: the cradle with his sister snuggled beside him. His parents looking down. Joe, much younger. Grandma Dolley. The cabin where they lived. The sire of their current collies.

And then he wasn't a baby anymore. He was—something else, something low beside the splashing waters of the river. It was night and he was moving quickly in the grasses. He was trying to get somewhere—a warren. His home. He saw it ahead. He heard a surge of wind above him, darted to one side, tumbled, then was suddenly righted and running toward the opening, into it, safe in the darkness . . .

Slash's eyes had shot open. He sat for a moment, breathing rapidly.

Gert was standing a respectful distance from the shaman, who was still in his trance. But she was not so far that her twin couldn't see the look of deep gratification on her face.

Remembering the pelt, Slash snatched it from his head. He rose and shook it at his sister.

"What did you powder this with?" he had asked.

"Shhhh," she had replied, motioning him away from the shaman.

Slash padded toward her, glancing back at the tree. It did not appear as if the medicine man's creased, leathery hands or face had moved. Though there was no breeze, just the rush and splash of beaded water, the feathers seemed to stir.

"What is the trick?" he had repeated.

"There is none," she had said. "You were skin-walking."

"An Indian myth, a trick," he had hissed dismissively.

Gert had pointed back at the shaman. "He is aloft. That is why his feathers are moving. They are his spirit wings."

Slash clutched the fur, put it to his nose. He had expected to detect the odor or effects of a plant or mushroom. There was nothing but the slightly musty smell of cured rabbit skin. His arm fell to his side. He circled wide around the tree. Nothing had been burned there, no dream-inducing leaves. Slash returned to his sister and looked back at the pelt.

"If I put this on my head, would I—would I be a rabbit again?"

"You might," she said. "The air around Chicon is like the thunderclouds. But instead of lightning, there is a menagerie—"

"A what?"

"A garden of animals, of their spirits," Gert had patiently explained. "When the shaman is an eagle, soaring, all that he sees is nearby."

The pelt had suddenly seemed neither innocent nor as dead as it had first appeared. The fingers clutching it tingled. Slowly, carefully, and with greater respect, he had handed it back to Gert.

"This is yours?"

She had nodded.

"An eagle." Slash had glanced back at the medicine man. "I felt as though he would have killed me. I was *afraid*."

"That is because you were new in your skin," she had told him. "In time, you would have learned that there is no lord in the abode of the spirits. The rabbit can see and smell what the eagle cannot. The wisdom he learns from the earth, about the earth, becomes part of the Great Knowledge."

Gert moved both hands as if to encompass the sky. Her brother might have thought that she had lost her mind—had he not just lost it with her.

They went home, but after that day he came often when she was in the Pechanga camp. He listened to the shaman when he spoke to the young of the Great Knowledge. He and Gert always sat off to the side, where she could quietly translate his words—though the expressive hands and expressions of Chicon often told the story without need of a spoken language.

Slash did not skin-walk again after that day. Even Gert admitted that she rarely partook in the magic art, because she found it increasingly difficult to leave that world of tranquility and beauty. A world, Chicon assured his people, that awaited them upon the death of their bodies.

The O'Malley boy felt he could wait until then to find out more about this Eden. Right now, his life and the survival of Whip Station depended too much on his being alert and fit and able to carry a hunt to the place where the animals lived. He did not want to become brother to the fox and pig. They were prey. Like this afternoon, with the wild turkey.

Was that just a few hours ago? Slash thought incredulously.

All of that passed quickly through the young man's mind, like a stagecoach made of memories. But it brought him to a surprising station. One in which he thought how useful it would be, just now, to become a spirit eagle and fly high over the terrain so he could see the place to which they were headed—and those who might already be in pursuit, trying to stop them.

Perhaps Chicon should be riding shotgun, not Slash O'Malley, he thought.

Or maybe Gert should be in the box. Why not? Clarity Michaels was riding with his grandfather. Gert could put on her rabbit pelt and run back, listen for plans, alarm the horses, create clouds of mischief to befuddle the enemy.

The young lady was a genuine worry to her parents and grandfather, and Slash could see both views.

Whether or not she became squaw to some brave—
and he could see that happening—she was already
combative about the old ways of doing things. She
resisted the calling of doctors instead of shamans.
Bottled tinctures and elixirs instead of burned or
pasted herbs. Wars over ideas instead of hunting
grounds. Boats that belched black smoke instead of
gliding along by the power of a man's arms. Alcoholic
spirits for strange visions instead of animal spirits.

Slash understood some of that. But he also saw
things the way the older O'Malleys did. They were
strangers in a new and often inhospitable land. If
they did not pull together, they might very well
perish. How often did B.W. proclaim that the nation
had been nigh on Armageddon because of blood-
shed over differences instead of cooperation over sim-
ilarities.

If not individual tribe members, the Indians themselves were a potential threat, as were many Mexicans,
white bandits, hungry, desperate former slaves who
had come west alone or with new families.

As Mr. John Butterfield himself had written in a
letter that accompanied the charter for Whip Station,
"There is stren'th in union of purpose, but erosion in
the consistent flow of dissent."

To which letter, of course, Gert ascribed an inter-
pretation contrary to the stated message. In her mind,
the Indians and their bond with land and sky was a
true union. The O'Malleys—whom she loved and
ultimately, stubbornly obeyed—were the dissenters.

B.W. interrupted Slash's thoughts.

"Someone ahead about—I'd say three hundred yards," the driver said, pointing along his own side.

Slash was instantly watchful, the long gun leveled in the direction he had pointed.

There was a man, no doubt of it, and he was not hiding. He was standing openly along the trail, a saddle over his shoulder, a rifle in his right hand pointed toward the ground. The man was tall, of broad shoulders, and wearing a tattered, wide brimmed sun hat.

The man was black. Either a former laborer from the North or a freed slave from the South. In either case, Slash thought, not a likely enemy but a potential ally.

"What d'you think?" B.W. said.

"What's the rules?" Slash asked.

"We don't stop for strangers, even if they can pay," the driver said.

"Y'ever do it? Stop, I mean?"

"Twice," B.W. admitted. "Once was a squaw injured by whites. Second was a white tied to a tree by Injuns."

"What do *you* think?"

"God loves a cheerful giver," B.W. said. "I ain't exactly cheerful, but . . ." The man's voice trailed off.

Slash kept the gun raised. "His gun ain't aimed our way. Could shoot us from cussedness if we pass."

"And there could be more of 'em hiding. My granpap was waylaid and kilt by robbers in such a way."

Slash looked across the mostly flat, treeless terrain. He didn't see anyone.

"Let's stop and talk," Slash said. "That can't hurt."

B.W. had obviously been considering the same

thing. His foot was already on the long brake arm. He pressed it forward.

The horses strained for a moment as the wheels resisted, then gave in to the tug and slowed. The stagecoach rocked to a swaying stop in front of the man. Slash leaned forward so he could keep the barrel pointed in his direction.

"Keep the cannon pointing the way it is," Slash said.

"I got no cause nor particular stren'th to lift 'er," the man replied.

"Freed slave," B.W. whispered to Slash, hearing his Deep South accent.

"I'd'a guessed such from his attire," Slash replied.

The man was a vision straight from some folktale, like the puppet Rowdy Patchwork Ma used to tell them about. His clothes were a patchwork of cotton, canvas, and mismatched pelts that had been used as patches. On his feet were moccasins that he did not appear to have made himself as they were too large and stuffed with moss.

"You're quite a sight," B.W. said to the man.

"I wouldn't know," the man replied with a helpless shrug. "Been a while since I saw a glass or a pond."

"I'm Slash, the Whip is B.W. Who're you?"

"Isaiah," the man replied.

B.W. smiled. "Prophet of God, beloved by the Hebrews in captivity."

"That's what my ma tol' me when I was put in chains as a boy," the black man replied. "You gentlemen happen to have any water? I am one thirsty prophet."

"Sure," Slash replied.

The young man handed the driver his water skin.

B.W. held it out. The man set his saddle on the ground, walked over, and reached out.

"Thank you," the man said. He drank only a little and handed it back. "I'm in your debt."

"You kin have more," B.W. said.

"Too much'll make a thirsty man sick," he said. "But thank you."

"You learnt that in the fields?" B.W. asked.

"On a raft I built m'self," the man said. "Poled the Chattahoochee River in Georgia with cotton, other goods, before the War. During the War, I watched for Yankees. Couldn't go far, though. Them four years I stayed close to shore, listened mostly."

"Why didn't you leave?"

"Sentries posted way the current flows," he said. "Woulda shot an escaped slave."

"How long you been waiting here?" Slash asked.

"Got here this afternoon," he replied. "Saw the ruts, hoped someone'd be along presently. Heard your approach, knew what you was."

"What happened to your horse?"

"Long trip from Alabama," the man said. "He had enough of carrying me."

"You said you's from Alabama," Slash said.

"I said the river," Isaiah corrected him, courteously. "My master was just over the state line."

"He knows the geography all right," B.W. said from the side of his mouth. B.W. nudged his companion. "But brother, why you getting his life story? We gotta *move*."

Slash didn't disagree but continued to address

Isaiah. He nodded at the man's rifle, the polished barrel aglow with moonlight. "Confederate?"

"Found it on the shore after a skirmish," he said. "Sounded the alert on the horn they gave me, then waited."

"You any good with that cannon? You keep it clean."

"Dirty gun cain't help no one," the man said. "And yes, sir. I'm more than fair. Good duck shooter."

"Not fowl that interests me," Slash said.

"Oh," B.W. said with sudden understanding.

Slash looked back. There was still no sign of pursuit and he took a moment to consider the situation. His grandpa used to say something that made sense now. "*You have your fear, which could come true. But you have reality, which is true.*" And the reality was, they had three times their armed number likely in pursuit and here was a free gun.

"We got some Rebs and possibly Injuns somewhere back there," Slash said. He jerked his head in that direction. "You care to ride north with us?"

The man smiled broadly. "Rest my dogs and shoot at Rebels? Mister, I will be many times in your debt."

B.W. turned to his shotgun rider. "Well?"

"I'm for taking the chance," Slash said to B.W.

"All we got is two dandies and a stone-silent Injun inside," B.W. pointed out.

"Exactly," Slash replied. "We could use a gun."

B.W. pursed his lips, nodded. The driver faced the black man. "Find room for your gear on top and let yourself in."

Isaiah used the back box to climb to the top of the coach. He lashed his saddle to a trunk, made sure it was secure, then lowered himself over the side. He opened the door.

There was no need to inform the passengers what was transpiring. When the coach had stopped, journalist Small pulled aside the curtain and stuck his head through the open window.

"Evening," the new arrival said.

When neither the reporter nor the reverend moved, Isaiah settled in beside the shaman. The Serrano took his headdress from the seat and put it in his lap to give the newcomer room.

"Kind thanks," the man said to the Indian as he shut the door and gently set his saddle-sore backside into the thinly padded seat.

With a jolt, the stagecoach resumed its travels. Slash craned around and kept his eyes on the horizon to make sure that no one had gained on them during the delay. He looked for a long minute, scanning the arid, flat landscape through dust they kicked up. He could really use those eagle eyes now, or even his own big rabbit ears. He wondered if he shouldn't have been so smug, back at the station. If he had brought Gert's pelt, he might have heard things no human could hear.

"Anything?" B.W. said over the rattling of the coach and rig.

"Not so's I can see," the young man replied.

"That's real good," the driver said with an ominous deepening of his voice.

Slash faced him urgently. "Why?"

B.W. pointed ahead with his whip and replied, "'Cause we may've been had."

The young man turned fully forward. Ahead, in the

road, too distant yet to reveal any details, was another figure. This one was also black. The person was on horseback in the middle of the road. A riderless horse was beside him.

As they neared, one thing more was evident.

Like Isaiah, the dark figure was armed.

Inside the coach, Isaiah sat with his rifle propped against the closed door. Across from him, Reverend Michaels had withdrawn a handkerchief and used it to cover his mouth.

"Sorry," Isaiah said affably. "Been a while since there was a river for bathing."

"I—I mean no insult," the reverend said.

"You prefer the rose scent they sold you back in Saint Louis," Fletcher Small said. "Two sprays for a penny, last you the entire journey. You could have had five sprays for two pennies but you didn't think you'd need them."

The preacher made no comment. But he was thinking that the protective scent was fading and a nickel would have been a good investment.

The reporter was busy studying the new arrival. He had fastened the curtain to the side to admit not just ventilation but moonlight.

"We are all soiled travelers," the journalist said. "My name's Fletcher, this gentleman beside me is Reverend Merritt Michaels, and the fellow beside you is the Serrano shaman Tuchahu. I heard you say your name is Isaiah . . . ?"

"That's right," the man said. "Isaiah Jesus Sunday."

"Your mother was devout," the journalist replied wryly.

"As the sainted Mama Mary herself." Isaiah smiled. He was looking at the journalist's waistcoat in the dark. "You don't carry a derringer," the black man noted.

Small chuckled. "Carry a gun, you could get shot. I leave that to others." He looked fixedly at the new arrival. "Is there a reason I should have one, in here, among my fellow passengers?"

Isaiah laughed right back. "Ain't room to level 'er. Stock'd have to be in the rear box."

"That's just one impediment," Small said. "I've studied these conveyances." He rapped gently on the wooden wall behind him. "The carriage was constructed for speed first, durability second. You discharge that blunderbuss at this range, bullet's as like to pass through me, and the wall, and kill the horses."

"Wouldn't do nobody's ears any good, either," Isaiah said.

"True enough," Small agreed.

"No, sir, I wouldn't do such a thing," Isaiah confided. "But there is one thing you got wrong."

"Oh?" Small replied. "What's that?"

Isaiah replied, "You mentioned my mama. She ain't a 'was.'"

It took a moment for the reporter to understand what the black man was talking about. No sooner had he done so than a shot cracked from somewhere ahead and whistled by the window.

The coach stopped once again. When it did, Isaiah reached for the door without hesitation or explanation. He grabbed his gun and opened the door.

"I thought, sir, you were a man of integrity," Small said.

"You dishonor your names," Michaels added through the scented fabric.

Isaiah did not have time to explain as he stepped into the night.

Slash heard the door open but did not turn. He had his gun leveled at the mounted figure. The figure was a woman and her gun was aimed at him. He didn't think she would fire, however. The first shot had apparently been a warning not to try and run her down.

"Don't be rash," B.W. cautioned. "Empty horse is lame—no saddle."

"I saw," Slash said.

"What's going on?" B.W. called toward Isaiah when he heard the door open, felt the carriage rock with his exit.

Isaiah had his own rifle across his shoulders, like a yoke. His right index finger was on the trigger.

"No one move sudden, or stupid," the black man said. "Little trick I learned from an ex-slave in Texas. It's so's I can turn, aim with precision using my left eye, fire sideways real steady, and not offer much of a target."

"I appreciate the lesson," Slash said. "Now how about an explanation."

"We got another passenger," Isaiah said. "Gentlemen, I'd like you to meet my mother, Willa. C'mon over, Mama. It's okay."

A tall, thin woman, white-haired, urged her horse forward, tugging the other. The second horse was having difficulty keeping up. She wore a floral pattern dress, splattered with dry mud. A cotton cloak was draped on her bony shoulders. It might have been a dark leafy green. Slash couldn't be sure in the moonlight.

"Sorry for the ruse," the black man said as he walked toward the front box.

"You should be," B.W. said.

"We couldn't go no futher after my horse stepped in a gully—and I didn't know that you'd have room for two."

"We might not have had room for *one*!" B.W. said angrily. "What would you have done then?"

The black man shrugged. "I'd've tossed some bags from your back box," Isaiah admitted. "There's room for two back there. And Mama's strong of spirit."

"This is crazy," B.W. said impatiently. "Slash, we gotta get moving."

"I know. But we got an impasse." Deciding, the young man lowered his weapon.

"Isaiah, you know our situation," Slash said.

"Fully. Like I told you, Mama's strong. And she can shoot."

"What a crew," said an exasperated B.W.

"Y'ain't wrong," Slash agreed thoughtfully. "But maybe God knows what He's doing."

"Oh, He does," B.W. said. "I ain't so sure about us. This is the first time I had a trip with one replacement Shotgun, let alone two."

Slash took a moment, then replied quietly, "These are uncommon times."

B.W. regarded him. "You thinking something? I hear it in yer voice."

"I am."

B.W. eyed him a little impatiently. "What is it, boy? Out with it?"

Slash answered by addressing the black man. "Isaiah, you better get your mother and take my place riding shotgun."

"Him?" B.W. said. "What are you fixing to do?"

Slash replied, "I'm gonna borrow her horse."

CHAPTER 13

B.W. was all confusion as Slash hurriedly climbed to the ground.

"Leave the horses," he told Isaiah.

"But we got a good one—"

"I know," Slash said. "Ain't got time to explain."

Isaiah did not argue. He walked over to the injured mare, kissed her and said, "Thanks, Molly," then lifted his mother from the saddle. He gave her his strong right arm as he escorted her toward the coach.

Meanwhile, Slash took the reins of both horses. As B.W. watched with confusion, Slash walked the horses into the darkness, toward the open plain. There, he released the injured mare.

"I can't shoot ya, girl," he apologized as he removed the reins and bit. "Someone may hear and figger how far we are. You graze till you can't no more."

The horse moved its head up and down, a reflex to being liberated. But it almost seemed to Slash as if it understood.

An animal knows its own mortality better than a person, Slash told himself.

He stood there for a moment, considering briefly about what lay in store for this poor mare. A mountain lion or coyotes would find the animal soon enough and take her down. Or Injuns. They'd take a lame horse for the young to learn on, making it walk miles.

"Slash!" B.W. called in a loud whisper. "C'mon!"

The young man still hesitated.

Pa loves horses more than people, he thought. *What would he do?*

The answer was unpleasant but obvious. Drawing his long-blade Green River knife, Slash stroked the horse's muzzle with his left hand and, with a quick move along its soft skin, cut the old mare's throat. The animal whinnied from the sting, backing away. Almost at once, as a sheet of blood washed free, the animal wavered from side to side. Slash stood there caressing it as the blood splashed onto the ground.

Molly fell over suddenly, and for a few seconds more the head and legs moved slightly along the ground, the chest heaving dully. Then the big eyes shut and the animal shivered still.

Slash wiped his bloody knife on the scrub. He finished just as the still-draining blood reached his boot.

"I'm sorry, girl," the young man said softly as he mounted the other and rode back to the stagecoach. Isaiah was just shutting the door and climbed into the front box.

"What'd you do with Molly?" the black man asked.

"She's at peace," he answered, then regarded B.W. "I'm gonna double back along the trail. Anyone coming after you, I'll slow 'em down."

"A shot will tell us how far they are," Isaiah said. "I used ta gauge distance that way on—"

"He won't be shooting," B.W. interrupted.

Isaiah was about to ask "*What then?*" when he noticed the sheaths on Slash's legs. Slash adjusted his hat against the high bright moon, then gave the animal his heels and went back into the lowlands.

B.W. eased the brake back and started the rig rolling.

"Knife fighter, eh?" Isaiah said.

"'Tween Saint Louis and the Yerba Buena Cove at trail's end, I never met one better," the Whip replied. "There's something I have seen plenty of, though."

"What's that?"

"Liars," B.W. said, giving the word bite. "Lord doesn't approve of 'em and I don't much care for them myself. Don't ever tell tales again."

"I apologize sincerely," Isaiah said.

"Now tell me true—that shoulder thing with the rifle," B.W. said. "You telling me that works?"

"No question. You lean your head forward a little, eye lines up with the sight," Isaiah told him. "Recoil don't blow back into your shoulder. Quicker t'get off a second shot."

B.W. shook his head. "Learned something new, and from a Colored man. That dust the Lord God used t'make us—I always believed it had all shades of earth in it."

"I like that," Isaiah said. Then he coughed and spit.

"Ya gotta keep yer teeth closed in the front box," B.W. advised him. "We got bugs at night, right smack into 'em."

Isaiah pulled the remnants of a powdery moth from his tongue, spit out the rest.

"You was apologizing before we got off the subject?" B.W. reminded him.

"Yeah," Isaiah said. "Colored man learns to try and put folks at ease, make sure they know that he don't wanna rob or kill 'em."

"But ya set us up just the same," B.W. reminded him. "And it was only yer elder ma on a horse! How 'n blazes was *that* gonna give us a fright?"

"Two riders on horseback? In the dark? In the middle of the road?" Isaiah said, his voice sibilant as he tried to get the hang of speaking with his jaw locked in place.

B.W. considered that. "Fair point. And—well, you was looking out for your ma."

"All I got left," Isaiah said.

"Your pa?"

"Died with a chain around his ankle, turned his raw skin green. I got a wife and son but they somewhere else. I don't know where."

"Out west, though?"

"That's why we come," he said. "Master took 'em when Alabama, Georgia, the whole region was afire. He had boats, used one of 'em to run, to flee like the mouse he is. He separated son and mother so she would have to follow. Has property out here somewhere."

"Name?"

"Bonita and Joshua—"

"The mouse, I mean."

"Brent Diamond."

B.W.'s teeth opened. He quickly clopped them

shut. That was the man who had been chartered to run the Vallicita Station.

"You're probably tired," B.W. said. "Why don't ya get a little shut-eye while you can. I'll wake ya, I hear or see something. Slash behind us—I feel a lot safer."

"That's a fine idea," Isaiah conceded. "I gave my ma the same advice."

The big man—who looked bigger now that he was in the box, at least six-foot-three—snuggled into the seat, his rifle across his chest, and shut his mouth and eyes. Isaiah probably did not feel it, B.W. thought, but there was a big, fat Indian blanket of silence that fell over the coach. The driver was now faced with a Solomon-sized dilemma. Did he tell this man that he knew where his wife and child were, or did he warn the fiftyish, puffed-but-slight Diamond on the way east—when Dick Ocean was back in his perch—that there was a freed slave looking for him? B.W. was no friend of the Alabama jackanapes, who still dressed the part of a plantation owner but treated his maid like dirt. The place was a dump. Diamond always seemed like he had one foot somewhere else, like he didn't expect to be where he was for very long.

B.W. didn't trust him. But that didn't give him the right to want him beaten bloody or massacred. A head taller, Isaiah looked like he could do it. Especially if Diamond was the man who shackled his pa to death.

Dear Lord Jesus, the driver thought plaintively. *What do I do?*

Before B.W. could consider it further, something reached his ears that he had never heard from the cabin of the stagecoach. Even Isaiah, who had shut his eyes and relaxed, shot alert.

Then he laughed.

"What *was* that?" B.W. asked.

The black man settled back and replied, "Kinfolk."

Fletcher Small had looked at the woman across from him as she settled in. She was wearing a house-dress that was torn and ragged. She had on a shawl that was made of wool or cotton—he couldn't tell which, but was in better repair than her dress. No doubt it had come from the house of whoever had owned her. She had on a small red bonnet, a mop hat. The frayed strings hung at its sides.

The woman's teeth were yellow, but most were present. The stren'th came from a diet of tough meat, cow and horse, and the color came from grits. Her eyes sparkled in the moonlight—bloodshot from dust but alert. Her fingers were bony but nimble. A house slave, no doubt, who had darned, did laundry—judging from the shattered nails—and did not cook, from the lanky look of her. Kitchen slaves always sampled what they served.

The gun she had used to fire over the top of the stagecoach sat upright, between her legs. Although there was a regulation on the Butterfield books that forbade passengers from carrying firearms, it was not enforced. On several occasions, passenger weapons had forestalled attacks from savages or outlaws.

"Madam, it is a pleasure to welcome you," Fletcher

Small had said. "I admit being abuzz with curiosity about what you are doing out here."

The woman then laughed. "Abuzz!" she had repeated. "Never heared a man who thought he was a bee."

The Indian sat still, the reverend was lost in reflection, and the reporter was amused by her innocent unfamiliarity with the term.

"It's a figure of—" Small had started, then said, "it's merely an expression. It means that a man is eager for something, the way a bee is eager for nectar. In my case, I am eager to hear more about you."

"Why?"

"I'm a reporter," Small had said. "I write for newspapers."

"I cain't read," she answered without apology. "Neither does my boy."

"I am gravely sorry to hear that, but what I am interested in are peoples' stories."

"'Gravely sorry,'" she repeated. "'Gravely sorry.' That sounds very serious."

Small smiled benignly. He gave up trying to get any more from the woman just now.

And then, suddenly, the shaman had raised his hands, cupped them beside his mouth, and howled. That was the sound that had alarmed B.W. and roused Isaiah. To both the reverend and the reporter, it was a reason for sudden and deep consternation. But to Willa, it was cause to join in.

She slapped her knees, tilted back her head, and made a noise using throat and cheeks that sounded like an owl. Then both she and the Serrano looked at each other in the dark and laughed. It was the most animated the medicine man had been since beginning this journey.

"Can you explain?" asked Small behind a nervous smile.

"Is an explanation even possible?" asked Reverend Michaels, still shaken and turning toward the window for air.

"Brother Moon, Sister Sky," Willa replied as if it were obvious. "The wolf and the owl." The woman dropped the shawl from her right shoulder to reveal a white feather sewn to the sleeve of her arm. It was missing large chunks and others were soiled. But she looked at it admiringly. "It's to watch over me and my family when I sleep," she said. "A custom from my African mother."

"And how did the shaman know about it?" Small asked.

She touched a slender index finger to her temple and made a face. "He know! That's all. He know."

The parson made a tsking sound. "Superstitious nonsense," he muttered.

"Superstitious, yes," Small agreed. "Nonsense, not necessarily."

"Oh surely, Mr. Small, you don't believe any of that," Michaels said.

"I am neither religious nor anti-religious—"

"*Religion?*" Michaels exclaimed. "You call this . . . this black magic a *religion?*"

"They have their talking owls and wolves, you have tempting snakes and a man dwelling inside a whale," Small replied.

"You, sir, are a blasphemer," Michaels said. "'For as Jonah was three days and three nights in the belly of a huge fish.' That is the work of God's mighty hand!"

"Mighty indeed, and surely strong enough to make kin of the wolf and the owl, if He so chooses," the reporter replied.

"Madness," Merritt Michael huffed, and turned back to the window.

The Indian and freed slave had settled back into their previous composure, though each wore the hint of a smile, a new and relaxed fellowship.

The reporter decided not to continue his pursuit of another story. He had the main one to consider, the Butterfield account, and the two Colored passengers had additional color. He took out his notebook and marked it all down, thinking for certain now that Willa Sunday herself was a better story for *Beadle's* than for the *Daily Missouri Republican*. The magazine that published his stories "Mrs. Calderwell and the Cussing Cowboy," "Master Melville and the Maverick Mule," and "Mr. Rockefeller and his Randy Rooster" should be proud to publish "Mrs. Sunday and the Serrano Shaman."

After he finished making his notes, the tired journalist leaned against the side of the cabin and shut his eyes. He knew he wasn't likely to sleep, though coming up with opening lines for his story helped him to forget where he was.

B.W. wondered if the Good Lord might be testing him.

There was a freed slave snoring beside him, his mother—an owl—inside, her Serrano companion—a wolf—beside her, and a Rebel unit on his trail. The two white men aboard were useless as defenders and the one man who could help protect the stage was headed off in a direction *opposite* the one they were traveling.

Dear God, I pray that I am strong enough to bear the burdens you have placed upon your humblest of servants.

That was when the Whip heard another sound. A sound he knew. One that sent fire up his back.

It was a snap, sharp and quick, and it was followed by a clattering.

The spoke that had been coated with pitch had broken, the pieces tossed away by the spinning wheel.

There were thirteen more rods, but supporting the entire wheel wasn't the problem. Every time it turned and pressure hit that unsupported spot it would weaken.

Eventually it would break.

The question was whether that would happen before they reached the next station. And then he was facing a two-hour delay—time enough to be caught.

He nudged Isaiah. The man started awake.

"We got a decision to make," B.W. said.

"What's that?"

B.W. gently, carefully applied the brake. When the coach stopped, he faced the black man.

"We got a missing spoke," the driver said. "Need to lighten our load, less'n the wheel come off. Then we're dead."

Isaiah didn't like what he was hearing at first. B.W.

could see it in his expression—and knew he'd mis-taken the driver's intention.

"The bags, the saddle," B.W. said. "Everything's gotta go."

The big man relaxed. "Oh. Okay."

B.W. looked around. "Let's put it somewhere off the trail—there, that patch o' scrub."

"Good spot. No one likely to see it till the sun comes over the mountains eastward."

"Exactly."

B.W. climbed from the box and told Michaels and Small to come out. He explained why.

"Our belongings?" the reverend said. "All of them?"

"It's just temporary," B.W. informed him. "Either that, or we risk a full breakdown."

There was no further discussion. Isaiah was already on the top of the coach and he began handing bags to B.W. With the preacher and the reporter they formed a chain to the patch of tall grass. For her part, Willa went to the back box and began undoing the crisscrossing straps.

"I am grievously disappointed in the way we have been treated," Michaels grumped. "Medicine men, picking up stragglers on the road, my own sister leaving the journey to fight Confederates with an old man—"

"Your sister is gonna learn more from that 'old man' than she ever has learned in her life," B.W. said. "And she's safer with him than she is anywhere west of the Mississippi."

"I hope you're right," Michaels said. "I pray to God that you are."

"You do that," B.W. said. He cast his eyes heavenward. "And I most sincerely wish you better luck with the Almighty than I have had of late."

"Will there be time to get anything I might need?" the preacher asked.

"Not at present," the Whip told him. "We keep the mail in the back box and send a cart from the next station to collect everything."

"Why the mail?" the preacher demanded. "That's got weight!"

"It do, and we need some traction," B.W. replied. "Your things will get to you, I promise."

Unless Injuns get to it first.

The nine bags and grips were higher than B.W. had anticipated, but there was no time to do additional arranging. While Isaiah helped his mother back inside, B.W. shooed the two men back to their seats. He shut the door, then joined the black man in the front box. B.W. made sure his Bible was still in its place, then carefully released the brake and gently flicked his whip. The horses started up. God no doubt had His reasons for testing the Whip, but B.W. loved his Jehovah no less.

God is giving me His sacred attention, B.W. told himself. *In a way, that could be a sign of heavenly love and affection.* His heart swelled with the thought.

The stagecoach felt strangely light, almost rickety without the weight of the luggage. He hoped he had done the right thing. The team was used to pulling more and he had to rein them a little to make sure they didn't rush ahead. That would be as bad for the wheel as the heavy bags.

He decided that it would do no good to worry, so he did his best to just guide the stage through the night, taking comfort in the parts of the territory that were familiar and the fact that each moment brought them closer to safety.

CHAPTER 14

General Rhodes Guilford was sitting at his large desk in the fort, smoking locomotive-steady puffs from a cigar, drinking a whiskey—two shots was enough, for now—and waiting. He was waiting impatiently for two things.

One was the return of the two Mission Indians he had dispatched to the O'Malley family's Whip Station. The two men he had sent to the previous stop in Vallicita had already returned. The stage had stopped there, the shaman Tuchahu was aboard, and it left for Whip Station on time. Malibu and Sisquoc should have returned by now with news that the coach had reached the O'Malley place late with the shaman no longer aboard.

Everything depended on that. Kennedy and Hathaway knew it. If that had not occurred . . .

That left the other thing he was waiting for. Word from those two Eastern functionaries. A dispatch . . .

No, "*information,*" he reminded himself. *Civilians don't call it a dispatch or intelligence or orders. They call it information. News. They write it on a piece of paper without formality or regimental detail.*

"Bloody brown," he muttered, blowing smoke and using the expression he had uttered so often during the War. It was a short phrase that described the rivers and streams his men often had to cross during the War Between the States. Waters turned from clear to brown by the bleeding bodies within the cool flow or on the uncaring shores.

General Guilford was waiting for information. He had been waiting since sunset. Now, nearly eight hours later, he was restless and tired. It was a bad combination.

The other thing the fifty-one-year-old officer was waiting for was the event that would follow. The abduction of Tuchahu was just the start. The war against the Indians . . .

He pulled on his cigar and drained his glass and resisted the desire to refill it. He had to stay clear-headed, at least for the next several days. Maneuvers had to be done carefully, as they had been against General Lee.

Of course, Andrew Johnson and his macaronis on the Potomac were not the adversaries that Lee had been. For one thing, they were not in the field, had no idea what was really going on. For another, they were fools. They could never imagine what was coming. The greatest event in the four centuries during which white men had trod upon this land.

One of the greatest events in the history of the world.

The honored Civil War officer was not a patient man. That was one of his greatest strengths. Short of stature, with a neatly clipped beard he nonetheless commanded a room with his barrel chest, penetrating, pale gray eyes, and a voice that could be heard over cannon fire. It had been tested time and again as his troops pummeled Confederate positions with ball and bayonet, sometimes with fist and teeth.

Men served Guilford. They wanted to please him. They did what he ordered.

They would do this.

The stocky man rose and walked around the ornately carved mahogany desk. He went to the open window through which a muscular breeze blew. Fort Yuma had no stockade. It sat on a high hill, was open to the elements that came from east and west, that rose from the Colorado River. Day and night came the sound of boats. The fluttering of the flag high atop its tall, white pole. The regular rattle of the stagecoaches that charged along the Butterfield route.

Fort Yuma was the most important stop along the line. Here, any substantial repair or reinforcement could be made. Arms could be purchased if an accident or carelessness had claimed a firearm. Medical care was available. So was a bath, for those who had had enough of dirt and sweat.

A woman could also be had. Some drivers, like "Maggot" Reynolds, even had a second wife here and a third in San Francisco, though none knew about the others. The men kept this knowledge private because Maggot's brother was the quartermaster and bribed them with liquor. They didn't think Guilford knew, but no good general is ever without sources of . . .

"Intelligence," he said out the window. "Good, solid military intelligence with able and reliable informants."

The lights of lanterns and a few torches spotted the

terrain. Above, the stars were few, obscured by the brilliant beacon of the moon. Guilford was not a Westerner by birth. He was from Connecticut, the son of a hatmaker. But in the two years he had been here, the general had fallen deeply in love with the scope of the West, its rugged geography that challenged a man to be better. Its leather-tough inhabitants. Even its Indians, who had courage and accepted whatever came, defeat as well as victory, death instead of life.

He inhaled deeply. As he did so, he heard a rider racing along the dirt road that wound up the hill from the west. At that pace, the horseman had to know that route well.

General Guilford flicked the cigar out the window. He retraced his steps and sat behind his desk. He always wanted to be ready, at his command post, ready to respond, when a dispatch—*news*—arrived.

The officer knew exactly how long it would take for the courier to be brought to him, what sounds his boots would make on the eight-year-old planks. He took fresh paper, moved the inkwell closer, picked up his Esterbrook steel pen.

He smiled at the tableau. In Washington, *this* was power. Out here . . .

His aide-de-camp, Lt. Bernard Anthony, knocked on the general's door.

"Enter!" Guilford bellowed.

The knob turned and a young courier walked in. He doffed his hat, sandy hair spilling out, then stopped before the desk and saluted smartly.

"At ease," Guilford said.

The general extended his hand just as the youth removed the folded paper from his pocket. He did not have to ask the young man if he had read it. There was honesty in his clear eyes and boyish cheek.

Guilford scanned the pencil message, then put it in the center drawer of his desk.

"See to refreshment before you leave, trooper."

"Thank you, sir."

The boy turned smartly and left. The orderly shut the door. The general reflected on the message.

"Bloody Kennedy," he said, creating a new denunciation. If Guilford had not needed a patsy, he would have selected a man with greater skill. Even Hathaway seemed more capable—though perhaps not in Washington. That required a different kind of competence.

Fortunately, there were still enough men from Brent Diamond's ad hoc unit to see this through. They didn't know what the true objective was. All they knew was that, for now, they were required to take orders from the Easterners.

"For now," he said aloud.

Guilford rose and selected a fresh cigar from the humidor cabinet that stood beside his desk. He took a stick match from the dish on top and lovingly touched flame to tobacco. He drew on the cigar, held the smoke for a moment, and then blew it out slowly.

He was disappointed but he was calm. Despite the setback, the general took consolation that Dr. Peterson would soon be in the field with them, making sure that events unfolded according to plan.

The general smiled.

"My plan," he said. General Festus Williams had contributed thoughts about covering the territory to the north, where Fort Mason had jurisdiction. But the main area of contention would be the south. To the north, the desert made military actions a severe challenge.

"Hold!"

Riding slightly behind Joe O'Malley, Clarity had been admiring the play of moonlight on the terrain. They had entered an area of high grasses. Joe had explained that underground springs keep this land fertile during spring and summer, after which rot feeds the birds and insects.

"Jackson built his irrigation plan after what nature thought up out here," he had told her. "'Stead of running ditches from the nearest water, he dug down and stuck in cloth that draws it up. Lay that under the plantings."

It was a clever idea, Clarity had to admit. The constant, mineral-rich water source no doubt explained why the carrots Sarah had served at the station had been so good.

They had been riding in silence for quite some time, stopping only to water the horses at a small pond. The frontiersman had taken them across terrain that had no trail. It would intercept the stagecoach line at a point some six miles north of the station. B.W. still might get there first, given his head start. But the road Joe and Clarity rode was shorter.

Clarity walked her horse beside Joe and listened.

"Someone's coming from the east," she said.

"A stampede o' someones," Joe agreed. "Sticking to the trail, riding hard, likely the Rebs."

Clarity circled the horse around, looking for a place where they could take cover. There was nothing. Not around them, not as far ahead as he could see. The land was just arid, low hills and brush. Even the rocks were small. That was one of the reasons the stagecoach came this way. No effort was required to make the trail.

"What're you doing?" Joe asked.

"If it's the Rebels, we went to watch them, don't we? Pick them off?"

"Yeah," Joe said.

"That means them not knowing we're here, right?" Clarity asked.

"Girl, they'll know we're here first time we fire," Joe said.

"Of course," she replied.

Clarity felt suddenly, strongly aware of her own limitations. The land made her feel small, but Joe's instant grasp of situations made her feel almost childlike.

"They followed the stage trail to overtake the coach, and because it's a flatter, cleaner ride at night," Joe said. He sat there, staring at the ground, doing mental calculations. "Juncture between us and the trail is about two miles. Stage can't be that far ahead, maybe another two miles. And that's if they haven't stopped for any reason."

"Why would they?"

"Breakdown, Injuns, road coulda fallen in for a stretch. A lot of reasons. Wherever they are, we want to get between them and the Rebels and slow the pursuit. Maybe get the Confederates to bump up against the Apaches, if they're out here, too. Then they can kill each other. But that ain't a plan, it's just the start o' one."

Joe said that almost as if he were chastising himself. In a sense, he was. He had been riding these many hours, knowing this moment was coming, and he still hadn't figured out exactly what to do.

"We can't lie flat again with nowhere to hide the horses," Clarity said.

"No," he agreed. "And we don't want the horses shot."

Joe thought for a moment, looking to the west. He held up a finger, then said suddenly, "Let's ride!"

The frontiersman exploded forward at a gallop, Clarity falling nearly three horse len'ths behind before she kicked into motion. With effort, she caught up.

"What's the plan?" Clarity yelled as she was near enough to be heard.

Joe half-turned and answered, "To beat them just short o' where our paths are gonna cross and make sure they stop."

Sarah O'Malley knew she would not be able to sleep. She had not even tried. With Gert, she had taken turns sitting with Dick Ocean and keeping an ear turned to the plains.

Jackson had fallen asleep in the rocking chair. That had not been his intention, but Sarah knew that needs do not often yield to wishes. Because of his injury, her husband had to work twice as hard to keep even with what Slash or Joe could do. He didn't ask for favors but how he pushed himself, she thought both proudly—and with sadness. He had never been quite the same after that fall. His will had not broken but something about his spirit had.

Sarah did her best to try and act as if nothing had changed, but it had. And they were all too busy to try and find ways to make things better, either by picnicking or traveling to San Diego or just reading by the fire.

Jackson had tried. The book was on the floor.

The woman had made coffee and took it out to Sisquoc first, then Malibu who was still in the loft. He came down when he saw her so that she would not have to climb up.

"Thank you," he said when she poured him a cup.

"You're very gracious, since it is I who should be thanking you," Sarah said. "Mr. O'Malley—Jackson— Gert and I would not have been able to do this alone. Not as well as you two have."

"Happy to help family of Joe," he said, sipping gingerly. "We know him from before."

"I know," she said. "He has spoken of you, always as friends—even when there was conflict."

"Brave honor brave," the Indian said.

"You came here to make sure the shaman was safe," she said. "I heard you talking with Joe earlier. Is this what you expected? Something like this?"

The Yaqui considered the question before answering.

"Strange things have been happening," he said. "Many couriers between the forts. Mission Indians sent out, all of them. Never before like this."

"Surely not because of a few Rebels."

"I agree," Malibu said. "Surely not."

"Do you have any ideas? Any thoughts about it?"

Malibu was silent again. He drank for a spell and then said, "I have not seen enough. But I have spoken with other Mission Indians in the field. We are all—"

He stopped and made a sign, pointing to his forehead and dragged a hand across his eyes.

"You can't see . . . think . . . confused?"

"Yes," Malibu replied. "Something is being hidden. Ask Sisquoc. He sees it, too."

"I'll leave him be," she said. "There isn't much we can do about it."

Sarah offered him a refill but Malibu declined. Thanking her again, he returned to the loft.

The woman thought as she walked back to the station. Gert was standing in the doorway.

"How is Mr. Ocean?" Sarah asked.

"Asleep again," Gert said. "Quietly, though. His fever seems to have gone down a little." She smiled. "Father is asleep."

"It appears *The Last of the Mohicans* . . . will last."

"You can go to bed, if you like," Gert said. "I'm fine."

"I don't think I could, now."

"Why? Isn't everything all right?"

"I don't know," Sarah replied. "Malibu says there is something—well, mysterious going on at the forts. He hasn't many details. It seems to be just a feeling."

"Indian instincts are always good," Gert said.

"That's what concerns me, a little," Sarah admitted. She reached the door and kissed her daughter on the forehead. "Maybe I will lie down. Please wake me if you need anything."

"Of course," Gert said.

Standing alone now, with only the wind and the creaking timbers of the station for company, Gert suddenly turned and went to the root cellar. Moving quietly so she would not disturb Dick Ocean, the young woman went to a small oak chest in the back and removed its contents.

Minutes later, sitting behind the station over a small brazier of burning arrow weed, she began to pray. It was a Pechanga ceremony to Wi'áaşal, the Great Oak, the source of all life and wisdom. She prayed not for herself but for the man at the center of this dangerous pursuit—and the men, and woman, risking their lives to protect him.

To the east, the makeshift unit of former Confederates crashed through the night like the fabled soldiers of Quantrill's Raiders.

Kennedy and his fellow Union bureaucrats had always despised newspaper reports of men like that. They hated the Raiders because of what he himself was feeling now. Fearless, dashing, filled with grim purpose. Who would not want men like these galloping to their rescue or rallying around their cause? The Union had masses of men but they did not have units that were intentionally flamboyant. They were the living embodiment and avenging devils of the Southern aristocracy.

Neither Douglas Kennedy nor Jessup Hathaway was William Quantrill.

The two Easterners were in the rear. For the first

two or so miles, they had struggled to maintain a heroic front. They rode as hard as their fellows. But Kennedy had never done more than take Sunday rides in nearby Virginia. And Hathaway was an Appalachian boy. He could fish and possum-hunt with the best of them, but his riding consisted of a dray horse he and his pa used to haul timber cut by local lumberjacks. This pace—and this discomfort—were entirely new to them.

Kennedy couldn't help but think that much of this gallop was spite and not devotion to duty. Except for maybe Doc Peterson, the unit was interested in a payday, not the extermination of the savage population. The doctor was difficult to understand. He was professional in his dispensing of medical care. But he was contrary, at times argumentative, and seemed unhappy to be among them.

Surely, out here, a man with medical skills could find employment elsewhere. It did not make sense to Kennedy. Fortunately, it did not have to. As soon as the Indian shaman had been taken prisoner by parties unknown, and murdered where the savages could find him, the War of Extermination would begin. The only loose end, the O'Malleys, would not be a problem for very long. On the way back, they and their station would be destroyed by Apaches.

At least, that was the tale the soldiers from the San Diego Barracks would tell. They were the ones who would find the tomahawks, lances, bows and arrows left behind in the ashes. It had always been part of the plan to incite outrage and a call to arms by burning the Whip and Diamond Stations. But only Brent

Diamond was in on the plan. It was the reason he had never done repairs on the Vallicita outpost. He would only have had to rebuild it, eventually. This was, after all, his plan. Diamond grew up in Tennessee with the president. It was said that if not for the War, Diamond would have been as powerful down South as then–Senator Andrew Johnson was up North. Kennedy could see it, when he met Diamond for the first time just the other day—this was a rivalry between the men. But it was the kind that had the side benefit of building nations.

These raiders, Diamond's men, loved that home-steader. The few times his name was mentioned, it was done so as if they were talking about General Lee himself.

Kennedy had to admit to envying that a little. Perhaps, though, when the West was cleared of Red Men he would have that achievement to carry him to political glory and whatever wealth a smart man could wring from that.

The riders slowed now and then to allow their horses a respite. There had been no full-out rests, no impediments, nothing surprising.

"Whoa!" one of the men in front said. "Barricade—"

Before he could finish, before anyone could stop, the road, the night, and two mounted men vanished.

Lying in bed, listening to the silence, Brent Diamond had to acknowledge that he was a clever man.

He had been the son of a dirt farmer who, one day, when he was still a boy, up and rode a log down a river and established a shipping empire at the other end. Before most of the landed patricians of the South met him, the young man was already dressing like them, acting like them, was every bit as good as the cotton farmers and tobacco growers.

What's more, they had needed him. There was increasing population up north and greater-than-ever demand for goods produced on Southern plantations. Diamond had built his fortune on that mutual need.

Then hell was unleashed and Diamond fled. His boat line was among the first targets, since it was a means of getting much-needed black market income for goods. The Union motivation was simple: Why pay for what you can now legally steal as spoils of a war of rebellion?

He sailed west until it was necessary to join a wagon train. That was how he met John Butterfield, who had an interest in all overland operations. Though Butterfield was a Northerner he was a lifelong stagecoach driver. He knew and loved transportation. His affection for the men who worked in that field transcended politics and boundaries. To a stagecoach driver or boatman, boundaries were simply a means to charge tariffs. They were artificial, needless, and proudly ignored.

Butterfield practically gave the native Tennessean the Vallicita Station with the promise that Diamond fix it up as soon as he recovered financially.

Diamond had recovered financially months ago. In addition to the money from Butterfield, he earned a good deal from items sold to travelers. These were made by his girl Rosa and her seven-year-old boy and included hand fans, fruit-scented water that he called perfume, and combs made of squirrel ribs. But he had not used that money to repair the station. He had used it to begin making much, much larger repairs.

It seemed strange to be in such peaceful surroundings at the station, his servant and her son abed in a locked room, knowing that so much was going on miles beyond.

It's almost decadent, he thought.

The man's long face showed the hint of a smile. It was the first one he had known in well over a year. But that was exactly right. After an arduous journey across the country with a slave—former slave, as she kept reminding him—and her sullen boy, this was the first time he felt as he once did. That the world had been righted and he was on the top of it.

He thought briefly of Bonita and Joshua. He had never molested her, as was his right—as was the way of so many slaveholders. He had beaten the boy, but only when he failed to keep the master's boots polished or brush the dust and grasses from his pants. Even so, that was less than other slaves received. And out here, they worked no less and no more than any white woman or squaw living on barren scrub. He kept the door locked at night, not because he feared violence against his person but because he was afraid they would flee on a foolish mission of their own. Diamond heard her prayers at night, asking God to keep her husband and his mother safe.

That man, Isaiah, had been a red-hot bastard. The slave, an uneducated son of an equally ungrateful slave, had an easy job. His wife and mother had easy jobs, and yet he had tried to escape and take them with him. Now, his damnable woman wished to do the same. Diamond would not lose his only two companions, two very able servants, and have to replace them with Indians or Mexicans who did not even speak his language.

It was as if the insanity of the War had not yet subsided. The Colored race was still mad.

When this is over, they can leave, he told himself. Then he would have position, power—all that he had lost, and more.

Part of him was very curious to see how far they got. Love and devotion made people blind and stupid. On foot, without survival skills, she would not last more than a few days.

She should thank me every minute of her miserable life, he thought.

Brent Diamond fell asleep with the baying of a wolf somewhere in the distance.

Chapter 15

"They're gonna see us," Joe called over his shoulder as he rode toward the trail, watching it to the south. "The trick is to make sure they can't *get* us."

Riding at a pace that threatened to exhaust the horses, Joe and Clarity reached the stagecoach trail when what seemed like a long line of horses appeared in the distance. They were about a mile away, a shifting line in the moonlight followed by a low blossom of dust.

Joe flew from his horse before it had fully stopped.

"Take the rein," he ordered Clarity.

The woman reached the empty saddle a moment after Joe had jumped down. Clarity did as she was told without comment. She watched as Joe started kicking together tumbleweeds, then bent and pulled scrub and bushes out by the roots. He bunched them together on the trail, creating a line of dry weed leading to the tall grasses that surrounded them. Then he hurried to the other side and created another line of . . .

"Kindling," Clarity said very softly.

"The birds and pests'll just have to look elsewhere for a meal," Joe said.

When he was finished, he still had time to do one more thing. He ran up ahead, away from the oncoming riders, picking objects up from the ground.

"What are those?" Clarity asked.

"Patties dropped by the stage horses," he explained. "Dung for fuel."

He placed them strategically throughout the bramble, then plucked the flint from his shirt pocket, knelt, and waited behind the pile.

"Back away some," he told Clarity. "Horses ain't gonna like this."

Which was the point, she realized. It wasn't just about delaying the riders, it was about them being thrown, injured. It was brilliant in its sinister way.

The line of riders neared and she could see now that they were the Confederates. They were racing ahead, heedless of any danger, until they were nearly upon the tumbleweeds and one of the men called urgently for them to stop, and then Joe struck the spark.

The wall of brush burned low along the trail for a moment and then erupted as if Satan's own forge had been fired up underground. Joe ran to where Clarity had led the horses. He not only wanted to put distance between them and the pursuers, he did not want to be standing where they were likely to fire—once they got their wits back.

He reached his horse and pulled himself into the saddle in time to see two men flailing horribly on their bellies, aflame from boot to scalp. Their horses had bucked back, colliding with the riders behind them, causing a general panic and collapse of the line.

There were no gunshots yet. The men were too busy restoring order in the face of a twenty-odd-yard sheet of fire. But the fire would not burn so high for long.

"Let's go!" he snapped at Clarity, as they turned and picked up the trail toward the north.

Joe pushed his horse, whipping it with the reins side to side, and checked to make sure the woman was keeping up. She was, though he knew it wasn't long before bullets punched through the blaze. The first thing to do was get out of range. The second was to get out of sight. It wouldn't be long before the Confederates went through the fast-burning fire or around it. Joe and Clarity needed to be far enough ahead to get the first shots in at whoever came after them.

The trail went straight for about a quarter-mile, after which it followed the northwest curve of a deep, wide ravine. It had been created by an earth fall years ago, a tremor that shook the area and just swallowed down whole sections of the prairie. When Joe was scouting out the route for the Butterfield line, he suggested building a bridge instead of going out of the way like this. But money was deemed more important than a short detour. The ravine closed up about a half-mile ahead where the trail resumed its northward passage. The walls of the ravine were too steep for Joe and Clarity to go down and up again. And if they made a stand there, they would have no place to retreat. A line of Rebs could fire from the edge and cut them down.

If the night had been darker, the Confederates might not know it was there, Joe thought regretfully. Many a rider under a moonless sky had tumbled to the death of himself and his horse in that pit. But unless they were blinded by the smoke and too angry to think, that was not going to happen.

Until they rounded the bend, Joe had been able to keep track of the size of the blaze by the glow it cast, by the len'th of his own shadow. Just before they turned, he could see that the fires were dying fast. He wasn't surprised. Dry scrub and horse patties burn hot but not long.

"They're coming!" Clarity shouted from behind him.

"I hear!" he shouted back.

There were a few loud voices, indistinct but mostly shouting one or two words that sounded like reorganization. That did not surprise Joe. Veterans of a recent war, still in fighting form, did not suddenly surrender their survival skills. They would leave the dead behind, as was done during battle, and collect them later. They would not make the mistake of running into another ambush or impasse. Most of all, they sounded determined to mount an immediate pursuit and catch the perpetrators.

The ravine was to his right and he watched as it narrowed. To even attempt jumping it, they would have to back off a considerable distance to the left for a running start. And even then, he wasn't sure he could do it, let alone Clarity. He considered leaving the horses, running down, and clawing up the other side—but there wasn't time. The Rebs would be here before they could get up. And the men in pursuit would round the end of the ravine before Joe and Clarity could get away.

All the two had going for them was a head start of maybe a quarter of a mile. Back at the station, some of those boys had the new Winchester muskets. They had a good hundred-yard range. If any one of the Rebs broke out and closed the distance, Joe would have to stop and cover Clarity's escape. Using tactics he had heard about, they would leapfrog, one past the other, so they could keep up a constant fire while their brothers-in-arms reloaded or moved ahead. They didn't give their quarry an opportunity to breathe . . . or, more importantly, to return fire.

Just then, Joe heard whoops behind him. The enemy wasn't mourning. They sure weren't celebrating. It was a battle cry. It was how Rebels spurred themselves on in the face of the devil's own odds.

"Girl!" Joe called over his shoulder. "Switch places. Anything happens to me, you keep going and pick these skunks off. Gotta protect the stage."

"I can cover you from the other side of the—"

"You can reach them, they can reach you!" he said. "No. The coach is what matters!"

"I understand."

Clarity pushed her tired animal a little harder while Joe fell back a few paces. He immediately began looking for a place to put himself along the roadside.

Flatlands or ditch, he thought.

There wasn't much choice. He would have to sacrifice the horse to take down as many Rebels as possible. If he was lucky, he could get one of their animals.

If you are lucky, you will survive, Joe reminded himself.

Nothing in life was guaranteed. Out here, that was especially true.

At the bottom of the slope were piles of rough-edged rocks that had fallen when the crevasse was created, and cracked again when they hit bottom. Ahead, however, was a spot where they had piled high enough to reach nearly to the top. The rocks at that level were still fairly intact.

That was where Joe would make his stand.

Dismounting as he slowed, and grabbing his rifle from the sheath, he swatted the horse toward the south. The Rebels would likely not shoot it, since they could always use horses. If Joe needed the mount again, it was likely not to wander past the nearest spot of grass. Gunfire was likely to keep away any of the cats or coyotes that might otherwise trouble it.

As he hurried to the rocks, Joe could feel the hoof-beats on the ground. He could also feel his heart whamming in his chest. He was a tracker and a hunter, not a trooper. He had to think of these men and their horses as charging varmints—winter-starved foxes or wolves, both of which he had faced in his time.

You see something alive—shoot it, he told himself.

He jumped to the nearest flat surface, some three feet down, then got to the west of it, opposite the direction the unit was coming from. He lay the long, brass muzzle flat on the rock, realized it shone in the moonlight, and backed up so he could shield it with his shoulder. Not as steady a shot, but it would have to do. He knew that he would only get off two, maybe three shots before they knew where he was. He had to make them matter. More than the lead man would have to be in range, which meant letting them get closer than he would have liked. He also knew he had to cover the area between the men and the ravine. Wouldn't do for them to get in there with him, where he couldn't see because of the rocks.

He watched the turn in the trail with held breath.

No. Breathe, he told himself.

He got into a steady rhythm, lowered the gun to wipe his perspiring hands on his jacket, then raised the gun again. His body calmed but his head was active, like it had a family of squirrels running around inside of it.

He thought about Dolley, about Jackson and Sarah, about the station he was here fighting for. Butterfield? He would benefit, but his well-being never entered into it. This was about their home, their land, the O'Malley family. That was what a man had to be ready to risk his life for. It was the lucky man—and so far, he had been damned lucky—who did not have to do that too often out here.

Though it's an unfair way for a man of seventy to be earning his keep, he thought with at least a hint of a smile. The smile was for himself. He knew he would not have it any other way.

Well, he thought after a moment, *there are two things I wish was different.*

One was that his Dolley would be waiting for him, still. Wherever they were living, that was reason enough to endure any hardship, reason enough to get back home.

The other was that Clarity would get safe away. He was glad that she was still riding west with her back to the site of the upcoming strife. She did not want her to see him die, if it came to that.

Just get away, he thought, stealing a quick look at her and the retreating horse. *Get to the other side and run like a deer.*

A deer with a gun. He was grateful, at this moment, for having met such a remarkable woman. He didn't want to wish his granddaughter were more like her but that's where his heart and mind went.

The vibration of the rocks under his legs and chest brought him back to the matter at hand. The Confederates were coming into view around the bend. They did not come stupid. There were five of them and they came at him abreast, behind a wall of gunfire.

Joe swore. In the moment he had before dropping behind the rocks, he saw that they were in a wide formation with two out front and three behind. Even a scatter gun could not have taken them down. They would have to be targeted individually—while they were firing back. His other immediate tactical regret was that he couldn't tell the Rebs from their dandy leaders. The Confederates were the real danger.

The good news was they could not just keep him hunkered down and ride past in pursuit of Clarity. The Rebs could not afford to have him at their back. The shots were coming in waves, men reloading while others fired. There was no window when he could show himself to return fire.

Ya gotta risk it, he told himself. *Even if you just get one or two of 'em—*

Gunfire sounded fiercely from the other side of the ravine. It couldn't be Clarity, who was still on this side.

There were three loud bursts, each successive shot more forceful than the one before.

Someone was coming closer from the north. It couldn't be the Apaches. They would still be south of here.

Within seconds, the gunfire from the Confederates had stopped. There were shouts, some from pain, and then the shooting was redirected—but only briefly. There was chaos on the southern side of the chasm, the disorder of a surprise attack and from the sound of it an enemy that no one could see.

Joe risked rising a little so he could see over the north side of the crevasse. A rider was approaching, fast. He fired quickly, then moved suddenly in a different direction, then fired again before he had turned. Whoever it was, the newcomer was a good shot and a better rider. Joe looked ahead and saw a Confederate on the ground, one horse dead, and the other men still firing—though they appeared to be retreating. It was difficult to say, with the rock half-blocking his view and the dark blocking some more.

Joe didn't want to show himself. Not yet. He didn't know who the other man was. Savior he appeared to be, but he could also be gunning for everyone out here. In his frontier days, Joe had seen everyone from put-upon prospectors to loco hermits to renegade Injuns cut down anyone who came into their land. If this man was one of those, he . . .

The shooting stopped suddenly. It ended first on Joe's side of the ravine. There were a few more shots from the north, nearer than before. Cautiously, he lifted his head a little more. The Rebels were already rounding the bend, headed south.

Joe shifted his eyes across the chasm.

There was a man on horseback about fifty yards east of Joe's position. He was sheathing a carbine with his right hand, still holding a six-shooter in his left. He wore a hat and rode a horse that was too dark to make out. That was all the older man's eyes could see.

Remembering his companion, Joe turned and looked to the west. Clarity was just rounding the far end of the big gully. She had to have heard the gunfire . . .

She did. She stopped about four, five hundred yards away where the stagecoach trail came around again to the northeast. Joe couldn't tell if her own rifle was drawn but he suspected it was. Clarity just sat there for a long, long moment. After apparently assessing the situation, which she had heard but not seen, the woman kicked her horse forward, slowly. The moon glinted off the barrel of her gun, which was held shoulder high on the right while she seemed to maneuver the horse with her knees.

Helluva woman, he could not help thinking.

Just then, the new arrival turned his horse in the direction of the woman. He moved slowly and came forward several paces. Nothing aggressive, just a slow walk. Joe watched them, fearing that one or the other of them might be a little hot-kettled after what just happened. He didn't want either of them doing something stupid.

The man was nearly opposite Joe's position now. The men were still probably just out of range of one another. Inhaling—and feeling the stiffness of his legs as he called on them to rise—Joe stood.

"Hello!" he called across the rocky break in the ground.

The man stopped his horse. He raised his arm in greeting.

"Hi, Grampa Joe!"

The Rebels stopped running. They had not left as a unit but as a disordered group of men, each unsure who his companions were.

Kennedy was the first to stop. Marcus Stone was the second. Dan Ridgewood was the third. Jessup Hathaway was the fourth. A fifth had fallen from his saddle after they had rounded the turn in the trail. His horse stood idly beside him.

Spotting the animal, Ridgewood rode back. He returned a moment later, stopping between Kennedy and Hathaway. The two Easterners were facing south, the way they had originally come.

"It's Mute," the former Confederate said breathlessly. "He's shot up but alive."

Kennedy was also breathing hard. He looked over his shoulder. Not at Mute, but at the trail.

"You say that as if we're supposed to *do* something," the leader said.

"We're *supposed* to go back and help him!" Ridgewood yelled.

"How do you know that gunman isn't waiting for us around the bend?" Kennedy replied.

"He's on the other side!"

"Not him," Kennedy said. "Whoever was in that

hole-in-the-ground. And—you saw the lady riding off?
I'm guessing that was Clarity, which makes the man
behind the rocks Joe O'Malley. He may be waiting for
us to come get Mute!"

Ridgewood rose in his saddle and drew his Colt.
He aimed it at Kennedy. The Easterner was too beaten
to move.

"I oughta shoot you for a coward!" he snarled.

"And I ought to shoot you for mutiny," said a thick
voice from behind him. It was Hathaway. He had
raised his own rifle and was pointing it at the Rebel.

"You want to go back, go back," the Easterner said.

"Let's just cool down here," Stone said more rea-
sonably. "I happen to string with Ridgewood but a
minute more or less won't help Mute. We gotta know
what our next move is, and it's still four against three.
I say we go after 'em, finish the—"

"Shh!" Kennedy interrupted.

Everyone fell silent. There was nothing but a faint
wind and the distant, soft moans of Mute.

"Jess, you hear that?" Kennedy asked, pointing
south. "Out there?"

Hathaway listened. "I don't hear anything. What
was it?"

"It sounded like a horse," Kennedy said.

"Where?" Stone asked him.

"Down the trail somewhere," Kennedy told him.

The men all listened.

"Who in hell would be out there?" Ridgewood said.
"No more coaches and nobody travels at night what
knows better."

The irony of what the man had just said was not lost
on Kennedy, but he let it pass.

"Any Indian tribes out this way?" Kennedy asked.

"Not here," Stone replied. "Closest is back near Whip Station, and those Pechangas is peaceful. Apaches are southeast, have no business out here."

"Marcus, maybe you should go off-trail and look," Kennedy suggested.

"We should stay together," Ridgewood said.

A whistling sound split the air.

Almost in the same instant, an arrow split Ridgewood's chest.

CHAPTER 16

"That was unexpected."

The speaker, Fletcher Small, had pulled aside the curtain for air when he happened to notice a glow fill the southern sky. He watched for the nearly full minute that it burned.

Reverend Michaels, resting his head on the opposite wall, stirred but did not ask what he was referring to. Rest was more important than fellowship and curiosity right now. As long as they were not being shot at, he was content to remain ignorant.

"What'd you see?" Willa asked.

"Fire out there," he said. "A big one, but brief. There was no lightning strike, so I'm assuming it was purposely lit."

"I hear there're places where fire just shoots up from the earth," she said.

"Those are volcanoes and there are none out here," the reporter informed her. "At least, not that I've read."

"May be that anyone who saw 'em got burnt up."

Small could not dispute the logic of that statement.

"You could be right, madam, but this was more like a wildfire that flared and died."

"Then that's likely what it was." She shrugged.

Again, Small had no reply to the woman's logic. He thought of Slash's departure, wondered if he had built a fire to distract or delay the Rebels. They had crossed no bridges, so that would not be the object of such an inferno. It seemed more like dry brush flaring then dying.

He hoped, in passing, it was not their luggage. It was only a ruddy glow, not flame. There was no telling how distant it was.

"In any case," Small said, "I'm relieved that we have someone covering our rear."

"And you got my boy up top," she said. "He's a 'sperienced lookout."

"So he said."

"All for a wicked cause and a wickeder man," she added. "I hope you write about that in your newspaper."

"I shall," he promised. "Though I assure you, it has been written about extensively, especially in papers up North."

"I cain't read so I have to trust you," she said.

The coach jolted over a series of small rocks, which caused the carriage to simultaneously shift from side to side and up and down.

"River travel is better," Willa noted. "Isaiah, he wants to get to the ocean. See if there's something he can do, knowing boats 'ng water."

"That's a sound idea," Small said.

"I see different," the shaman spoke. It was the first time he had said anything since they left the station.

"Welcome to the conversation, Tuchahu," Small said, evincing surprise.

Willa looked up at the taller man. "What do you see—Tuckahoo? Is that right?"

"I see through eyes of young girl," the shaman replied, his eyes half-shut. "At station. I see her—with you." He nodded slightly toward Willa.

"You having visions?" Willa asked.

"I . . . see," he replied vaguely.

"Tell me something, Mr. Tuckahoo. Can you see a vermin name of Brent Diamond?"

Small froze. It took him a moment to find his voice. "What was that name, madam?"

"The one I just said? Brent Diamond."

"That's right," he said. "What about this man?"

"He ain't a man," she said. "He's a thing, a creature, a hog. I even hate t'say it aloud or even *think* it. He was the man we was slaves to. He broke up our family. We want to find it. And Isaiah wants to kill him."

"He sounds bad," Small said, unable to think of a better word at that moment. Less than a day before, he had eaten chicken and corn at that man's table. It had been prepared by a Colored woman and her boy. The problem was, he dared not tell his riding companion. She might alert her son who, armed, might force B.W. to turn the stagecoach around. While that would give him an incredible story, it would put them running right into the hands of the Confederates. Small feared gunfire. In the dark, anyone could be killed.

Willa turned to the shaman. "I hope I didn't interrupt your dream."

"Vision," he said. "I still see."

"You say you saw—see—Willa with someone at Whip Station?" Small asked to make sure the topic stayed changed. "The young woman, Gert?"

The Serrano grunted in acknowledgment.

"A young lady . . . with me?" Willa said. "I don't know any young ladies. A white lady?"

"Yes," the shaman said. "You will know her."

Willa sat back. "Well, that is something."

"What else do you see?" Small asked.

He put no credence in native mumbo jumbo but Tuchahu certainly did as would any of the Indians they might yet encounter.

"She prays for me," he said. "There is no more."

"Well, that is a kindly thing to see," Willa said. Her alert eyes shifted back to Small.

"You don't seem right," she said.

"The ride," he apologized. "It doesn't agree with me."

"Is that it?" Reverend Michaels said, stirring beside him.

Small fired him a disapproving look. "I assure you, it is."

The pastor looked over at the woman. "God did not spare His own Son, nor shall I a sinner. I have met the man you seek."

"Reverend, this is not the time," Small said. "We must continue on our journey."

"And we shall," Michaels assured him. He looked back at the woman. "When we reach our next stop, I will tell you where you can find the one who kept you in bondage."

"You *know*?" Willa said. "You're not lying to Willa?"

"I am not," the preacher replied sanctimoniously.

"Where is he? Near?"

"Not afar," Michaels answered in his soft, reverend voice.

A dread silence filled the cabin. Willa slumped back in her seat and Small could not see her face very well. He had no idea whether she was thinking about the sorry past or the bloody future or a potential re-union with her family.

Probably all of that, he decided.

And then Willa screamed, a cry the likes of which neither man had ever heard. It came from a place of suffering so deep that Small wasn't sure it would ever stop.

The stagecoach, however, did stop.

"Go ahead, I gotcha covered!"

Joe O'Malley waved back at his grandson as he walked to where his horse had wandered. He did not think the Confederates would come back around the turn, but he couldn't be sure. The Rebels were now outgunned, unless it was both Hathaway and Kennedy who got shot. He wouldn't give a penny for either man's courage.

Joe mounted and took a brisk ride in the direction Clarity had gone. He arrived at Slash's side shortly after the woman did.

"Who's watching the coach?" Joe asked with an open mix of surprise and concern.

Without taking his eyes off the bend—except to tip his hat to Clarity when she arrived—Slash explained what had happened. Although strictly speaking Joe did not approve of the boy having left his post, the older man was glad that he had.

"You probably saved my life," Joe admitted.

"Reason enough, though I think you'd've probably cut 'em down," Slash said.

"I mighta got some of them," Joe agreed, looking across the ravine. "But we oughtn't tarry. The survivors are still out there and we likely have Apache on our tail."

"While you were riding out, did you come up with any idea what all this fuss is about?" Slash asked.

"I didn't think about it much," Joe admitted. "But I wouldn't say anyone's worried about keeping the shaman safe, 'cept us." That made him think about the two former slaves. "Slash, with this thing so fulla mystery, you sure this ma and son you picked up are square?"

"I ain't sure of anything 'cept my family and my knife," Slash said. "But he seemed so to me and B.W."

With a final look across the chasm, the three turned their horses north and continued along the trail. It suddenly hit Joe just how exhausted he was when, riding in the rear, he shut his eyes and jilted awake as he started to tilt off the saddle. He took his deerskin and dribbled water into his eyes, feeling it a worthwhile expense. A drink wouldn't help if he fell and cracked open his skull.

You aren't twenty, he reminded himself. *It's good to hold tight to the usefulness of your life. But you also have to hold just a little tighter to the reins.*

He stayed alert by considering the question Slash had posed. There was nothing he could think of that would have Easterners, Rebels, and Apaches working to the same purpose.

An Injun leader gets east just fine, meets with the President of the United States, and suddenly folks want him hogtied, he thought. *For ransom? Maybe. Or his death could sure start something. An Indian uprising, maybe. But who would want the Red nations to join and revolt?*

Except for being tired, which kept creeping back on Joe, the ride wasn't difficult or unexpected.

Until, after a time, Slash raised his arm and slowed. Joe saw his grandson looking ahead. His own view was blocked by the two riders in front of him, so Joe came around Clarity . . .

And saw what had made Slash stop. Its one lantern lit and hanging very still from the front box, the stagecoach was motionless under the moon. There was no sign of distress, no one was outside, and the horses were still rigged.

Joe moved beside Slash, leaned toward him.

"We're a fat target here," the older O'Malley whispered. "We should spread out."

Slash nodded in agreement and moved his horse west. Joe motioned for Clarity to stay where she was as he went east. The woman had already determined that something might be wrong and had unholstered a Colt. She held it pointing down so as to be threatening, but also to be ready.

They were still out of range of most guns but Joe would rather not find out for sure. He looked to Slash for their next move. This was the boy's ride, and the stagecoach was still his responsibility.

Slash clucked with his cheek and urged his horse forward. He stopped only moments later when he saw motion in the driver's box.

Slash's horse whinnied. He tightened his thighs and his hold on the reins, bracing for a shot.

Instead, he heard a man's voice call out, "Walk him in, Slash. Slowly."

After Willa screamed, B.W. slowed the team as Isaiah looked around in the dark. There was no one out there.

"She prone to fits?" B.W. asked.

"Nah," he told the driver. "Nightmares, sometimes—who can blame her, what she's seen." He called back without turning. "Ma, what's wrong?"

"Diamond!" she wailed.

Isaiah's jaw locked, the strong line of it frozen in moon glow. The rigidity in his muscles was visible all over his body, even in the dark.

"Stop the coach!" the shotgun rider demanded.

B.W. reluctantly, slowly applied the brake. He didn't think the woman and her son were up to anything, but he was alert for a trick. His left hand settled on his holster.

When the rig had stopped clattering, Isaiah half-turned and shouted back. "What're you talking about?"

"The pastor!" she cried. "He say he *seen* Diamond."

"Where?"

"Out *here*!"

The horses had not fully settled before the freed slave had leaped to the ground and was running toward the door. He yanked the panel open and stuck his head in. His expression was raw fury, the likes of which neither Fletcher Small nor Merritt Michaels had ever seen.

His eyes rested briefly on his mother, who had huddled against the unflappable medicine man. Then they darted to the pastor who was tucked into the front corner on the other side of the coach.

"Where did you see him?" Isaiah demanded.

The reverend was too frightened to speak. His eyes between Isaiah and the shotgun clutched tightly in his right fist.

The black man pounded the side of the opening with his left fist. The entire coach shook.

"I asked you *where*?" Isaiah shouted.

"He—he runs the stagecoach station in Vallicita," Small said with a tiny voice.

"Where is that?" the man demanded.

"I—I don't know, exactly."

"It's a day's ride to the south and east," B.W. told him. The Whip had left the box and come up behind him to see what the shouting was about. "You mean to tell me the proprietor is this man you're hunting?"

"He ain't no man and I don't mean to 'say' anything," Isaiah said. He backed from the stagecoach and shook his head slowly. "What I mean to do is turn this rig around and kill that slave-driving *viper*!"

"Isaiah, come back to the box with me," B.W. said. "Let's talk this through."

"Talk?"

"Yeah, talk," B.W. said. "Or anyway, just listen. Let's say we was to go back. You kill him, then you have to kill everybody who heard you out here. 'Cause when the marshal asks, we have to testify at your trial what we heard. And they will catch you. You got two forts overcrowded with veteran trackers. You got plainsmen like Slash's granddad who know this area. And you got some good sheriffs and marshals between here and Frisco. They will see to your being caught and hung."

"I don't care. Diamond must and will die."

"Maybe, but if you die your old ma is alone. And that's not all."

Isaiah glared at him. "What do you mean?"

"Come up and talk to me," B.W. urged. "There's more to tell."

That caught Isaiah's ear. He looked back at his mother in the dark coach. She was sobbing into the Indian's shoulder. Tuchahu did not move other than to put a hand on hers. He did not dislodge her.

Isaiah kicked the door shut with such anger that the frame cracked slightly.

"That's gonna whistle now," Small muttered.

Isaiah climbed up first, stomping so hard that the horses nearly bolted. The reins were hanging from the side and B.W. had to grab them, steady the team while he dug his boot heels into the earth. When they were calmer, he climbed up, settling in beside the big man.

"What do you got to add?" Isaiah asked.

"I'll get to that," B.W. said. "This fella down in Vallicita—first thing you gotta consider is that he didn't break any laws. Not where you're concerned, anyway. Owning slaves and even killing slaves was legal."

Isaiah turned on B.W. and the driver recoiled slightly at the ferocity of his expression. The black man thumped the Whip's Bible with a rigid finger.

"'Thou shalt not kill,' driver."

"Them's God's laws, but as you brought that up I would say that there is also God's justice."

Isaiah glared at B.W. in the darkness. "Is there? Is God watching out for my wife and son, is he?"

"No," B.W. said very carefully. "Diamond is."

"You've seen them?" Isaiah asked with sudden realization.

"Your wife and your son, both."

That quiet remark caused Isaiah to pass through a succession of emotions, as if clouds were passing in front of the moon. His face started with surprise, then shaded to disgust, then deeper revulsion, then pain, and finally he screamed into the night.

B.W. looked around, making sure no one was coming down the trail. He thought he saw a dust cloud in the distance. His gut began to burn. At least, in his current state, Isaiah would madly have at any Confederate who showed a hint of gray.

Isaiah settled when reason regained control. Now tears formed in his big, clear eyes.

"Are they all right?" he asked.

"They look healthy," B.W. assured him. "They're dressed fine, they work in the kitchen and wait on the guests. They don't say much . . . though the lady . . . she smiles at the passengers from time to time."

That caused Isaiah to grin and weep at the same time. "Bonita has such a nice smile," he said. "And my boy. Joshua?" he asked eagerly.

"Tall and straight. He's with her, helps out," B.W. told him.

Hearing that, Isaiah heaved forward and broke down. He put his face in his free hand and sobbed out years of suffering and worry.

B.W. looked back. There *was* a dust cloud catching moonlight.

"Isaiah, I don't wanna intrude on this moment, I truly do not," B.W. said. "But we got some men coming after us."

The freed slave looked up. "We have to turn around," he said. "We *must* go back!"

"Did you go deaf just now?" the driver asked.

Isaiah cocked the shotgun. B.W. hoped it was to stave off an attack, not to enforce the black man's will.

"I heard ya," Isaiah replied. "We're turning around."

"And what about the Injun? These other folks? If those are Rebs back there—"

"Then they will all die!" Isaiah vowed.

"And if they don't? They're veterans, man. We caught them by surprise before. They will not be tricked again."

Isaiah was visibly tortured. "But my *wife*!" Isaiah said. "My son."

"They'll still be there once we deliver our passengers."

"How do you know?" Isaiah asked. "How can you be sure Diamond won't hear about us looking for him?"

"There's no way," B.W. said. "No one but Slash saw you."

"An' he rode back that way," Isaiah said, jerking a thumb to the south. "He may say something without realizing it!"

B.W. did not know what to say. The man was not wrong.

"Don't make me force you," Isaiah said. His hand tightened on the shotgun. "Don't make me."

"Friend, if you shanghai this coach you are as good as hanged. Butterfield got his own men, good men, dangerous men, an' they don't wait for trials. Like I said about your ma, what happens to your wife and boy if you swing? You want them to *see* that? You're found with them, they will watch you die. After all you been through, is that how you want things to end?"

Now Isaiah had no answer—other than to consider what B.W. had said and then kick the bottom of the box hard. That caused the horses to jump again and B.W. being forced to steady them once more.

That was when, from somewhere behind them, they heard a horse whinny.

Isaiah and B.W. were both immediately tense. Motioning Isaiah to sit still, B.W. ducked low and stole a look back. Then he sat back up.

"Three riders," he said.

"How many Rebs was there?"

"More 'n that," B.W. said. "But who knows what their strategy is or if these are even them."

"They got horses, though," Isaiah said.

"Of course, but—" B.W. began, then stopped. "I see. We go one way, you go another."

Isaiah nodded gravely.

"But brother Isaiah, that don't change nothin'," B.W. said. "You kill Diamond, you die."

The black man said thoughtfully, calmly, "I gotta go where my wife and son is. That's all I know."

Then, half-turning so as to be heard, he told the riders to come forward slowly.

CHAPTER 17

When the arrow struck Ridgewood, Kennedy and Hathaway both scurried from the dead man as if he were a lit keg of black powder. They had no destination in mind, other than to get away.

Their instincts were good even if their execution was not. Almost at once, arrows struck the ground where they had been just moments before. Kennedy heard them penetrate the ground, hard.

With no cover, Hathaway belly-crawled as low as possible while Kennedy tucked his arms in and rolled.

Away was all the Indian agent thought. *Get away.*

There was nothing but survival in Kennedy's head until he tumbled into a ditch. The long, grave-like hole had been part of the earth fall that created the crevasse. All that Kennedy cared was he fit inside. He stayed there, facedown, panting, listening. He heard Hathaway's scrabbling off to the west, his shoes and the knees of his britches on pebbles, his breath coming in short busts. Then Kennedy heard hoof-beats. He could not be sure how many or where they were headed, exactly, other than they were coming in his direction.

He heard the *whoosh* of more arrows flying wide. He heard no cry from Hathaway. If he hadn't been so concerned about his own fate, he would have hoped a little stronger that his partner was still alive.

The hoofbeats stopped. The silence was miserable. Kennedy imagined the Indians were listening. He pushed his face down into the ground, his lips pressed on cold, dry dirt, hoping to stifle his breath. He sucked air through his nose. He also waited for the anticipated flash of pain, imagining that a lance or tomahawk would pierce his spine or shatter his skull. Savages were nothing if not brutal . . . and quiet. A quick death or scalping was what he would get if he were lucky. If these were Apache, it might amuse them to take a day or more killing him with knife and fire . . .

The horses suddenly charged, but not at him. They were racing around him, ahead to the north. The sound, and the trembling of the ground, receded. Then there were other sounds, other hooves, and the vibration of the earth started again. With those came the clatter of metal on leather.

A full canteen, he thought, recognizing one sound. *A sheath? For a saber? Pray God, was that a bugle? Cavalry?*

What sounded like a small herd of horses drummed past him. One actually jumped the pit without stopping on the other side, apparently not knowing he was there. He turned his face up, saw flashes of blue in the moonlight, and laughed with relief.

It was the United States Cavalry.

The relief and the big, involuntary smile were short-lived as Kennedy realized he would have to explain the dead and dying and whatever Confederate markings were on the other men . . .

Dying, he thought, thinking of Mute. The last thing he needed was a simple man telling the soldiers the reason they were out here.

Kennedy pushed off on his hands and knees. He remained kneeling and looked around. He saw a soldier helping Hathaway up, another two riding over to Ridgewood, two more headed over to Mute. And an officer—a major—seated on his horse, circling around and looking at the carnage. He was probably trying to reconstruct the battle.

It was he who spotted the Indian agent in the ditch.

"There!" the major shouted.

Others looked on as the officer rode over. He dismounted at the north end of the pit.

"Major Howard out of the San Diego Barracks," he said as he bent and extended a strong, helping arm to Kennedy.

The Indian agent took it gratefully.

"Doug Kennedy of the Bureau of Indian Affairs," replied the man as he half-stepped, was half-pulled from the ditch. Kennedy looked up at the officer's shadowed face. "The other gentleman is my associate, Jessup Hathaway. I—we—thank you, sir, for coming to our aid."

"I'm glad we were here, though it was happy chance that we were so," Howard said. "We were on patrol and saw the bodies of these unfortunate men. Who attacked you and where did they go?"

"There were three Indians, I think," Kennedy said. "I could not see any attire or markings, or if there was war paint. They rode north—when they heard you, I suspect."

"So the tracks indicate," Howard said. He took the canteen from his horse, offered it to Kennedy. "And you, sir. What were you two doing out here? And with these Confederates?"

Kennedy poured a palmful of water and used it to clean his face. He also used it to buy time to think. As he did, his gaze caught that of Hathaway. From the other man's frozen expression, it seemed as if he, too, were waiting for an explanation.

As always, Kennedy thought, *something closest to the truth works best.*

"We were passengers on the Butterfield stage," Kennedy explained. "Our assignment was to escort a Serrano medicine man home after his meeting with President Johnson."

"A Redskin met with the president?" Howard asked.

"He did indeed. It was a show of support for our humble efforts out here," Kennedy said, touching his chest. "Something for the press."

"I understand," Howard said. "Printer's ink is as good as gold."

"That was the plan, anyway," Kennedy said. "We were—put off the stage, left to die out here by men we met at the last way station. O'Malley, I think. Wasn't that their name, Jessup?"

"Joe O'Malley," the other man agreed.

Having two men confirm a story was better than one, Kennedy thought.

"I'm not from around here," the major said. "I don't know him."

"From what we were able to figure, their job was to deliver the shaman to these Rebels," Kennedy went on. "What they wanted him for, I cannot say. But it could be that the Indians who shot at us thought we were helping them—I don't know."

"I see," Howard said. "Where is the stage now?"

"North, maybe an hour away. Two at the most."

Howard watched as his men gathered the stray horses. He took a step toward them. "What about those men?" he yelled, pointing toward the nearest of the fallen.

"Both dead, sir," a soldier reported.

"Thank you, Private," Howard replied.

Kennedy exhaled. Hathaway's expression relaxed.

Major Howard removed his white gloves and slapped them in an open hand. "Chasing Redskins is dangerous enough in daytime," he said. "They could lead you into an ambush. The thing about the medicine man concerns me, though."

"Why is that?" Kennedy asked, washing out his mouth with a slug from the canteen.

Howard regarded him in the dark. "You being a government agent and all, I guess it's all right to say."

"If it has to do with the Indians—"

"That's what I mean," the major said.

Hathaway walked over then and, with Howard's permission, Kennedy passed him the canteen. Behind the major his men were busy gathering stones to temporarily inter the bodies.

"I saw a message at our camp regarding a stagecoach station and Indians," he said. "There was something about night pursuit as well."

The two Indian agents were both alarmed and intrigued.

"Who was the message from—and who was it to, if you don't mind my asking," Kennedy said.

"It was from a doctor and it was to a general," Howard replied.

"Was the doctor's name Peterson, by any chance?"

The major shot him a look. "It was, yes. You know him?"

Kennedy nodded. What he did not know was why Peterson was delivering secret messages to a cavalry encampment.

"You don't have to tell me any names, but the message," Kennedy said. "It was to an officer locally?"

That was right at the tipping point of confidential. "I am not at liberty to disclose military details."

"Of course," Kennedy said, affecting embarrassment for having asked. In reality, he was damned curious. Peterson should not have been in communication with anyone, let alone a general.

"One more question, if you don't mind," Kennedy said. "Your being out here had nothing to do with that message, did it?"

"Not directly," Howard said. "We had no instructions for the night. I don't like for me or my men to sit around. That's how dust gets in your soup."

Kennedy smiled politely at the expression. If anything, he was frustrated by this simple man's sense of duty. There was a war at stake here.

"Agent Kennedy," Howard said, slapping his gloves against his thigh now, "would it help the Bureau if my unit and I were to ride you out to the stagecoach? Even if we don't catch them on the road, we will certainly meet them when they lay over at Oak Grove. If this O'Malley has broken the law, we will detain him until he can be turned over to the San Diego County Sheriff. They have a nice cobblestone jail there."

"That is certainly where the renegade belongs," Kennedy said. "He's a rough man, a liar. The driver, a decent man named Beauregard Lafayette was genuinely afraid of him."

"That will stop," Howard announced. He looked from Kennedy to Hathaway. "Gentlemen, are you able to ride?"

"I would welcome it," Hathaway said as he returned the canteen to the major.

Kennedy simply nodded his assent as the major left to see to the departure.

Hathaway sidled to his partner. "There are loose ends in that ribbon you just tied," he said. "The girl, whoever was shooting at us from the other side of the ravine, the passengers—"

"It will be our word against theirs," Kennedy assured him. He nodded toward the major. "Who is that government employee going to believe? A grizzled old man or two solid citizens who have the same superior as he does?"

"Fair point," Hathaway agreed. "But what about Peterson?"

The stocky man nodded. "That has me perplexed. I never did trust him."

"Nothing to trust," Hathaway agreed. "Always contrary. And he just up-and-left Crane, it sounds like. Not even good doctoring."

"No. For whatever reason, seeing Major Howard was more important. I'm thinking," Kennedy went on, "it could have something to do with people he met during the War. Maybe he has a separate operation."

"Not the surgical kind," Hathaway said, not trying to be witty but clarifying.

Howard and his men were mounting up and the two men from Washington did the same. One of the cavalrymen peeled off and headed south.

Probably to alert the rest of the column of their plans, Kennedy thought. It reminded him of Washington protocol with young pages and interns running this way and that bearing messages. It was a wonder they didn't confuse things with all their rushing and criss-crossing more than they straightened them out.

Within minutes, they were rounding the ravine to pick up the trail of the stagecoach—and Joe O'Malley.

"It's Slash O'Malley, Isaiah."

The young man spoke clearly as he rode, unafraid, toward the stagecoach.

"Who's with ya?" B.W. called back.

"Me, Joe," the boy's grandfather shouted. "And Miss Clarity. Where's all your goods?"

"Weakened wheel, hadda leave it. Slash, what're you doing back?"

"Met and unhorsed the Rebs," Slash said. "Those that didn't run."

"Bless the Lord for that," B.W. said. "Glad we don't have to run no more."

From the carriage, the preacher yelled, "Can we go back for our belongings?"

"We still got a schedule to try and keep!" B.W. hollered back.

Isaiah stood in the box, one hand on the cabin. "Slash—bring my horse. I'm gonna need it!"

While Slash approached, Joe kicked his horse forward and Clarity followed.

"What's the urgency?" Slash asked. "An' why are you stopped?"

"Our new friend here was once owned by Brent Diamond," B.W. said. "The woman and child who work for him—they're his."

Joe swore. He had learned that, in life, there was always a way you wanted something to work out, and there was the way it eventually did work out. They were hardly ever the same. He had an aching feeling in his chest that this would not end well for the figures involved.

Especially you if you get involved, he reminded himself.

But it was complicated because he only knew Brent Diamond as a courteous neighbor who sent over two barrels of water when his own well went dry during a torrid summer and who sent a letter, by stage, complimenting Sarah for pies she had made with cherries he'd sent over on a previous run.

"*They reminded me of my childhood home, a memory for which I owe you dearly,*" he had written.

As someone who had been held by Comanche for three weeks years back, forced to carry rocks just for the hell of it, he had no gut for the enslavement of any man, let alone a woman and child.

But times wasn't always what they are now, he reminded himself. *Many a time that's why wars get fought, to correct things like being free states instead of oppressed colonies, or booting a tyrant from Mexico out of Texas.*

Years back, Mexicans would've been his blood enemies. Southerners, too.

Now they weren't. But where revenge was concerned, time was rooted where the seeds first fell.

By the time Joe and Clarity reached the stagecoach, Slash was already swapping places with Isaiah. The reverend would have gotten out to embrace his sister save for Isaiah being in his way. The big man held off mounting long enough to insert himself into the cabin and hug his mother, and make a vow.

"I'll bring my wife and son back," he said.

"Make sure you come back, boy," she replied sadly but sensibly. Her spindly arms clung tight around his big neck.

As the farewell played out, Joe was trying hard to think of something to say, not that Isaiah would listen, and B.W. was holding his Bible as though a perfectly right passage would jump from its pages to his mouth. But it was Clarity who spoke and surprised everyone, uttering words Joe had heard before.

"I'd like to ride with you," she said to the man she just met.

The freed slave held up. He looked her over in the pale light. She appeared feminine enough but she was armed like she was ready for war.

"Why would you do that?" Isaiah asked.

The door was still open beside the big man and, with just enough room, Reverend Michaels leaned out.

"Clarity, the man is right!" the pastor yelled. "This is not your affair!"

"Neither was this," she added, nodding toward the stagecoach.

"Sister, you could *die*!" Michaels said, choking out the word.

"True enough, but I can also live the way I think I was meant to," she replied. The woman turned back toward Isaiah. "These other men will attest that I am a dead-shot and have no stomach for men who bully women. Or children."

"She's all that," B.W. heartily agreed. "Seen it with these very eyes."

The black man used his knee to shut the door, jolting Reverend Michaels back into his seat. Then he climbed into the saddle. Isaiah sat so hard it was as if he was intent on joining man-flesh to horse-flesh.

"You know the way to Vallicita?" he asked.

"It's directly back the way we came," she said. "If we ride through, we'll be there early morning. I can let you know before we come into view."

Isaiah pursed his lips as emotion rolled up into his throat. He coughed to clear it.

"Then I thank you and accept your generosity."

"Clarity!" Michaels half-sobbed, finally finding his voice as they vanished into the dark. "Clarity, what's wrong with you, woman?"

"Absolutely nothing," Joe answered, as heartfelt as he had ever uttered anything. Then he raised his voice and said, "But just a minute. Everybody had their say, now I'll have mine."

The eyes of all, save the reporter and the Indian whose eyes were lost in the dark of the cabin, turned toward the speaker.

"I admire your gumption, Miss Clarity," Joe began, "and your devotion, Isaiah. But has either of you stopped to consider what happens if anyone other than a Red Man happens on a Colored man and a white woman riding alone in the wilderness? Isaiah is shot or lynched, prob'ly both, before he can state his purpose."

There was a pall of silence that was covered by a finer blanket of something else—a sense of guilt. From Joe to Isaiah, everyone experienced a withering of purpose under the hot sun of reality.

"Now, Miss Clarity—you can say you'll shoot anyone who tries," Joe went on, "and maybe you could. Then you got bodies behind you and a posse in pursuit. That's the way it is and everyone here knows it."

Isaiah did not allow another moment to pass. He hurt to get on with his business.

"Mr. Joe is right and I'm sorry he is," the black man said to Clarity as he ended the brief partnership. "I thank you again."

"You just follow this trail," she told him quietly. "You'll get there."

He tipped his flimsy hat and, drawing the horse toward the south, gave it his heels and rode off.

CHAPTER 18

The stagecoach resumed its journey with Joe in the shotgun position and both Clarity and Slash riding behind.

"You had some day, y'old cactus," B.W. said.

"True enough, though I prefer mine to any of the men lying back there," he said.

B.W. nodded. "'For he that soweth to his flesh shall of the flesh reap corruption,'" he said.

"They accomplished that," Joe replied.

"That glow on the horizon, earlier?" B.W. asked.

"Their reaping, my sowing," Joe answered. "Little wildfire to set the Rebs back. Thought it'd burn longer than it did."

"Funny how that is," B.W. said. "When you don't want 'em, they blaze for a prophet's age."

"Fire don't know when it's need or not," Joe said. "Just is."

B.W. nodded sagely at his companion's prairie-born wisdom. Then he went right into shaking his head. "That preacher—he's a gnawing canker."

"I don't much care for him, but that's a little strong, seems to me."

"You ain't religious," B.W. said. "It don't affect you. There's a difference between being devout, reading the Good Book, and being sanctimonious."

"You lost me with that word."

"Holier than someone else without actually being pious," B.W. said after thinking about it.

"I see. You know, I do believe in God."

"Of course," B.W. said. "How can you look around you and not believe?"

"I suppose," Joe said. "I also see how a man like the reverend'd rub your cheek wrong."

The men fell silent. "You can rest if you want to," the Whip said. "I'm watching things."

Joe shook his head. "There are still those Injuns I'm concerned about. The ones I met at Civil Gulch. They was riding out this way."

"Well, you know those savages. They won't come after us directly. They'll skulk and watch."

"That's what worries me," Joe said. "All this stopping and starting you've done, they may have found time—or a way—to circle 'round us."

"We'd still have the advantage of a pretty good road while they were crawling over rocks to the east and high grasses to the west."

"I'm still not at peace even with all that," Joe replied.

He cradled his carbine in his arm as the stagecoach bounced forward. It was an interesting feeling, the lighter ride due to the loss of the baggage. It was almost like going down a river rapid in a canoe, just a sense of moving ahead.

"Maybe more like a bird," Joe said aloud.

"What?"

"Not having anything to weigh us down."

"I thought that, too!" B.W. enthused. "But I wouldn't wanna be one of those Pony Express boys. I had the chance, y'know."

"I didn't know."

"Yeah, both started at the same time, roughly. Hell, same route. I see 'em shoot past sometimes." B.W. shook his head. "That pace ain't for me."

Joe didn't answer.

"Something wrong?" B.W. asked.

"Why?"

"You look like you're cloud-gazing, only there ain't no clouds."

Joe shifted in his seat. "I was just thinking about Clarity."

"Impressive woman."

"She's that, but I was thinking—actually, it was about Gert I was thinking. I don't understand why two women, equally headstrong, should impact me so different."

"That's easy," B.W. said. "Gert is afly with all things Injun, not guns. But y'know, friend, it takes as much guts to ride out there to those savages, and trust they won't make you marry a brave or worse, as it does to ride into a shoot-out."

"Thing is, a shoot-out's something you try to avoid," Joe said.

B.W. snorted. "You joking me? Clarity was itching

for it, like a coyote for a hare. Maybe she's still killing the one who wronged her or liked killing the one who wronged her but Gert—she goes out trying to learn things."

Joe knew better than to say there was nothing someone could learn from the Indians. They were an ancient people. Even when the Apache held him, their simple ways were not foolish ways. They were grown from generations of practice.

"I still don't like it," Joe replied.

"I understand that. I don't much care for a lot of Injuns myself. But not liking them and not liking her for liking them is two different notions."

Joe's mouth twisted. Unlike Gert, he didn't especially like learning new things. Especially when they conflicted with old, old things. This would require some consideration. He could not imagine tolerating Injuns who weren't working for the cavalry, but once, he wouldn't have been able to imagine meeting a lady gunfighter, either.

What do you think, Dolley? he asked.

She had strong opinions, too. But they were born of her hard upbringing. Survival was more important than anything. But securing that, she was more open than her husband to listen to others.

I guess I never felt that survival was ever secure, he thought, half-apologizing to Dolley for his ever-present stubbornness. But fate had proved him right. It took his girl. That was why he had never trusted anything, since, except for those of his closest blood. He counted the O'Malleys of Texas among them. Though he had no regrets, he couldn't help but wonder what life would have been like had they thrown in with that bottled lightning side of the family.

"This peacefulness is getting to me," B.W. said suddenly.

Joe had been half-drowsing with his thoughts. His eyes opened slowly. His thoughts collected slower.

"After all that, back there, I can't believe everyone just gave up," the Whip went on.

"Even Injuns gotta sleep," Joe said. "Me too."

"Sorry," B.W. said.

The driver fell silent again. It was strange. B.W. and Dick Ocean were always alert when they were between stations. There was always a sense that something could go wrong. What B.W. felt now was with fire and gunplay and a broken wheel behind them, they had earned a rest.

"I want to chew something over with you," Joe said suddenly.

"Is it something that's going to rattle my new-hatched sense of well-being?" B.W. asked.

"Quite likely," Joe admitted.

"Dammit, Joe." B.W. held the reins in his right hand, took up his Bible in the left and clutched it to his chest, like a preacher about to address a revival meeting at a river crossing camp. "Awright. I'm ready."

Joe settled back. "What I need you to do is help me think this through," Joe said. He held up fingers one at a time as he spoke. "First, we got Rebs working with two Indian agents fresh from Washington. That figures because, second, they wanted to kidnap this big headdress among the Indians. The government can't be involved in that. Hell, they wanted him so bad they was willing to shoot a Butterfield stage. Powerful man to upset. That would also upset the Serrano, but here's the thing that gnaws. It would also rally Indians who ain't Serrano. We already seen that happen with three, Apache wanting to catch you."

"That alone is troublin'," B.W. interjected.

"Rightly so," Joe said. He paused. "Where was I?" he asked, then looked at his fingers and held up another. "Fourth, with Indians uniting, likely attacking settlers, outposts, the stagecoach, the army has no choice but to move in on reservations, break treaties. In short—"

"Wipe out the West Coast population," B.W. said. "I been thinking something along those lines since Miss Clarity shot her first Confederate west of the Rockies. But, Joe, it don't figure."

"Why not?"

"We was witnesses. There was a newspaperman—"

"Because their plan to stop the stage in the gulch failed," Joe pointed out. "Kennedy and Hathaway, they could've continued riding on. But the Rebs made a decision to come 'n' get the Injun. The two agents backed their play because they thought it would succeed. And you're right. We saw them. The reporter saw them. We all would've died. The station would've likely been burned—the first acts of an Indian rebellion."

"But the Indians wouldn't have killed that Tuchahu fella," B.W. said. "That's bad medicine whatever tribe you're from."

"Betcha that's not how the papers would've reported

it," Joe said. "He'd've been found somewhere visible with Indian wounds."

"Why?"

"For making peace with the White Chief," Joe said. "President Johnson."

B.W. put down his Bible and fished jerky from a pocket. He offered some to Joe, who accepted. Both men chewed thoughtfully.

"So you got a Cavalry-Injun war," B.W. said. "Washington ain't dirtied by it. The flats are safe. The railroads can finish crossing the land. We're dead."

"All of that's true," Joe said. "And I can see how it made sense in a sneaky sort of way. If it failed, Rebels and a small barrel of Indian agents would've taken the fall. But how do those turtledoves from the East benefit, whipping all this up? They can't boast about breaking the laws of man and God."

"They would have to have orders."

"From someone who was in a position to give 'em," Joe agreed. "Someone close to the president if not the president himself. Why I think that is, they brought this Indian to the heart of our newly put-together nation, celebrated him, then shooed him away."

"Make him big chief totem and then cut off the head," B.W. said.

"It's a ripe possibility," Joe said, taking a fresh bite of dried beef. "But here's the other thing. Washington does that, the army has to know. They have to be armed. They have to have horses. They have to be ready."

"Right," B.W. said. "Tuchahu takes a slow trip by river and land, couriers take a fast message west.

Supplies follow. I was talking to Jackson earlier about those Spencer repeating rifles. May not have anything to do with this, but Butterfield was helping to arrange for transport of crates of 'em on special stages."

"When?"

"Oh, about last month," B.W. said. He shrugged. "Regular swapping out of old guns. Army does that all the time. You know that."

"I do," Joe said, gripping his carbine. "Got a lot of their hand-me-downs over the years."

"Always figger Injuns are gonna get their hands on some. Last thing we want is those guys who can sure ride also being able to shoot faster, further, and better."

"So fifth," Joe said assertively, "you got cavalry units spread across a wide area that by plan or happenstance has replaced old Civil War, 58-caliber muskets with real killing power. These Blues ain't just ready to pick off Injuns and Rebel marauders. They are muscled up for war."

Both men reflected on that for a moment. The flight of the stagecoach through open road made both men feel like eagles soaring over the land where everything is all laid out for the hunt. Only in this case, mountains cast shadows over key hunting grounds.

"Is that wrong?" B.W. asked. "That an army be prepared to fight?"

"Can't say it is," Joe answered with a yawn.

"I have t'say, it'd be nice not having to worry about getting an arrow in the shoulder while I'm in the box," B.W. continued.

The men were quiet again.

"Maybe we're not looking at this thing right," B.W.

said. "Let me ask you this—call it 'six.' What would *you* do with an army out here?"

There was no answer and the Whip looked to his left. Joe had nodded off again. B.W. picked up the piece of jerky that had dropped from the old man's hand to his lap and poked it in his mouth. The Whip grinned as his companion bobbed from side to side.

"Funny," B.W. said quietly. "That's kinda what I thought you'd do, y'old bull moose."

Riding side by side, Slash and Clarity let the stage-coach gain some distance. There was no reason to keep up and tire the horses. Anyone pursuing the shaman would still likely be coming from the rear. It would take only a minute for the two riders to catch up. If an attacker came from another direction, Joe was there. And not just Joe. Tuchahu carried no weapons, and Small and Michaels might be no use, but Willa seemed as if she was able and willing to handle a firearm.

"I wonder where she learned," Slash said over the dull clop of the hooves.

"I'm sorry?" Clarity answered.

"I was thinking of Willa," Slash told her. "Isaiah said he was a duck hunter. But how'd an old slave woman learn to use a rifle?"

"I suppose it was during the War," Clarity said.

Slash snorted. "A master giving his slaves guns? Why wouldn't they just up and shoot him?"

"It may be that the devil you know is better than the devil you do not know," Clarity replied.

"What's devils got to do with anything?" Slash said.

"It's a figure of speech," she said.

"You lost me, girl," Slash admitted.

"A saying," she said.

"Hmph. You make that saying up?"

"Hardly." Clarity laughed. "I heard it when I was a child. It made an impression."

"It sounds nice," Slash conceded, still wrestling with the meaning of the phrase. "But I don't know if it's true. 'The devil you know.' How . . . *why* would a slave defend her owner from the people who come to set her free?"

"The Yankees came with fire and cannon," Clarity said. "I know, I saw them coming through. Maybe Willa saw other freed slaves who were fleeing, scared, wounded. Or maybe she wasn't treated as bad as others, preferred a place to sleep. She seems as if she had been fed . . . Isaiah, too."

"Lotta 'ifs' there," Slash said.

"It could also be that her master deserted her when he ran off with her son's family," Clarity said. "Could be Isaiah had to choose between pursuit or staying behind to protect her. He may have showed her how to shoot so they could survive."

Slash nodded. "That, what you just said, makes sense."

"Thank you," Clarity replied, bowing her head slightly.

Slash looked her way and frowned. "Was that a real thank-you?"

"What do you mean?"

"It didn't sound like one."

"How is a thank-you not real?" she asked.

"When it's a little . . . like what you just said. Syrupy," he said.

She laughed. "Now your turn of phrase has got me. I only use syrup on freshly baked biscuits, not on friends. What do you mean?"

Slash's horse acted up a little and he patted it on the side. The young man sat a little straighter, turned his ear slightly toward their rear.

"What is it?" Clarity asked.

"Horse got spooked," he said. "Could've been a snake."

Slash heard nothing. The animal settled under his hand. He thought back to what he was saying.

"What I meant was, there was just something funny about the way you said 'thank you,'" he told her. "Maybe I just imagined it."

"That could be gratitude you were hearing," Clarity said.

"For what?"

"Respecting what I had to say," she replied. "Since I first stepped from the stage back at the station, I haven't heard anyone tell me anything I said was a good idea."

"Hold on—that ain't entirely so," Slash said. "Everyone liked you shooting those Rebs—except maybe the Rebs and those two agents."

"'Everyone' approved *after* I did it," Clarity insisted. "Before, when we were sitting around the table and first turned our ears to those scoundrels, my brother was hissing at me not to get involved, it wasn't my affair."

"So why did you?" Slash asked. "That Injun hadn't spoke more'n two words to anyone since he got there."

"Mercifully," she said. "I preferred his silence to Mr. Small's jabber. But it wasn't for Tuchahu I took that carbine from where your grandpa kept the stack. It was for your mother and your sister."

"I figgered it was because you liked shooting!" Slash said. "You didn't know Ma and Gert before you got there."

The innocence of this boy was both astonishing and endearing. She had to remind herself that he had probably spent most of his life around no one but his family.

"I didn't know your mother and sister, Slash, but I know fear," Clarity went on. "Your mother especially was trying to do their duty and see after us, make sure we were at our ease. But I saw in the tight smile, the way she would pause for a moment and listen—they were scared for you and your pa and grandpa. What I did, I did mostly for them."

"Hmph," Slash responded. "It's like what men do, but—women."

Clarity's mouth twisted as she tried to work her way through that statement.

"You only know your mother and sister, don't you?" she asked. "Women, I mean."

"No, I met others," he said. "Injuns. My cousins back in Texas. Once in a while, a lady who comes on the stage. Before you, though, I never got to talk to them, other than to say 'Howdy, ma'am,' or 'Yes, miss.' They're too busy working their fans, trying to breathe with all they got on. About all they ever take off is their hats. Why d'you ask?"

"I was just wondering."

"Am I doing something wrong?" he asked suddenly.

"No, no, no," Clarity quickly assured him. "I was

curious—you know, about who you get to meet out here."

"Miss Clarity, you saw 'em all, 'cept for our livestock."

"Does that ever bother you?" she asked. "Isn't it lonely?"

"I think I'd like to have a sweetheart," he told her. He grinned. "I went to San Diego with my pa, once. He had to see a special doctor about his leg. I looked out the window while I was waiting, saw some ladies come to work in a dance hall across the street. They smiled so sweet. Walked real special, like no lady I ever saw. I thought about them a lot since then."

"Do your mother and Gert—do they ever laugh? Have fun?"

"On Christmas and birthdays," he said. "And Gert laughs with her Injuns."

"Is that all?"

"Sometimes after dinner," Slash said. "Grandpa acts out some funny stories when he's got some whiskey in him. Now let me ask you something."

"Certainly."

"If you don't mind me saying so, this sounds like more than 'just wondering.'"

"Does it?"

"You sound like Pa when he's talking to Horsehead Billy about buying an animal," Slash said. "Are you—would you—ever think of settling here?"

If it weren't night he would have seen her blush. She thought she heard more than a question in his tone. He sounded almost eager.

"Is there a church anywhere between Vallicita and Oak Grove?" she asked.

"Mexicans got a place west a bit, outside San Felipe."

"Where do you worship?" she asked. "Marry?"

"There's a traveling padre, sets up a tent every other Sunday about a mile east of Civil Gulch. On Christmas, we go to the Mission San Luis Rey outside San Diego. It's very holy there. We feel kinda sacred just showing up."

Clarity was about to speak when Slash held up a gloved hand beside the brim of his hat.

"Hush!" he whispered.

As she had done before when Joe had roughly urged silence, Clarity obliged. Despite her confidence with a gun, this was not her land. She did not know the rules or the possible fox traps. This was not civilization, like back in Murray, Kentucky.

Slash reined his horse to a stop, rose in the saddle. The animal was restless again. His rider half-turned and listened.

"Clarity, get back to the stagecoach," he said, settling back down and riding ahead. "We got company! Lots of it!"

CHAPTER 19

General Guilford lay in bed beside his wife, unable to sleep and unwilling to get up.

His mind was always engaged, relentlessly, whenever a battle was imminent. It could be days away but he was already considering the many things that could go wrong. It was said that generals had it easiest. They were not facing bullets and bayonets. But the soldier had only two concerns: advance and survive. The general had hundreds, often thousands of concerns. To see that each man was as prepared as possible to achieve those goals. And to see that the honor of the nation he was sworn to protect was unblemished.

General Guilford carried the tradition of George Washington and Andrew Jackson in his heart—and on his back. Their heroism and resolve gave him something to reach for, but it reminded him that war was imperfect and unpredictable. How many times did General Washington retreat before achieving final victory? How did it weigh on General Jackson that his greatest battle, in New Orleans, with its fire and death, occurred after the 1812 war had already ended?

A wounded soldier had only to heal or learn to live a different way. The general had to look into the lost and sorrowful eyes of every soldier who lost a limb or his sight or his brother or best friend.

A war was how a general tested not just his tactical skills but his conviction that this war, any war, was necessary.

That was what General Guilford was doing now. The maps were already drawn. The arms were already stockpiled. He had to make very sure that what he was doing was for country first and vanity second.

What does a place in history matter if it is beside the dishonored busts of Benedict Arnold, Generalissimo Santa Anna, or the benighted John Wilkes Booth? he wondered.

As his mind drifted from plans to risks to potential outcomes, Guilford was startled by a soft, respectful knock on the door. The officer was awake and staring at the torchlight playing on the roof of his quarters. The knock had already roused his wife, who turned her pale cheek toward him. He kissed it lightly.

"Rhodes?" his wife said groggily.

"I'm waiting for a report," he said as he flung off the light quilt. "This may be it."

"Don't be long," she urged sleepily.

"Shan't be more than a few minutes," he said hopefully.

Audrey Guilford cooed and let her head roll back into the deep pillow.

His poor wife. She tried so hard to look after him. After twenty-nine years, he would have thought the onetime nurse would know better. Perhaps she did. She also knew the demands and dangers faced by cavalry troops and officers alike. Maybe this was just a way to remind him that she cared. Whatever the reason, he always appreciated the effort.

Guilford grabbed a robe from a rack in the corner, was still tying the belt as he turned the knob on the three-panel timber door. Guilford was hopeful, even eager, but also concerned. According to the grandfather clock thunking in the corner, it was not yet three a.m. It was too early by several hours for the stagecoach to have reached Oak Grove where—he assumed—the next attempt would be made to secure the shaman. He had already considered that Kennedy and Hathaway would have tried an alternate plan, to take the coach between station stops. He did not know if the two men had that kind of courage, to ride at night. He had tried to calculate whether there would even have been enough time for the men to return to the mine from the failed effort at Civil Gulch, regroup, and catch the stage en route.

His gut burned to know.

The door opened and Lieutenant Anthony was standing there, chest out, breathing heavily but trying not to show it. He would have had just moments to wake, dress—on the run—and escort the two men standing behind him to the general's quarters. There were two other men behind him in the musty, narrow corridor. One was the oak-solid Sergeant Russell, a trusted veteran of several of Guilford's campaigns. The mustachioed man was holding the lantern to one side so that the forward side did not blind the officer. The solid orange glow lit the faces of the two other men along with the walls, covered with small paintings of bucolic scenes painted by Audrey.

The other man was a different courier than the one who came before. He stood a respectful distance behind the lieutenant.

The general stepped into the hallway and shut the door behind him, so as not to disturb Audrey. The other three men shuffled back awkwardly even as Lieutenant Anthony was in mid-salute.

"Sir," the lieutenant said, recovering, "Private Morgan from Major Howard's column in the field."

Guilford's gaze shifted to the man. Unlike the previous messenger, this man was covered with fine prairie dust. He had not come along the scrub-and-rock fields between Temecula Point and the fort.

"Come," the general said to the boy.

Lieutenant Anthony stepped aside and the youth stepped forward. He saluted.

"Sir, Private Morgan bringing the respects of Major Howard and his oral report," he said.

Guilford frowned. "The major did not have time to follow protocol?" he asked sternly.

"General, sir, my apologies. The major shared nothing but the dispatch I bring."

"Of course," Guilford said.

He blamed no one, but security was ever on his mind regarding this matter. The fewer people who knew about this operation, the better he would sleep—when he slept.

The general looked at the other two men. "Sergeant— you may go. Set the lantern on the table."

"Yes, sir!"

"Lieutenant Anthony? Wait for me. There may be orders."

Both men saluted, did a smart about-face, and departed quickly.

The general regarded the boy. The courier looked anxious, having already disappointed the renowned general. Guilford forced himself to smile a little, benignly. His dark eyes twinkled in the light of the lantern.

The youth relaxed.

"Your message, son?" the general asked.

"Sir: While on night patrol, Major Howard encountered Messrs. Kennedy and Hathaway approximately eight miles northeast of his camp. The civilians reported two attacks. The first was by a civilian, Joseph O'Malley, and a threat to the Butterfield stagecoach. The second was an attack by at least three savages, their tribes being unknown. They fled at the approach of the column, which rode north to try and overtake the coach."

The boy had been looking past the general, reciting the message by heart. It was an incomplete confusion that told him very little. Major Howard was not privy to Major Guilford's plan, nor to the mission of Kennedy and Hathaway. The general did not know whether this information helped or hurt the advancement of the operation.

The young man had no doubt recited every word he had been told. Hopefully, the private saw more.

"Did Kennedy and Hathaway accompany the major?" Guilford asked.

"Yes, General, they did."

"Who were the dead men?"

"I only know that they were Confederates, sir," the courier reported.

"How was the other victim lying?"

"On his back, sir."

"His head facing which way?"

The courier thought for a moment. "North."

That likely meant the Indians had come up from the South. Apaches were the only ones who routinely rode at night.

They were not in pursuit of the column, or they would not have arrived before, Guilford thought. *Were they out for mischief or were they after the stage, perhaps the shaman?*

Guilford hadn't realized he had been holding his breath until he exhaled.

"Was there any other information about the stagecoach or O'Malley?" Guilford asked. "Speak freely. What else did you see or hear? Anything at all."

Private Morgan thought hard. "We put the dead under piles of rocks, sir. I heard mention, General, that this Kennedy and Hathaway were Indian agents."

"Anything else?"

"A name," the young man recalled. "Someone said a name—Peterson. I don't know who he is, sir. I think it was Major Howard who said it. I wasn't facing him."

"Could he have said it to the Indian agents?"

The young man thought harder. Guilford could see it in his young face, an eagerness not to disappoint, to prove himself, to remember without embellishment. If it was possible to be proud and frustrated in the same moment, the general was both.

"I can't exactly say, sir. They were back there with the major but I didn't hear a response."

The general nodded. "You've done very well and I thank you," he said. "Go to the mess and remain here."

"With respect, sir, I was instructed by the major—"

Guilford stopped him with a look. "As you say, Private, he is a major."

"Yes, sir!"

The young man saluted again, turned sharply, and left.

It was not just the health of the private that concerned Guilford. He was young, and young soldiers were regularly ordered to push themselves. What concerned him was the fact that Indians were abroad. Guilford did not want a lone cavalry rider with highly secretive information riding through the plains at night. Such men were known to put the barrel of a gun in their own mouth rather than be captured by Apache.

The general took a few steps down the corridor, walking lightly so the floorboards didn't creak. His eyes fell on a miniature Audrey had painted of her husband many years ago when he was still a colonel. She had hung it next to the arbor scene she had painted from memory. The spot on the Hudson River where he had proposed.

"Lieutenant!" Guilford said in a loud whisper.

The man emerged from the small secretary's office where he had been waiting. "Sir?"

"Please have Colonel Burke in my office in fifteen minutes. I'll dress there—field uniform."

"Yes, sir."

Anthony picked up the lamp and General Guilford followed the tall young Pennsylvanian down the corridor to his office headquarters. The lieutenant set the one lamp on the desk and was set about lighting the other desk lamp. Lieutenant Anthony then went to the wardrobe where he efficiently removed the general's uniform from between a frock coat and surtout coat. He hung it on a brass hook inside the door. Typically, he would stay to brush cigar ash and dirt from the fabric. But an order took precedent over protocol. He left at once through the courtyard door to rouse the colonel.

The glass bowls of the lamp cast a warm, welcoming light through the stuffy room. The windows would remain closed to keep from attracting moths. It wasn't only the inconvenience of the pests but the indignity of a general trying to give orders while constantly being distracted and swatting.

Guilford went to a washstand in a small alcove and scrubbed his eyes. Then he walked over to the wardrobe. He eyed the brass buttons as they gleamed in the light, touched the stars on the epaulets. He was about to set matters in motion—matters that depended on the loyalty of his officers and men to him, personally. Matters that would not have the benefit of events having unfolded according to plan.

"But this is too big, too important to stop," he reminded himself softly.

As if he needed a reminder. There had been little else on his mind for months. It was more a matter of reminding himself that it was unfortunate things had not gone according to plan. Guilford had wanted to minimize civilian casualties. It was equally unfortunate, but not wholly unexpected, that it should be so.

Kennedy and Hathaway had the credentials to gain access, but they did not possess the experience to pull off the maneuvers that had been necessary. He always suspected that the Fort Sumter moment, the flashpoint that would start the War, would fall on him.

Now it had.

Moving his burly arms and shoulders like a bear, Guilford shucked his robe and hung it in the wardrobe. As he slipped from his pajamas, he wondered if the two Indian agents ever had any idea what the true goal of their activities had been. They did not seem to possess the vision or imagination. And Peterson would not have said anything to them.

That doctor, though a Southerner, was an angel of God Himself. He had toiled for the Union, had saved the life of his precious Audrey and others at the fort when their own doctor was seconded by the Union once again. Peterson had been headed west to seek a new life and stayed. They shared war stories, Guilford of the Confederates who came out here during the war trying to recruit Indians, Peterson of the Northerners who forced him into servitude.

"If saving lives can be called such," Guilford had mused.

"When they heal and attack your neighbors—it can," Peterson had answered. He had not said it with bitterness but with sadness.

Well, war is sadness as much as it is glory, Guilford thought then, and now.

It was Guilford who, one night, suggested a way they could both help fix the blight that continued to afflict the North, the South, and the West—even though all were supposedly at peace.

"I am for anything that preserves life, anywhere," Peterson said.

"Does that mean Indian life?" Guilford had asked.

It had taken a long moment before the doctor answered. "If they would allow us to live, I would wish the same for them."

"But they do not," Guilford had said.

That truth had saddened Peterson. Expansion and growth were not always equitable masters, especially where young nations were concerned. That did not need to be explained to Peterson.

"Sometimes legs must be sawed off to save a life," the doctor had responded.

Guilford had gone on, then, to talk about how the North and South would always be at war. Their ideologies were nowhere near the same and defeat would only arrest the Confederacy, not kill it. The South was less a place than an idea that would never die, a way of life that could not die.

"The muscle of the North, its desire to build and transform, to control and rule, could also not be stopped," the general had said. Then added, "Except by one thing."

He went on to explain some of what Peterson already knew, that the Confederacy had lost the War because while it had the will, it had neither the industry nor manpower to resist the Northern war machine. There was nothing for the North to struggle through except Rebel soldiers. Landscape, towns, even proud cities were no match for Union numbers and torches.

Guilford had learned from that war. For four years he had fought with that colossus as it strode through the South. He had studied dispatches and red-taped files of maps and newspaper reports. They were unanimous in pointing him to one obstacle the Union Army could not have beaten.

"The mountains and canyons, rivers and deserts that separate East from West are similar to terrain that has challenged the finest generals from Hannibal to Napoleon," he said. "The ocean that separates the West is formidable as the waters that thwarted the great Spanish armada. We, here, are safe from any attack save through narrow corridors of foreign lands."

Peterson had regarded him with dawning realization.

"That's right," Guilford had said. "The geography I just described will make the Western States of America impregnable."

Guilford had outlined his plan to a riveted Peterson over a bottle of whiskey at this desk beside him. He saw, in the doctor's expression, a way to salvage the honor of his lost South without having to recruit the old, depleted stalwarts.

The general told him about a planned meeting between the President of the United States and the revered Serrano shaman Tuchahu.

"If anything were to happen to so revered a figure, the Indian population would go mad," Guilford had said.

A medicine man was not like a war chief who was expected to die in battle, who wished it. A medicine man was sacred. Moreover, Tuchahu was the son of Hanakwiche, a shaman whose place he had taken.

The death of the aged Hanakwiche was mourned throughout the Indian population.

"The murder of such a man would enflame the entire savage nation," Peterson had remarked thoughtfully.

The plan had been broadly laid out before sunrise though it was not yet ready to be executed. Meetings first had to be arranged with the commanders of the other forts out west. Most of them proved eager to join the general. To a one, they felt forgotten out here. They had fought a brutal war against the Confederacy. Now, there was no place an army was of any use except against the Indian. And to Washington, the Indians were far, far away. Even that very real war was one that Washington was loathe to fight. Popular opinion in the big cities was against it. Without the cause of slavery to embrace, the people of the northeast were without a banner to raise.

To fight and eradicate the Red Man, a wide-scale uprising was required. The seizing of Tuchahu and his assassination by Confederate renegades. Guilford and Peterson had suspected that Kennedy and Hathaway would be easy to recruit. They were low-paid but high-living bureaucrats in positions where there was little hope for advancement. The two conspirators confirmed their essential, greedy natures when they came west to collect the shaman. As a matter of course, they stopped at Fort Yuma.

The victim, its perpetrators, and the subsequent war were set. That was all anyone but Guilford, Peterson, and a few key generals had been told.

"And when the enemy is destroyed," Guilford had

told Peterson on that humid July night, "what will there be for an army to do?"

"Your new nation," Peterson had said with clear understanding.

"Exactly so," Guilford had said.

"But can you be sure?" Peterson had asked.

"You know soldiers who are injured on the outside, but not men who are wounded inside," the general had said. "Offer an officer a flag that stands for something great and he will fight to the death. To such an officer, that ideal would be a land free of bureaucrats and dandies. A rich land with fertile hills and fields, and an ocean for commerce." Guilford remembered having leaned into Peterson, who was sitting opposite. He had leaned into him and said conspiratorially—it was treason, after all—and said, "How will the United States or the broken Confederate States reclaim that land if the bulk of their veteran army is in charge of it?"

From the very next morning, Peterson had proven himself the right man to do the "gopher work," as Guilford thought of it. Stay underground, organize with Kennedy and Guilford to arrange a small, mercenary militia of former Confederates. Such men were plentiful out here, and hungry.

"But do not tell any of them the full plan," Guilford repeated before Peterson joined Kennedy and Hathaway on the stagecoach, their first trip to collect Tuchahu. "These are not the kind of men to become engaged by an idea. I have it from the Mission Indians, who seek a secure life for their families. These men who are still in rebellion will do anything for money."

Peterson broached the subject, and carried full payment in gold to back it up. The chest of gold coins was left at Fort Mason, to be collected when the men returned from Washington and thence back to San Francisco—without Tuchahu. The general at Fort Mason, Lars August, was an old West Point comrade of Guilford's. Unlike Guilford, who saw the Indian as simply an excuse to field a massive army, August genuinely hated the Red Man. In fairness to the Indian, August typically saw them when they were lawlessly drunk along the Barbary Coast, their passed-out bodies littering the streets of San Francisco.

But the reasons didn't matter, Guilford knew. Only the results.

The Indian agents did not know about the new nation or that they would be leaving behind their money, which was simply borrowed from the army. It would remain at Fort Mason to begin the first federal bank of the WSA. The men would make no complaint, of course, because once the War of the Pacific had begun they would not want to be known to have had a hand in it. Not when they were back in the arms of the enemy and could be hanged for treason.

Guilford angled the two doors of the wardrobe so the mirrored insides allowed him to check his uniform. He pulled a brush from the top shelf, began dusting it himself.

"The supreme idiocy, of course, is that neither of those buffoons have managed to do the one thing for which they were engaged," Guilford said.

The outside door opened. The lieutenant was just returning.

"Did you say something, sir?"

"Nothing, Anthony," Guilford said. "Please get me

the coast map—the desk size map—and go back to bed.
I will be with the colonel quite some time."

The man hesitated near the fireplace. "Coffee,
General?"

"I'll light a fire if we require it," Guilford said.

The lieutenant walked over to a wide, low cabinet
in which the regional maps were stored. He withdrew
a large sheet and lay it on his extended right arm
while he carried it to the desk. Guilford did not like
his maps folded, unless he was in the field. Too many
details like Indian encampments—signified by a
tepee—and the location of wells could be lost in the
creases.

The map was laid out, the lamps moved closer, and
the lieutenant departed. The door clicked shut loudly
behind him. Tonight the air was still, but on many
nights when the gates of the fort were open and the
wind swept in, the heavy door had a way of rattling for-
lornly. On those nights, even the new iron latch failed
to steady it entirely.

The sound reminded Guilford of whitened bones
lying in a plain, being knocked together by the wind.
They could be animal bones, it did not matter. The
death rattle was a sound no soldier liked to hear. It
meant that a life had been forgotten.

"And yet . . ." he thought as he replaced the brush
and walked to his desk.

Like a fort or a command, a nation was a living
thing that constantly required repairs. When they
took too long, the cracks pull that nation to pieces.
Guilford had read his history. Civil war was not the

exception since nations were first founded. It was the rule.

"But it will not happen in the WSA," he vowed.

Bureaucrats were the ones who eroded the good intentions of nation builders. Politicians needed money and votes before they would act. One took favors and demanded constant, special attention. The other came about every two or four years. Between elections, repairs could be permitted to lapse.

"That house will not be divided when I am Supreme Commander of the Western States and Lars August is Vice Commander of the Military," he said. When things needed to be done, soldiers would be dispatched to do them quickly. And investors would come as well. They would come because they would know that what they constructed or founded would be safe from forces within and without.

Construction would be swift and robust. A navy would be built, at first using bought or confiscated merchant ships that routinely journeyed to the Sandwich Islands, Honolulu, Rio de Janeiro, and even Boston and New York through the Isthmus of Panama. Sailors? There were many of them who could be bought for coin or the promise of plunder. Andrew Johnson would send military vessels and they would be met and sunk. Even now, plans to blockade key regions were being drawn up by Captain Scott Campbell of the British ship *Albundy* from Glasgow. The former naval officer had been running guns to the South during the War. He was now forbidden a port of call in the reunited states.

It was a plan built on hard-won experience but also on men. Guilford knew each man and, better, had *read* each man who held a key position. In his lifelong military career, stretching back to the war against the Mexicans thirty years before, Rhodes Guilford had learned how to take the measure of a man in a moment. Were his eyes steady, was his speech slurred, did he react—not overreact—to sounds behind him? Did he care about his appearance before meeting a superior officer, even during combat? Were his shoulders straight, his posture erect even when he had not slept in over a day or just completed a forced march?

The general's successes, his very life, had often depended on the fitness of others. He did not permit men to serve who were not at their best. They had to be *the* best. If they were embittered, like Captain Campbell, were they still clearheaded enough and devoted enough to serve?

The wardrobe doors squeaked as Guilford shut them. He returned to the desk and selected a cigar from the humidor. He lit it, took a few slow puffs, then sat. He wanted to be relaxed. He wanted to appear— no, to *be*—at ease when he spoke to Colonel Burke.

Guilford looked at the map, his eyes agleam, the smoke curling up as if the terrain below had opened to release the first plumes of the coming fire.

Colonel Burke was a son of Dixie who had sided with the North. Guilford would not tell him the entire plan, not yet—only that a final war with the Indian was coming. Burke would serve that war without reserve. When the time was right, when victory was at hand, Guilford would reveal the larger plan.

"Yes," he said, looking over the map that stretched from Mexico to San Francisco. He could already see the legend at the bottom bearing the name of the new nation. He could visualize the star that would mark the military capital in San Francisco, where General August would be headquartered, and the national capital in Tucson, four hundred miles to the southeast of Fort Yuma. It would be important to form a quick alliance with Mexico not just for mercenaries to fight the United States—if more were needed—but for resources the new nation would require. Servant labor, for one.

"After all," Guilford said, "most of the Indians will be dead."

His eyes narrowed slightly, and not from the smoke. Once more, his thoughts returned to the present.

All of this, all of his plans, depended upon one thing that remained to be done. The shaman Tuchahu *had* to be taken and he had to be slain. That meant the stagecoach had to be stopped before it reached San Francisco. Major Howard was not likely to detain it but to see it to its next destination. Perhaps he would dispatch troops to ride with it to their base fort. Howard was a good but simple man in that way. He occasionally showed initiative. The fact that he went out tonight, to show the Red Man a presence at unexpected hours, was evidence of that. But he still stayed strictly within regulations. And he had indeed met the Indians.

So doing, he had given Guilford a reason for his own next move.

The Indians who killed a white man tonight were making war. They had to be stopped. Riding out with the entire garrison—a justifiable response, however excessive it might seem to some in the East—Guilford would do that. And in the process, Tuchahu would die.

It almost didn't matter who did it, as long as he was white. Preferably a Rebel, so the army would not be blamed. For the next few weeks at least, Guilford still required the full assent of Washington and the press that influenced public opinion.

There was a firm knock on the door and General Guilford told Colonel Timothy Burke to enter. A tall, lantern-jawed, clean-shaven man walked in, his gray eyes pale in the light. He was dressed smartly, despite having been abed just a few minutes before.

"Pull over a chair, Colonel," Guilford began. He motioned to a comfortable armchair diagonally from the desk. "Sorry to wake you, but I have received a courier with distressing news."

The colonel sat leaning forward with an intense and attentive look.

"It appears," Guilford announced, "there is a large-scale Indian uprising afoot."

"Do we know how large, General?"

"The largest we've seen," the general replied. Then he, too, leaned forward and said with certainty, "It will be crushed."

The braves rode in the encampment with horses that were so exhausted, so driven that two of them died after stopping. While on the way from the plains, Baishan had to stop and light a fire under his own palomino. It had laid down not far from their destination and refused to go any farther. Rather than slow one of the other braves down by riding with him, he scorched the horse's belly to get it back on its feet.

He was the first of the two horses to fall to its side. Baishan would miss the steady mount. He fully intended to take another one, a better one, from the pony soldiers.

The camp was roused by the whoops of the three Apache. A committee consisting of the braves, the war chief, and the tribal chief was hastily arranged. It was held in the open, around the dying campfire, which the men encircled.

Baishan explained to the tribal leaders what he had learned from Joe O'Malley and seen in the flatlands. He believed that the intent was to harm the Serrano and turn tribal wrath against settlers.

"They will burn with a fire that only blood can quiet," he said. "And the blood will be our own."

The aged chief, Eskinospas, stood with his arms clutching a staff decorated with pelts. After listening, he shut his eyes to commune with his spirit animals, the fox and wolf.

All was silent, save for the low crackle of the fire and the occasional movement of the horses.

"The guardians speak," he said. "They say that the Serrano people should take to the plains and prevent the attack on our brothers."

Tarak, the war chief, said he would take twenty braves and left to organize their immediate departure.

"Wait!" the chief said, raising the staff. "The eagle of the shaman has a voice. It tells us to wait for the sun, when he can provide us with eyes."

Tarak heard the words and nodded. Baishan knew that the war chief did not like to delay, feeling that quiet blood was fit only for old women—and for aged storytellers like the chief, who believed that the land was made unfertile by war.

But when a great Indian, even a Serrano, was threatened, that could not be ignored. And when the son of Eskinospas's sister came with the kind of urgency that Baishan displayed, even the ancient pelts must fill with fire.

At least there was time to ready the horses, arrows, spears, and guns before riding out, to gather the best warriors. Baishan was confident that Tarak would be prepared for this struggle.

"Before you ride you must rest," Eskinospas told his nephew. His aged eyes briefly sought the other two men. "You and the others, your good friends and companions."

"We will go to our tepees, Uncle," the warrior said.

The younger men all made a sign of respect, touching their hearts and sweeping their fingers toward the chief. Then they departed and the camp returned to its previous silence.

Eskinospas did not tell the real reason he had permitted fox and wolf to have their say.

He looked up at the stars, saw a few that shot through the heavens like cold arrows. Later, he would ask his own medicine man what the falling lights meant. But the Apache suspected that he already knew.

As the firmament comes asunder and the stars fall, so do the Apache fall, he thought ruefully.

For many seasons now, the numbers of Apache and Pechanga and other local tribes had been dwindling. Since the Great White War, the hunting grounds had become fewer and fewer, the rivers dammed, the noise of wheels more frequent. The era of Man was at an end. It was the time of Wood and Iron. The chief permitted them to go because none of them would have a place in what was to come.

"Better to die in battle with an enemy than to live under his boot."

With his spirit heavy, heavier than even the greatest young wolf could bear, Eskinospas returned to his tent.

CHAPTER 20

"Stop the coach!"

Slash was riding alongside the right side of the box, near B.W., and shouting loud enough to be heard over the clatter of the hitch rail. They were on a slightly weather-beaten section of the trail due to a low grade to the north and runoff from weather.

"What's wrong?" B.W. shouted back as he braked.

"You got a whole lot of riders coming up," Slash said. "Seems like more'n we shot down before."

"Any idea if they're Apaches?"

"Couldn't say, but the cloud they're kicking up is considerable." He dismounted as Clarity rode up beside him. "Grandpa, I'm thinking Clarity should take the shaman's place and I should go off with him eastward. We got the big Salt Creek not far off—places we could hide there."

"Do it," Joe decided. He climbed down.

"You want me back in the coach?" Clarity protested.

"This is not the time for a squabble," Joe said urgently as he peered to the south. He could see, just barely, glints of white light moving along the ground.

"They're soldiers, judging by what the moonlight's saying," he said.

"What would they be wanting?" B.W. asked.

"Either they're headed to Fort Mason or they want us," Joe said.

Slash hadn't bothered to contribute to the speculation. He was a man who dealt with things that presented themselves now, not later. He had already opened the coach and told the Serrano to come out.

"What's amiss?" asked Fletcher Small.

"I'll let you know after it isn't," Slash said.

The shaman didn't move. He was holding Willa's hand in his and she was asleep. Slash reached in past her and made an expression that implored cooperation.

"Tuchahu, if these men are after you, Willa and the others could be hurt," Slash reminded him.

With reluctance, the medicine man gently placed the woman's hand on her lap and picked up his headdress. He could not help brushing against her and rocking the coach as he left, though the woman slept through it.

Clarity steadied her horse as Tuchahu climbed easily into the saddle. Mounting the paint was easier than settling in the saddle.

"You rode before, yeah?" Slash said.

Tuchahu didn't answer. He sat tall but stiffly and Slash realized they might not reach the large body of water as quickly as he had hoped.

The two men rode off and Clarity entered the cabin, gun-first.

"We best start out," B.W. said, looking back. "Them riders is only a mile or so distant."

Clarity boarded, Joe shut the door, and Slash and the shaman rode off on the rocky plain.

"What do you think?" B.W. asked as he released the brake.

"I think we put on some speed to draw whoever it is south as far as possible," Joe replied. "Other than that, Tuchahu's horse knows as much as I do."

The stagecoach rolled on, bouncing hard. Joe fixed himself with his hip against the side rail so he could stay twisted backward and keep an eye on the trail behind.

Inside the coach, Clarity was angry at the new development—and she was angry at herself. She should have gone with Slash, even if she had to ride double with the medicine man. Tuchahu did not look like he could ride. That was going to slow their progress. And if he had to stop and make a stand . . .

You mustn't think of that, she told herself. *He is smart and he knows how to use the land better than probably anyone other than his grandfather.*

Reverend Michaels had awakened when the coach braked. He saw his sister and, still groggy, it took him a moment to make sure she was really there.

He was about to ask if everything was over when he noticed that Tuchahu was missing.

"Did—did someone take him?" the man asked.

"Slash did," Clarity answered, leaning forward so her voice wouldn't wake the old woman.

"My, that *is* a story!" the reporter said.

The pastor's pasty expression brightened. "If he's

gone, then the miscreants who have been pursuing us will have no further cause to do so."

"Unless they seek hostages," Clarity said.

"Would they do something so endangering?" Michaels asked.

"At least until dawn," Clarity said. "At sunup, they might be able to detect a trail. But by then, Slash and Tuchahu would have had a considerable head start."

"This is all so vexing," Michaels said, sitting back.

"I feel alive," Clarity said.

"Do you?" her brother said. "Even though you could be shot? We all could be?"

"What better time and reason to *feel* alive?" she asked. "Merritt, I feel reborn out here. I don't think I will be continuing with you to San Francisco."

Michaels and Small both went very still.

"It's the full moon," Small said finally. "Affects people funny, I'm told."

"Sister, you are joking."

"I am not at all, not a word of it," she replied. It sounded, even to Clarity, as if she was in the process of very quickly convincing herself. "I want to live here and I hope you will stay. They don't have a church here. They need one."

"Well, Parson," Small said, finding his voice—and a chuckle. "Looks like God has been working in His own wondrous way."

"Clarity," was all the suddenly forlorn preacher could say.

The reporter continued, "I see, sir, you have learned not to argue with a lady whether she is armed or not."

The pastor had shrunk to a portion of his former

height, his eyes sinking. "Clarity, I have a new parish. I have made a commitment."

"You sent a letter ahead to your old seminary brother saying we were coming," Clarity told him with growing agitation.

Before Michaels could answer, Small spoke.

"No time to wait for a reply, I'm guessing," he said.

Clarity looked at him, edged her carbine very slightly in his direction. "This is a private matter, Mr. Small, unfortunately being aired in a public space. I ask for you to be decent enough not to interfere."

Small held up a palm and nodded. But Clarity was already stung by the ricochet reference to what she had done.

"Merritt," the woman continued more sedately, "the reality of our situation is, all you've got is hope."

"'All'?" the preacher said with disbelief. "Clarity, my entire life is based on hope, on faith! Without that, without trust in the divine providence of God, we have nothing! None of us!"

"I believe in God," Willa rasped, suddenly awake. She curled her bony fingers around the shotgun, which now stood barrel-up between her legs. "But I also believe in my own self. At the risk of earning this here girl's unfriendliness, I say you should let her be."

Clarity smiled at Willa. "Your wisdom would never offend me," she said.

That ricochet hit Fletcher Small squarely.

Clarity looked softly at her brother. "I have been looking for something my whole life, Merritt. You know that. This may be it. I have to find out."

"Isn't it possible, Clarity, that you could find this in San Francisco?" he asked. "Even if I am unable to get a position at first, we know someone there, someone of connections and influence."

"*You* know someone," Clarity said.

Willa waved her free hand in front of her impatiently. "It's the boy, you blind mule," the old woman said. "Your sister is in love with her cowboy."

A velvet-thick silence dropped on the group.

"Oh—I don't know that," Clarity said, just as suddenly and blushing again.

"You an' your brother the only ones," Willa replied. "Except maybe the cowboy. He seems to lack general awareness."

"No, Willa," Clarity began, then went in a different, slightly flustered direction. "I don't know. I *do* know what I am in love with, and that's the life out here."

"Barbarity and primitive conditions," her brother said imploringly. "How could anyone be in love with that?"

"Son, you don't know barbarity and poor conditions," Willa said. "Let the girl be. I didn't have a choice in my life till recent. You have no idea what that feels like!"

Before the conversation could continue, several shots cracked from somewhere behind the stagecoach. As one, Willa and Clarity both reached for their guns.

"Is this all people do out here?" Reverend Michaels screamed, and immediately folded his hands in prayer.

B.W. turned to Joe. The former plainsman was still looking back.

"What do I do?" B.W. asked.

It was a moment after the shots before Joe answered. "Damned if I know why, but it's cavalry," he replied. "Don't see as we have a choice but to stop."

"Butterfield oughta figure out how to make one o' these that can outrun bullets, or at least can't be stopped by 'em," B.W. grumbled as he braked once more. He slowed his hardworking team gradually and allowed the riders to catch up.

"Do you need help?" Small called through the open window. "We have ladies who seem keen to shoot something."

"Y'all just sit tight," B.W. said. "It's troops."

Joe and B.W. exchanged looks as they waited. Joe was considering a number of possibilities. The most likely were that it had something to do with the medicine man or the men who got shot back at the ravine.

"Rotten luck if they was out on patrol," Joe said.

"Huh?"

"Nothing," Joe replied.

The column encircled the coach, with a major leading. When the stage was enclosed, the officer doubled back and approached the Whip. Behind him were two men Joe had hoped never to see again.

"Kennedy and Hathaway," B.W. muttered. "Scoundrels on the hoof."

"Did you say something, driver?" the major asked.

"Nothing, Major," B.W. said. "Just chewing fat with my Shotgun."

"I am Major Alexander Howard out of the San Diego Barracks," the man announced.

"Welcome to the Butterfield Trail, sir," B.W. said.

The officer regarded Joe. "Are you Joseph O'Malley?"

"No one but," Joe replied.

"You are not the regular Shotgun," the major said.

"My family and I run Whip Station, south of here," he answered. "Why are you asking, Major Howard?"

"I will address that later. At the moment, I want you to hand your weapon to Sergeant Wayne, beside you."

Joe didn't move. "I assume you got a reason for that request?"

"It wasn't a request—"

"I am not a pony soldier," Joe interrupted. "You want to take it, you're welcome to try. You want me to give it over, I want a reason."

"Because I will, trust me, sir, have you shot. Until proven otherwise, you are a renegade and will be treated as such."

"On the say-so of him?" Joe pointed the gun at Kennedy.

"Now, Mr. O'Malley!"

Joe handed the weapon to a private who reached for it. Howard's eyes shifted from Joe to the Whip.

"The men behind me are Indian agents who are authorized by the Bureau of Indian Affairs to take charge of one of your passengers, the Serrano named Tuchahu," Howard said to B.W. "You will surrender him at once."

The driver was sitting with his right hand still on the brake, his left forearm resting across his knees and he relaxing on top of it.

"I can't do that, Major," B.W. said.

"Company policy does not outrank military jurisdiction in this state," Howard assured him.

"I was schooled in such things before I was hired," B.W. answered. "Doesn't change the fact that I cannot oblige."

"Why not?"

"Because, sir, the gentleman you referred to, Mr. Tuchahu, is not presently aboard."

Major Howard ordered two men to check the coach. They dismounted, went to the door, and opened it. One of the men asked Joe to pass the lantern down from where it was suspended from the cargo rail. The shotgun rider obliged. The private handed it to his companion, who thrust it in the cabin. The trooper stepped back suddenly.

"Cooper?" the major said.

"There are more weapons, sir," the private answered.

"Collect them," Howard ordered. "And bring the Indian out at once."

The private gave the lantern to his companion who stood close behind him. Cooper approached more cautiously now. After a moment, he came back out with his arms full of two shotguns, Clarity's two handguns, and a .22-caliber pistol he confiscated from Fletcher Small, a seizure that made Clarity laugh.

"Where's the Serrano?" Howard demanded.

"Sir," replied Cooper, "there is one gentleman, one priest, one woman, and one Negro woman. No medicine man."

"Shut the door," Howard ordered his men.

"What if we're attacked?" B.W. said. "You're leaving us defenseless."

"Mr. Cooper, place the weapons in the rear boot,"

Howard said through his teeth. The men obliged, the major's eyes returned to B.W. "I notice, Brother Whip, that you are carrying no luggage other than the mail. Where is it?"

B.W. indicated Kennedy with the hand holding the reins. "Broke a spoke running from this prairie-rat. Wheel acted up so we had to ditch the baggage."

"Where?"

"Back on the range about three miles," B.W. said. He wanted to say that he used the bags to build a lodge for Tuchahu. But when the lantern was rehung and he saw the major's expression, he thought better of it.

Howard came a little closer to B.W.

"Where is he, this Tuchahu?"

"He departed of his own free will," B.W. said.

"On foot?"

"On horseback."

"Whose horse?" Howard demanded.

"It belonged—I lost track, but I think it was the one belonged to the old Colored lady, Willa."

"You 'think,'" Howard said. "Who else had a horse out here?"

"Her son," B.W. told him. "He rode south to look for his kin."

"Did *he* leave alone?"

"Yes," B.W. said.

"And Tuchahu?"

"No, Major," Joe answered. "My grandson Slash is with him."

"'Slash,'" Howard repeated, looking at Joe. "He also had a horse?"

"He did."

"Which way did they go?"

"They was headed eastward to start, though I don't suspect they stuck to that path," Joe answered.

"Why not?"

"Because Slash ain't a dope," Joe said, making a point of looking at Kennedy—whose face was a taut, ugly mask. "He figured somebody might ask me that question and I would have to give an answer, far as I knew."

Howard was clearly unhappy with that explanation. He gestured behind him.

"You seem to know these gentlemen," the major indicated.

"I sadly do," Joe replied. "The big log is Kennedy and the grub-line cayuse is his partner in crime Hathaway. Reason I'm here riding shotgun, like B.W. said, is because their Rebs shot up the reg'lar man, Dick Ocean, back at Civil Gulch. When their mercenary posse rode in to Whip Station to take the Indian at gunpoint, Kennedy and Hathaway joined them. The only reason they departed without their man is the lady your Mr. Cooper mentioned, the white girl with the gun, chased them off."

"A girl," Major Howard said.

"A dead shot," B.W. assured him.

Joe said, "That Miss Clarity? If you hadn't relieved her of her gun, she could shoot my seat through my chest from where she's seated. I've threatened Apache but I would not take my chances with her."

Several of the troops smiled. Major Howard was not among them.

"That's quite a tale," Howard said when it was finished.

"If they was honest men, the two finefied dirtbags would back it up," Joe said. "But they ain't."

"And *you*, mister, are a liar!" Kennedy charged.

Howard turned on the Indian agent. "*Did* you threaten any of them, Mr. Kennedy?"

"I certainly did not," Kennedy said, riding forward. "And I've had enough of their hollow talk! Major, this man is the Rebel lover. We shot one who was working with him, the man you saw dead. The Indians took care of the other fellow shortly before you arrived."

"Finally, a word of truth," Joe said.

Kennedy ignored him. "Joe O'Malley has been obstructing Bureau business since we stopped at Whip Station. I don't know why, maybe to incite an Indian war, but I demand that he tell us where the shaman is bound and that the Indian be immediately apprehended."

The major took a long moment to consider the situation.

"Sergeant Wayne?" he shouted.

"Sir!" the man answered, riding over.

"Take Cooper and Locke and escort the stagecoach back to Whip Station," the major said.

"Aw, Jiminy!" B.W. yelled. "My schedule! The mail!"

"I'm sorry, but as Mr. Kennedy has told you there are two dead men four miles back and a missing Red Man of keen interest to our government," Howard said. "Since Whip Station was the start of this, and since this Slash O'Malley lives there, that is where we are going." He looked at Joe. "Mr. O'Malley—and passengers!" he shouted the last. "You may retain your weapons. However, anyone who uses one to countermand my orders will be shot." His eyes remained fixed on Joe. "Is that clear?"

"As the sinking moon," Joe said.

"What about the Indian Tuchahu?" Kennedy demanded.

"Sir, the rest of us are going after him," Howard said. "We'll go back a ways and head east, since they left before we spotted the coach. It will be light in about an hour. We should be able to pick up a trail."

The three-man detachment took up positions to the side and rear of the stagecoach and, with a deep, unhappy sigh, B.W. turned the conveyance around. In just a few minutes, the Butterfield party was headed back to the south and the rest of the cavalry unit was headed east.

B.W. leaned toward the shotgun rider.

"You want to get off and figure out some way to help your grandson?" he whispered.

"If there was some way to catch them, I would."

"One o' those troopers' horses?"

"Thought of it," Joe replied. "As likely to get the horse shot in the arse or me in the back. This bear of a sergeant—he looks like the type to do it."

"So what do we do? Just ride back?"

Joe looked longingly to the east where the cavalry column was riding hard after his grandson.

"I got folks at home I have to think about, too," he answered. "We lose our boy, someone has to avenge him."

B.W. thought about that, then nodded.

"How in heck did good folks like all of us get trapped in this quicksand?"

Joe replied, "'Cause even after this is done—I agree with your book," he dipped his head toward the Bible on the seat between them. "I have ta think the best of men or else why do anything but build bigger walls and gun down everyone you see?"

"I reckon that's true," B.W. said. "But since yesterday afternoon, it's been a whole lot less true."

Joe suddenly raised his arms straight up.

"You cramping?" B.W. asked.

"You haven't been watching ahead," Joe said.

"Naw, I been watching for ruts and rocks since we got a weak—"

As B.W. spoke his eyes rose from the road just below to the road beyond. He stopped talking. One of his arms followed those of his companion, while the other hand stayed with the reins.

"God A'mighty," B.W. said. "You fixin' to get to the back box?"

"Not in time, especially if we have to explain to those troops who are half-asleep in the saddle."

"Hey, Sergeant!" B.W. yelled down.

The man was riding beside him and looked up. "Yeah?"

B.W. pointed. The cavalryman swore and barked an order to driver and riders to stop.

"This is gonna be interesting," Joe said, his arms still in the air.

CHAPTER 21

Slash and Tuchahu rode through increasingly hilly countryside at a slow but steady pace. Although he didn't really wish that Gert were here, he could sure use her. This man was a mute mystery. He barely moved, he didn't speak, and if he was scared he didn't show it.

I really wish you could help me understand, sis, he thought. *Coupla lives could depend on that.*

The young man had briefly kept to an easterly course, measured by the stars—those he could see, that weren't swallowed by moonlight. When they reached a stretch of desert, he debated separating: letting the Indian continue east while he turned south. If there were two sets of hoofprints, anyone following them would have to divide their forces to follow both.

But that would still leave half of them on Tuchahu, he realized.

They stayed together. Slash was satisfied with the distance they were putting between themselves and the stagecoach. Hopefully, by dawn, they would have reached the shoreline of the creek. He had never been there, but he heard his grandpa tell it was a considerable body of water with a lot of gullies and underground caves.

Places where a man could hold off an army, Slash hoped.

His eyes were suddenly heavy, the perfect companions for his arm-weariness. He stretched them wide, looked up. The moon was setting and the sky was becoming pitch. The stars were coming out like bashful ladies who were now all dressed . . .

I should have stayed with Clarity, not ridden off with this Injun, he thought suddenly—and to his own surprise.

Sure she could handle a gun, and Joe and Willa were there. But who knew how many of what kind of men were coming. If they were anything like the band he shot at, they would be ruthless.

Hell, he thought. *They could stop the stage and starve 'em. Set it afire.*

The more he thought about what could happen, the more Slash wanted to tell the medicine man to just ride into the sun while he raced back to the trail.

But duty, he thought.

Joe and his own father had hit that into him since he was a boy, clunked on his head like he was a shoe on an anvil.

Defend the family, defend the station, defend the safety of those who come to it.

Who could deny that Tuchahu was probably in more danger than Clarity?

So why does it hurt my chest to think of her in danger?

Unless that wasn't it.

Might be that we're apart that's got me, he realized with the sudden cold-water shock of an icy river.

When they briefly rested the horses at a watering

hole, Slash considered turning around in a circle and heading back to the trail. Outrunning a pursuit in one direction was as good as running another.

Except they'll still follow you back, he realized. *It would've been better not to run at all, then. Just to fight it out.*

Almost as concerning as the danger, Slash was distracted by how much he was distracted by thoughts of Clarity. This was not like thinking about how to corner a wild turkey—

A little bit, but not exactly, he told himself upon reflection. *This is new.*

Ahead, the faintest light began to turn the low line of the sky purple. He began to see the silhouette of the land ahead. What's more, he thought—and then he was sure—he saw something else.

The slashing glint of light on the lowlands between the low mounds of hills.

The Salt Creek.

As the purple shaded to orange, pale yellow began to creep across the plain. It came at them faintly, then more boldly, like the changing tide he had watched with amazement on a beach in San Diego.

Slash looked back. He saw a point man against the flat horizon. Behind the man was a line of other men, visible when they writhed around a gully or stone or tree. As the sunlight crawled up the horse to the rider, Slash saw a patch of dark blue.

Cavalry. Slash almost preferred that it would have been Apaches. He knew they had contempt for peaceful tribes like the Serrano, but they weren't likely to kill one of their leaders. Cavalry worked for the government, Indian agents worked for that same government, and that could not be good. If troops had found Kennedy and Hathaway dead, they would have a pretty good idea who did the shooting. If they had found the men alive, they would know for sure who killed the men that were riding with them.

A shot boomed faintly across the intervening land, gaining in sound as it rolled through its own echo. That was a command to stop. Slash ignored it. The only possible salvation was ahead, and he pressed hard in that direction. He did not think the column would risk sending a rider or two ahead. The troops' only safety was in superior numbers.

That, plus the fact that Slash did not want to have to kill troops. He and his companion *had* to outrun them and hide.

Slash moved his horse closer to that of the Indian. The young man leaned over and—so as not to alarm the horse—he very gently inserted a gloved hand in the bridle.

"Listen, Tuchahu," Slash said. "I hope ya can understand but we gotta hurry. There's cavalry after us."

The Indian nodded once. He was otherwise implacable, his dark face turned to bronze by the rising sun.

"Hold the reins and just sit tight," Slash said. "I'm gonna run us to the creek ahead."

At that, Slash kicked his own horse and shook the bridle of the other one hard. Both animals set off, Slash using as much muscle as he owned to keep the two animals running together and side by side. From the start, he was afraid the Indian's horse might tug his arm from its socket, but the animal steadied soon enough and the two ran agreeably in tandem.

The water ahead was clearer now, glistening blue-gray with streaks of golden dawn. As they came closer, maneuvering around little outcroppings here and there, Slash had a better view of the Salt Creek.

It wasn't that at all. It was a lake—and the nearer they got it seemed larger than any lake he'd ever seen. Even on horseback, he could not yet see the other side.

But Slash could not afford to be distracted by the water, not now. The horses were nearing the end of their endurance. He had to find a defensible point somewhere on this side.

His keen eyes picked out sand, a curving shoreline, points of land stretching out here and there. He also saw what looked like long, grassy dunes—possibly the result of flooding or wind, maybe both. They were slightly to the northeast of his position. He made for it, thinking that behind that rise they might be able to hold the cavalry off. At least long enough to talk to them, see what they wanted.

Other than my scalp, he thought, finding it ironic that it was pursuing white men he was talking about and not Apache.

The body of water was not just wide, it was long, as Slash saw when they reached the shore. The horses stumbled a bit on the sand and, slowing, he bade Tuchahu dismount as he did the same. Leading both horses, Slash told the Indian to follow him toward the shore.

Instead, the tall Serrano dropped to his knees and bowed to the big Salt Creek.

"Not now!" Slash implored him, stopping and using his hat to swat the two steeds ahead.

The Indian did not move from that position. If he was praying, he was doing it silently.

"Aw, beans," Slash said as he flopped beside the Indian but facing away from the water, toward the cavalry. "Whatever water gods you're praying to—ask 'em to send a deluge of some kind."

"Not water, earth," the Serrano said.

"What?"

"I thank the earth for bringing us to this place," Tuchahu said.

"Figure you to finally speak and I have no idea what you're saying," Slash said. "Friend, we have troops charging down on us. I was hoping we might go to that ridge—see it to your left?"

His headdress askew, his beads tangled from the ride, Tuchahu stood and walked slowly toward the spot Slash had indicated. Another warning shot was pumped into the sky. The soldiers were close enough now that Slash was afraid to move. He didn't think they would shoot the Indian out-of-hand, but Slash did not know their intentions where he was concerned. He bellied down deeper into the sand. He had his rifle before him, his left arm beneath the barrel to keep sand from getting into the mechanism. He was glad there was no wind at the moment. The rifle would have been grailed up beyond redemption.

Like a desert mirage, the men rode into the sun, their images wavy. Slash was still looking ahead with both eyes, not aiming the rifle. He did not want to take a threatening stance unless it became necessary.

It was at that moment he realized how tired he was. What *was* his play? These were trained soldiers, not ragtag Rebels. What would he do if they ignored him, just wrapped up Tuchahu, put him on his horse, and sent some men off with him. The soldiers could outwait him. They could sit in the shade of a rock or one of the few big yucca trees that spotted the area. He couldn't stay put, buried to his chin while the sun rose and baked his back raw.

He would never hurt the Indian, but these men didn't know that. He needed Tuchahu as a hostage. That was how to get the men to talk instead of shoot.

"Dash it!" he said, bolting from the sand. Bent low, he went running after the shaman. Tuchahu was standing behind the ridge. The horses had stopped farther along, by the water. They weren't drinking. Not at Salt Creek.

"You, Slash O'Malley—*halt!*"

He kept running. A bullet spit sand not far from him. He was about ten feet from the ridge. A bullet struck closer—close enough so that the sand pelted his cheek.

Slash stopped running. He wanted to fight back— he did. Surrender was not in his blood. But neither was being heroically stupid, especially when there might be a better way. His back to the men, he dropped the rifle and raised his hands. If he hadn't been so tired, he would have thought this through. If he had been dealing with a normal companion, one who could cover him instead of standing there, do what he was told instead of stopping to pray . . .

"Turn around," he was told.

Slash did so. The sunlit cavalry was a small unit of perspiring blue, dust-covered and scowling. The man in front was a major. Alone among the troops, he rode tall. A few paces behind him, to the east, was the private who had been firing. His repeater was still pointed in Slash's general direction.

The major halted the column a few paces away. Slash now saw the vile Kennedy and Hathaway peeling off from the rear and coming forward. Of course they did, now that the danger was seemingly past.

"I am Major Howard," the man in front announced. "We've come for the Serrano Tuchahu and also to take you back to the San Diego barracks under arrest."

"What have I done, other than ride off with a man who was free to go with me?" Slash asked.

"The two Indian agents traveling with me believe that you may have been party to the murder of one or more people back at the Butterfield Trail," he said.

"It was two," Slash said. "I shot one. They was shooting at my grandpa and Miss Clarity Michaels."

Kennedy snorted. "He's as big a liar as the other O'Malley."

"You're lucky I dropped my gun, you mongrel."

"Watch your mouth, boy," Kennedy said.

"Brave now, are ya, with a mess o' cavalry," Slash said. "Last time I saw you it was your back, not your face, and you was running."

Kennedy made a sound as if he were thinking of responding, but the major angled his horse so he could see the Indian agent.

"These O'Malleys apparently don't think much of you, Mr. Kennedy," Howard said.

"Neither I nor the Indian Bureau care what they think," Kennedy replied. He looked toward the ridge where the medicine man was standing. "Tuchahu!" he called out. "We've traveled a long way together. Come. I'd like to get you home, to your people."

The medicine man did not move.

"Maybe he remembers how you threw in with

the Rebels to kidnap him back at Whip Station," Slash said.

"That was your plan, not mine," Kennedy alleged. "For ransom, I suspect?"

"You got gall the size of this lake," Slash said. "Major, I do not know what is up this card sharp's sleeve, but it isn't the well-being of the shaman, that is for sure. You let this dog have him, the Serrano, I suspect, will never see his people again."

"Not my people," Tuchahu said suddenly.

All eyes turned toward him.

"What was that?" Kennedy demanded.

Only Tuchahu's head and the top of his torso were visible behind the sparsely grassed outcropping of rock and sand.

"I not see my people," he said.

"What *do* you see?" Major Howard asked.

The Indian raised an arm and pointed toward the west and answered, "See Apache."

Major Howard and his men turned to see a line of Indians galloping toward them. They were not riding single-file as the cavalry had done, they were spread across the horizon, some twenty strong, guns and spears raised. Even at this distance, the sharp morning sunlight picked out the blues and reds of their war paint.

"Skirmish line!" Major Howard shouted to the five men in his unit. "Kennedy, Hathaway, I suggest you arm yourselves. Mr. O'Malley, would you care to join us?"

Slash picked up his gun and brushed it off with his

sleeve as he strode forward. The steel of his knife was hot at his side, wanting desperately to blaze a trail through Kennedy's false tongue. But that could keep. With luck, he would live long enough to see the Apache take his hair.

The soldiers lay their horses down and got behind them, facing the enemy. Slash did not join them on the ground. Nor did he raise his rifle. He had been with the Apache a few times when he went to fetch Gert. Maybe one of them would recognize him and know he wasn't their enemy. Or if not, maybe they would see that he didn't want to fight.

Like Slash the major was on his feet, standing at the northern side of the line. He was not holding a gun but his saber. The sword was a weapon respected by the Apache. It could not kill from a distance or from hiding. The man who held it must have courage.

The Indian agent and his colleague were lying in the sand, belly down, behind the troops.

"Don't fire unless we are fired upon," Howard said. "Mr. Kennedy, do you have any idea what they are up to?"

"They are supposed to be at an encampment north of Vallicita!" Kennedy said. "I don't know why they are here, making war!"

"Maybe to stop whatever you and your mercenaries are up to," Slash said. "Tuchahu!" he said suddenly. "Would you mind stepping from behind the ledge? Go where the Apache can see you."

The shaman fixed his headdress so it sat squarely, arranged his beads, then stepped proudly to one side. He was silhouetted by the rising sun, his shadow falling long and slender across the troops.

Almost at once, the charging Apache braves slowed. They came forward at a canter, guns and spears lowered but still at the ready, but there was clearly no intention now to attack.

"I will be damned," Major Howard said.

"Not today," Slash said.

"Troops, rise slowly, guns lowered, and get your horses on their feet," the major said. "Three on the left go south, right go north. I want an opening in the center."

This was done as the Indians continued to ride toward them. Major Howard walked to the space that had been created. As he passed, Kennedy and Hathaway were just brushing the sand from their clothes.

"Dirt goes deeper than that, you curs," Slash told them.

Howard made no comment as he walked ahead of the troops. One of the Apaches also broke from the line and rode a few paces before dismounting. The Apache advance stopped as the two men approached one another.

Major Howard saluted and introduced himself.

The Apache slapped a fist across his chest. "I am Baishan, blood of Chief Eskinospas of the Apache." He removed his fist and pointed to Tuchahu. "We come to see the Serrano father to a place of safety."

"We are here for the same purpose, then," Major Howard said.

"No," Baishan snapped. "Joe tell us of men hunting him. Grays. And two Indian agents."

"Another O'Malley lie!" Kennedy blurted.

"Quiet!" Howard half-turned and shouted back.

"My apologies, Baishan. When did Joe O'Malley tell you this?"

"This night just past," the Apache replied. "They blow up pass—one man die. Others, Joe say, in mine with red metal."

"Copper?" Major Howard asked.

"Yes. That was word Joe used. *Copper.*"

The officer thought back to the visit from Dr. Peterson. There was copper dust on his medicine bag. That could mean any number of things. Or it could mean just one.

Suddenly, Major Howard saw two more figures approaching from the west. They appeared to be— they *were*—riding on two of his own cavalry ponies.

CHAPTER 22

"You okay, boy?"

The unmistakable voice of Joe O'Malley traveled across the intervening countryside like a returning faith. At his side was Clarity Michaels. Slash smiled and made his way past the soldier, through the Apache.

"I'm fine, Grandpa! You?"

"Better than we feared," he said. "Baishan and his two cohorts recognized us from a little adventure at Civil Gulch yesterday. We just filled him in on what happened since. I told him that the two Indian agents who tried to take Tuchahu were out here. Didn't have to say no more."

Slash had been listening to Joe but looking at Clarity. The sun made her look like a princess in Gert's book of fairy tales. Only alive and full and . . .

"Howdy, Clarity," he said.

It may have been as stupid as it sounded to his own ears, but Clarity didn't seem to mind. She smiled back.

"Howdy, Slash."

Joe O'Malley left the two and rode toward Major Howard.

"You took those from my men?" Howard said disapprovingly.

"I only rode 'em," Joe said. "Baishan and his boys took 'em."

Joe dismounted in a sturdy leap. Then he walked over to Douglas Kennedy and sent him staggering backward with an uppercut that reached for the clear blue sky. The bigger man lost his footing and dropped.

"You shot at the station with my daughter and granddaughter inside!" Joe shouted, bending over the man, grabbing him by the lapels of his jacket, and hoisting him up. Joe kneed him hard in the gut, then spun him around, pushed him back to the ground. He was about to stomp on his chest when, at Howard's command, several troopers restrained the enraged older man. They held him under the arms, pulling Joe back as he swore a day's worth of fiery hate at the Indian agent.

"Come at me, you tub o' guts!" Joe said. "Get up! *C'mon!*"

Hathaway ran over and helped his partner up. The taller man seemed eager to strike back—though the presence of the major stayed his fist.

"I'll see you in prison," Kennedy vowed, coughing from the belly.

Howard stepped between the two. He faced Joe.

"Mr. O'Malley," the major said. "You have just assaulted a federal agent who is out here on government business."

"I hoped I wasn't being obscure," Joe snarled.

"You have committed a criminal action in front of—"

"A criminal action? I'll tell you what the crime is here!" Joe said. "Not the one against me but against our government, our land. Me an' B.W. figgered it out."

Joe had relaxed somewhat and the major indicated for his men to release him.

The frontiersman rolled his shoulders and approached the officer. "This creature wanted to rile the Indian nations with the death of this shaman." Joe pointed at Tuchahu who had remained standing before the climbing sun. "Kennedy and Hathaway and their Rebels and—well, I don't know who else, they wanted to use that to fire up the Red Man for a war of extermination."

"That's idiocy," said Kennedy, standing his wobbly ground.

"I wonder, Mr. Kennedy," Howard said. He spent a moment thinking—*remembering*—carefully before he spoke. "Late last night, a doctor came to see me at our campsite. He sat in my tent and wrote out a message to be delivered to General Guilford at Fort Yuma. It said something about an objective missed and someone being back on the road. There was also concern about Whip Station and Indians being involved."

Howard walked toward the Indian agents, who were standing shoulder to shoulder. Hathaway was glaring and Kennedy was breathing hard, a large hand on his belly.

"Do either of you know this man I'm speaking of, Dr. Peterson?"

"No," Kennedy said. "Why should we?"

"Because from what I've heard today, your actions fit the particulars of the message he sent."

"Then you should be talking to him, not to me," Kennedy said.

"I intend to do that," the major said. "You said the dead Rebels we found worked with Mr. O'Malley. How do you know?"

Kennedy pointed at Joe. "This lowlife and another ran off when the Indians arrived. You saw that."

"I saw the Indians," Major Howard agreed. "Get on your horses, all of you. You ride with us. The rest of my unit, mount up!"

As the command did as they had been ordered, Howard wheeled his horse toward the medicine man. He did not approach the lone figure, majestically haloed by the sun, but spoke out so that he could be heard by all.

"With the help of Baishan and the Apache," he said, "I would like to see that the Serrano father is returned to the stagecoach so that he may be taken to his people in the north. Does Tuchahu agree?"

The Indian walked forward without comment. Grinning, Slash excused himself from Clarity and ran back to get their horses. Mounting with Tuchahu, the men rode forward to join Clarity, Joe, the Cavalry, and the Apaches as they turned west.

"If I live to be as old as Salt Creek itself," Joe said with some astonishment, "I will never again see a caravan like this."

The troops at Fort Yuma had mustered with the sun, eager to be out of the fort and just as eager for action. Only General Guilford and Colonel Burke knew what the mission was, and both rode with the complement of twenty-four men, including a supply wagon.

The column headed out and to the northwest, full of vigor and resplendent in uniforms that were as sharp as Guilford insisted they be. Their mapped course would take them west along the foot of the southern end of Salt Creek toward Vallicita and then north to the Butterfield Trail.

General Guilford had not gone back to bed but he felt—*not rested,* he thought, *but settled, like a colt.*

After months of planning, the operation was finally in motion. The dream of a new nation was on the verge of being realized. He was a military man and understood that nothing in war was guaranteed. But he could not see how the conflagration could be stopped. Tuchahu was the match and he would soon be struck.

The officer could feel the fire in his men as they rode. Like a cannon that was fired too infrequently, men who drilled needed a challenge to test their skills. Fielding their new, powerful Springfields and surrounded by comrades-in-arms and a sense of purpose—for the first time since the War—these men were battle-tested and ready.

The blazing sun slowed the horses somewhat and canteens were lifted with regularity. Guilford had not set a limit on when and how much the men could drink. There were water holes and rivers along the way, and hardship would distract rather than toughen them.

There is a time to give and a time to withhold, he thought.

It was late morning when the United States Cavalry

was on the Butterfield Trail some two miles beyond the Whip Station, heading north. Guilford was looking ahead when suddenly, at his command, Colonel Burke halted the two columns.

"Glasses," the general said to Lieutenant Anthony, who was riding to his right, a pace behind.

The officer handed him a pair of binoculars. Guilford turned them north and focused. What he saw puzzled him. He did not know whether to smile or spit. Not yet.

Ahead, a column of cavalry was riding south on both sides of a stagecoach.

There were two men in the front box and . . .

"Christ, sir!" Burke exclaimed. The colonel was also looking through his glasses.

"What is it?" the general demanded.

From his vantage point to the right, the colonel could see part of the procession that was blocked by the stagecoach from the general's straight-on position.

"Sir, there are Indians with our boys."

Guilford could see the lead officer chatting with the driver. "They don't seem to be in trouble," he said.

"No sir, and the Indians—I think they're Apache— are not bearing arms. Orders?"

"Hold," Guilford replied. "Just hold."

The train approached, the officer—Major Howard— galloping ahead to meet the cavalry commander. Upon reining, he saluted.

"General . . . Colonel." His eyes took in the columns. "Is there trouble somewhere?"

"Perhaps you can tell me," Guilford said. "I received, as you know, a message from a gentleman named 'Gus' suggesting there was trouble. I decided to look into it personally."

"That was Dr. Peterson, sir," Howard said. "I was led to believe he knew you."

"He worked at the fort during an influenza outbreak."

"So he informed me," Howard said.

The general raised his arm, still holding the glasses. "What is all this?"

"The individual who concerned Dr. Peterson, the Indian Tuchahu, is aboard the stagecoach," Howard explained. "The Apache have volunteered to see him safely to his people, but as the shaman is still under the protection of the President of the United States I decided to withhold permission until instructed otherwise."

"Very wise," Guilford nodded.

The parade was now near enough so that the general could make out the Indian agents Kennedy and Hathaway. The men seemed broken.

Almost as shattered as my plan, Guilford thought. He knew, even as he had spoken, that disavowing any knowledge of Peterson's intent had been the start of its unraveling.

"Who else is with you?" Guilford asked.

Howard named the occupants of the coach. Guilford listened without comment. The O'Malleys ran Whip Station, where the wheels had come off this wagon. What they had witnessed would be enough to end the careers of the individuals involved. Perhaps worse.

The coach and its complement stopped just yards from the cavalry column. The general ignored the searching, imploring eyes of the head Indian agent. This was his failure. He and Hathaway would bear the responsibility alone. His stony expression informed them as much.

"Our presence here is clearly not required," Guilford said. He turned his eyes, and an approving smile, toward Major Howard. "I commend your initiative, Major."

"With the general's permission," Howard said, "we believe this Dr. Peterson is currently in the copper mines north of Civil Gulch. I believe, from what Joe O'Malley and another passenger have told us—that would be Miss Clarity Michaels, who you see riding off to the side—significant munitions including gunpowder are stored there. Some of that was likely used to bring down one side of the gulch."

"Yes, we saw the rockslide when we rode out," Guilford said. "Permission granted. I want you to report to me directly when your investigation is concluded."

"Gladly, sir!" Major Howard said. He was pleased that a mission undertaken hastily and with everevolving tactics seemed to have worked out so well.

At Guilford's command, Colonel Burke marched the column about-face and they retraced their route to the south. There was general discontent among the men, but none felt worse than General Guilford.

The Western States of America had just been stillborn.

The first thing Major Howard did upon returning to the stagecoach was to turn Tuchahu over to Baishan and the Apaches. Sincere farewells were made, though none more earnest than Joe O'Malley to the Indian brave.

"I am very happy to have fought this with you instead of agin' you," Joe said. He turned to his grandson who was mounted beside him. "You'll agree I said that when we see Gert, yeah?"

"Gladly," Slash said.

Baishan nodded once in agreement, then turned to the other O'Malley.

"Slash—we fight, someday." He made a fist. "Knives."

"Bone-blade so I don't kill ya, okay?" he said.

Baishan snorted. "Not kill. Not even cut."

"That'll be the day," he said.

The respective parties separated, the Indians to the north and the cavalry to the southeast. Only the stagecoach and the O'Malleys remained.

"I guess I gotta go back to Whip Station," B.W. said. "Seems to me I'm losing my Shotgun."

Slash grinned as he rode to Clarity's side.

B.W. sighed. "Dick Ocean warned me not to go without him. I shoulda listened."

Major Howard's unit rode to the copper mines, where their stay proved surprisingly brief.

During the ride, Douglas Kennedy had approached him. He spoke with a mouth that sounded as if it had gravel under the lower lip, thanks to Joe's punch.

"I want to make a deal," he said.

"About what?"

"I'll point out the mine where Peterson is if you let me and Hathaway go."

Howard turned to him. "That sounds almost like a confession, Mr. Kennedy."

"I don't care what it sounds like," the Indian agent replied. "The general was lying back there. Peterson will confirm that."

"The general was lying? Just like Mr. O'Malley was lying?"

"That was different," Kennedy said. "The general wanted us to seize the Indian. Peterson will confirm that."

"Will he? If the general did give such an order—why did you follow? You're a civilian."

"He gave us army gold," Kennedy said. "As payment."

"Where is this gold now?"

"At Fort Mason."

"Where they keep the paymaster's gold," Howard said.

"Yes, but they were only holding it for us. Peterson will confirm all of that."

"So it would be in your best interest for us to find him," Howard said. "Seems to me you have nothing to bargain with. If you don't show us where he is, you just confessed to something you'll have to face alone."

Kennedy's own distracted, careless speech flummoxed even the man himself. Beaten, he told Howard how to find the mine and they rode directly to it. As he had promised, Dr. Peterson was there with guns, powder, and a man who had died at some point during the night.

"Now there's a sight," Peterson said as the major and the Indian agent appeared in the mouth of the mine, the troops massed behind them. Peterson tittered.

"Your jaw's swollen, Douglas. You want me to look at that?"

"I want you to tell the major, here, everything you know about this operation, including the involvement of General Guilford."

"General Guilford?" Peterson asked. "I know him. He's a good man. I saved his wife, you know, when she was not expected to live. He was very grateful."

Kennedy seemed at a loss. And then suddenly he realized what Peterson had just said.

"He's going to protect you," the Indian agent blurted. "You're going to try and pin this on me and Hathaway."

"As well he should." The doctor looked at Howard. "The general received intelligence from Washington that an attempt might be made on the life of the Indian who had just been to visit the president, the medicine man Tuchahu. I was asked to keep an eye on two suspects, Kennedy and Hathaway."

"*Liar!*" Kennedy screamed.

"Him too?" the major asked.

"Yes! Him most of all!"

Peterson snickered. "My message to the General— through you, Major—was to inform him that the attempt had failed. You saw, in my note, that I believed it might be tried again."

"I remember," Howard said.

"This is madness!" Kennedy shouted, stalking back and forth in the narrow stone opening. "Jessup, say something!"

Hathaway looked at his partner, his own expression grave. "What is there to say, Douglas? We've been had."

Troopers attended to the body of Tod Crane—

who had apparently bled to death when his wound reopened. After posting two men to secure the munitions, Major Howard saw Peterson to his horse and had him ride apart from the Indian agents. Though Howard permitted Kennedy and Hathaway to ride without being tied to their horses, he warned them not to try and escape.

"I do not know if treason was committed out here, or whether a civilian court will hang you," Howard warned them. "I do know that I will shoot you myself if you attempt to ride off."

Howard did not know whether he would have fired on an unarmed civilian, but neither of the Indian agents knew that. Slumped in their saddles, they made no unexpected moves, uttered no words loud enough to hear, all the way to Fort Yuma.

CHAPTER 23

"There are three things we need to survive," Willa had once told her son. *"Air and water are gifts from God. Love is a gift from another."*

As he approached the long hut that was the Vallicita Station, Isaiah Sunday was a man sundered by conflict. In his heart was love for his wife and his son. In his chest was hate for Brent Diamond. These two things were tangled and he did not know how to settle one so he could deal with the other. It was that reunion which caused his heart to beat faster while the hate caused his belly to burn louder.

Diamond deserved to die. There was no question of that. He had killed Isaiah's father and other human beings, men and women that pieces of paper and links of chain called "slaves." Diamond had compounded his sins by enforcing servitude on two free souls, Bonita and Joshua.

But his blood would stain the hoped-for reunion with his family. Isaiah's violence against him might accomplish something even worse. It would show his boy that the kind of savagery that damned the South was somehow acceptable in the hands of another.

It wasn't. Willa had remarked on that over and over during their journey west. Isaiah hadn't heard her because he could think of nothing but finding his family.

Now . . .

The sun threw a new day on the old walls of the station. Isaiah was still a ways off, but he watched it like all the mountain lions he'd seen riding west. Those big cats were all eyes, nothing else.

Until they saw their prey and sprang, he thought.

Isaiah carried his rifle under his arm. He did not think it mattered whether he appeared threatening. A Colored man, approaching the house of a Southern refugee, would probably be shot on sight. If such a shot were fired, and missed, Isaiah wanted to have a chance to fire back.

There was no shot. Isaiah stopped when he saw a tall, gangly boy go out to the well on the approaching side of the station. The man resisted the urge to cry out, though he might not have had the voice if he'd tried. His lower lip trembled and his throat seemed plugged.

Isaiah kept riding forward. He had decided that he would not sneak up on the place. He would ride in, like the free man he was. His son would see that. His wife would see that. And most of all, Brent Diamond would see that.

Brent Diamond did see that, from inside the doorway where he had stepped to light a cigarette. Wearing a white bell-sleeve shirt and pale trousers, the station master was facing south and Isaiah was riding east. Diamond saw young Joshua reeling up the bucket, then suddenly let it drop. He saw the boy stare at someone riding in. Diamond looked over. Both saw that the man on the trail was Colored.

"Joshua?" the man on the horse said.

"Uh-huh," the boy replied quietly, nodding.

"Joshua, it's your pa."

Diamond ran back inside as the face of Bonita Sunday appeared in the window. She cried out.

"Isaiah?!"

Joshua charged forward, arms churning, and Bonita ran to the door. She did not make it. Diamond grabbed his Colt from the holster behind the door, then grabbed the woman around her slender waist. He forced her back to the window where Isaiah could see.

"Stop where you are or this Colored dies!" Diamond shouted in his familiar, soupy Southern voice.

"Ma!" Joshua shouted, stopping and turning.

"Stay there, son," Isaiah said. He stopped the horse, dismounted, but did not draw his shotgun. "Mr. Diamond!" he called out by wretched habit. "I don't want any shooting! All I want is my wife and son." He decided, on the spot. "Restore them to me and we will leave."

"I do not take orders from Coloreds!" Diamond replied.

"Then I'm asking you," Isaiah said. "Let her go and we all go."

"I need her! And the boy."

"Not more than I do," Isaiah said. His anger was rising.

"I will tell you just once, boy—get back on your horse, ride off, and don't come back, y'hear?"

"Go, Isaiah!" Bonita shouted. "We'll find you!"

"You will find *no* one," Diamond roared, "even if I have to chain you to the stove!"

Isaiah was no longer thinking. His arms and legs were moving, putting him back on the saddle of the horse.

"Pa!" Joshua shouted.

"Don't move, son," his father said in a dead monotone.

Slowly, quietly, Isaiah turned the horse around. His back to the station, he lay the rifle across his shoulders. And in one swift motion, he twisted, aimed at the window, and fired.

Isaiah had aimed wide to make sure he didn't hit his wife. But the bullet only struck Diamond in the right shoulder. He still held on to Bonita, even as he fell into the room, away from the window.

The former slave did not waste a moment. As soon as he saw he hadn't killed Diamond, he had spun the horse around and kicked it forward. The animal charged the station, shied as he neared the wall and tried to throw the rider.

Isaiah had expected as much and was already out of the saddle and charging through the open front door, rifle in his hands now. Diamond was wincing with pain, still trying to regain his feet, still clutching Bonita, still holding the gun.

"Drop it!" Isaiah shouted, aiming at the forehead of his former master. "Drop it or I will, I swear, forget that I am a human being!"

Diamond did not hesitate. He let the Colt fall to the floor.

"Let my wife go!"

Diamond obeyed. Crying from joy and fear, the

woman ran over and hugged her husband hard around the waist. She was smart enough, and seasoned enough, to bend lower than the barrel of the rifle.

"I love you," she said. "I never gave up hope!"

"Go outside to our boy," Isaiah said. "I got words for this fella."

She kissed her husband on his neck and ran out, scooping up her son who had kept the horse from running off and was standing beside it.

Isaiah's eyes burned into Brent Diamond.

"For more than two thousand miles I swore to kill you," Isaiah said. "Now—you don't seem worth the complication it may give me down the road. So here's what I'm offering instead. Go. Now. Take what you need, get on your horse, and don't come back, ever."

"No Colored comes into my own station and tells me to run!" Diamond shouted, causing blood to pump from the wound.

"You're thinking of slave-Coloreds," Isaiah told him. "There ain't no more of those. Not here."

Diamond didn't move. Isaiah came closer. "I'm giving you a chance to live," he said thickly. "That's more'n you gave my father."

With surprising swiftness, Diamond reached for the fallen Colt and swung it toward the man standing over him. Isaiah kicked it away and put his foot down on the man's wound.

He looked at the Colt and smiled.

"You better shoot me!" Diamond said fiercely. "I will come for you!"

"I know that," Isaiah said. "Reason I didn't put a bullet in you is there's something you are going to do for me. First—I'm gonna patch you up, like I used to do with your whipped slaves." Still looking down, he added, "This may hurt."

Outside, Bonita and Joshua were standing behind the well, with the horse, their backs to the station.

"It's quiet," Joshua said. "You think Pa's all right?"

"I guess we'd've heard if he wasn't," she said, more hopeful than certain.

More than a few minutes later they heard boots crunch on the dirt and turned. Isaiah walked over to his wife and son and hugged them both. Bonita held him around the chest, Joshua around the right leg.

"Everything's okay," he said quietly. "Our old lord and master is having a whiskey before he leaves."

"How's—how's Mama?" Bonita asked.

"Last I saw, she was safe with some nice folks from Whip Station," Isaiah said.

"The O'Malleys?" Bonita asked.

"That's them."

"Then she's fine." Bonita smiled with relief.

"Pa, will we have to leave, too?" Joshua asked.

"No, son," Isaiah said.

Bonita was pushing her cheek to her husband's chest, loving the feel and musk of him, when her face felt something crinkle. She pulled away. "What's that?"

Isaiah grinned. "Our future."

Whip Station had never seen so much activity without a stage being present.

The stagecoach arrived shortly after noon. Even

the hot sun could not bake away the invisible clouds of pride and new love that trailed behind.

Joe rode with B.W. and Slash sat inside next to Clarity, their horses having been returned to the United States Cavalry. Willa was beside the younger woman, fidgeting restlessly.

"Had that gun for so long, for so many miles, I don't know what to do with m'self," she complained.

Fletcher Small was uncommonly silent as he wrote fast, tight little lines in his notebook. Reverend Michaels was also silent, though he did nothing but sit and look out the window.

During the ride, Clarity decided to tell Slash about what had happened to Young Thunder. He winced at the news—but did not show more in front of the others. She took his hand. He squeezed it tightly.

"I don't ever want to hear bad news again without this hand to hold," he informed her.

"Then we will see to that," she replied.

When the stagecoach pulled up, Jackson, Sarah, and Gert ran out, unsure who would greet them . . . what news. Dick Ocean limped out on a crutch Jackson had made from a busted rake.

They all saw Joe right off and Sarah began to weep, even as she and the others sought Slash. The young O'Malley jumped from the coach like a deer and helped Clarity out. He was wearing the same smile he'd had on back at Salt Creek.

Slash hugged his mother, sister, and father and then Joe came over and did the same. Fighting back his own tears, he helped Willa from the stage. He introduced her to his family as Small and Michaels climbed out.

"Did my boy happen by here?" she asked of the three O'Malleys. "He was headed to some other station to get his family back."

Joe explained what she meant as Malibu and Sisquoc came from the posts they had held since Joe's departure. The old plainsman paused to shake the hands of both men, thanking them for their loyalty.

"What happened those from Washington?" Sisquoc asked.

"They've been taken to Fort Yuma where they will remain until their trial," Joe said.

While everyone was having their reunion, B.W. had made his way from the box, walked stiffly to the horse trough, and plunged his head inside. He returned looking and smelling like a wet dog, but smiling.

"It's been a day," he told Ocean.

"Where's the baggage?"

"Out on the prairie," B.W. said. "Gotta collect it on the way back."

Ocean shook his head. "Brother, I told you not to go without me."

"My very words not two hours ago." B.W. winked. "I vow I won't do it again. We need a good wheel repair. You be ready to ride shotgun in the morning?"

Ocean just smiled.

Breaking away from Slash and his family, Clarity walked to the back of the station. She had seen her brother go there and found him standing by the garden, staring at a row of beans.

"If you are staying, I am staying," he said without looking up.

"You don't need to do that," she said.

"We have been together for so long, endured so

much. I—I want to be a part of the joy and also whatever tribulations lie ahead. I want to know your children."

Clarity smiled broadly.

The reverend looked up, his eyes misty. "I want to be the one to marry you to the man you truly love."

"You can see it?"

"Clearly, sister."

The young woman threw her arms around his neck and hung there.

"God surely has His way of getting us where He wants us to be," the preacher said.

Fletcher Small was already at the table, reading back through his notes, when the others entered. B.W. looked at him as if, for a moment, he had no idea who he was.

"You been pretty silent for a while, Mr. Writer," the driver said.

"Been writing," Small said. He held up the notebook and smiled with a twinkle of condescension.

"What's your plans?" the driver asked.

"Oh, I'm leaving whenever you do," he said. "I intend to complete this fascinating journey for my article. Though I'm thinking it will now be articles, plural, and secure a more prominent place in our publication than I'd imagined."

"Corruption is carrion for sensational journalists," Gert remarked.

"And readers," Small said. "If they didn't buy it, we would not print it."

"Perhaps more would buy if you printed thoughtful stories?"

"Many men with lofty ideas have lost considerable amounts of money thinking like you."

Joe had gone in with the women, helped to get Willa settled in a comfortable chair—which she cherished audibly—then left when Gert and Small started up. He would talk to her about his experiences with Baishan, the Apaches, and Tuchahu.

"Dad, you have to eat, rest," Sarah said, laying a hand on his arm as he headed back out the door.

"I will," he assured her. "There's something I have to do first."

Joe went to the stable where Jackson had gone with Malibu and Sisquoc to saddle their horses.

"You'll eat before you leave?" Joe said.

"You have many mouths as it is," Malibu said.

"Yeah, an' most of 'em are moving too much, not with chewing," Joe said. "You come in and keep me company. I want to hear more about this Major Howard from the San Diego Barracks. You know him?"

"We do, but not well. He is higher rank," Sisquoc noted.

"Right, but you should try and—I don't know. Get transferred or something. I think there'll be some investigations at Yuma. Mud will splash."

The Indians thanked him.

"I also have a favor to ask," Joe said, and explained what he needed from the two Mission Indians.

"Of course, we will do this," Malibu said.

"C'mon, Jackson," Joe called over his shoulder as he put his arms around the backs of the two Indians. "The saddling's gonna wait."

"We're spoiling these boys," he said of the two horses. "This is prob'ly the longest they haven't had to work."

"Y'know," Joe said, "I do envy them."

As they crossed the dirt and hay floor, the four men flashed with sunlight that fell jaggedly through cracks in the old wood.

And Joe loved every horse-smelling, dust-spraying, eye-blinding step of it.

The sun was setting on as beautiful a vista as Bonita Sunday had ever seen in her life.

Her own place. A home belonging to her and Isaiah and Joshua. Her husband had convinced Diamond to sign over the deed in exchange for not revealing what he had discovered.

The gun Diamond had drawn had an ivory handle with the initials BIA engraved on the side. He had been in business with the Indian agent. Diamond could not have known, as yet, that things did not go the way the Easterner had planned.

"I do know that he has powerful forces who found him out and is turned against him," Isaiah had said. "You might not want to remain in these parts. There will be a reckoning."

Isaiah allowed him to take a carpetbag with gold coins and clothes. The former slave knew that the gold had been the product of his own labors but that was in the past. What mattered now was the future. He even let the man keep the gun, though he emptied it of all but a single bullet.

"In case you are of a mind to turn it on me," Isaiah told him, "Bonita will see it is your last killing."

As he saw the man to the trail, Isaiah left him with one more thought.

"If you return," he warned, "I will smell you coming. I will feel it. I always did, on the river. You get to know a skunk by more than just his stink. You come back and I will kill you. Day or night, sun or storm, I will know you and end you."

Isaiah did not know how much of what he said or how he said it had actually frightened Diamond. He did not know if the man would return some day. What he did know is that he would figure out a way to keep this station on the Butterfield route. The O'Malleys and B.W. would help him, he was sure of that. And he would see them soon, he was certain.

They had his mother. He wondered if she had ended up in San Francisco—and if she would decide not to come back. B.W. seemed an honorable man. He would see to her in Isaiah's absence. He would not seek out the O'Malleys, or news of Willa, until he was sure his wife and son were safe here. That Diamond was truly gone.

Isaiah had his answer to one of those questions when he went to join his wife by the well. Joshua had been playing with a frog he found in the creek out back when he came running around the station.

"Comp'ny!" he shouted.

Isaiah at first thought to get his rifle—then decided against it. He was no longer in the wild, on the run. He was a man of property with a right to be here.

"I'm going to get the rifle," his wife said.

Isaiah didn't stop her. Bonita was a wise woman with the instincts of a fox. She might be right.

The family stood there, side to side, as a family. It

had never been mentioned but they knew they would rise or fall in that unity.

Three figures were approaching with the setting sun to their back. The light was obscured by the oaks behind them on either side of the Butterfield Trail. None of the Sundays could make out any features of rider or horse, but the travelers seemed to be in no rush.

"Could it be some o' those Rebs you was talkin' about?" Bonita asked.

"They look whupped enough," he said, noting the rounded shoulders of the figures on either side.

With Bonita holding the rifle, her husband stepped forward.

"Isaiah—" she cautioned.

"We are hosts, now, and these are travelers," he said. "We have to get used to this."

He continued forward and then stopped. From where he stood, the sinking sun outlined a familiar spindle of a form, a rifle under her arm. Isaiah's eyes, then his mouth, then his arms went wide. He ran forward.

"Ma!" he cried. "*Ma!*"

Malibu and Sisquoc had been riding close to either side, the calico nudged between them, since the tired woman did not seem interested in actually directing her horse. The two Mission Indians stayed where they were, Sisquoc steadying Willa's horse lest the man's approach frighten it.

Barely slowing, Isaiah squeezed between the animals. As his mother reached out with one arm—the other still wrapped around the rifle—he ducked his shoulder beneath it and swung her into his arms.

Bonita arrived, shouting and sobbing, moments later, followed by a beaming Joshua.

Willa's stony exterior cracked, fast. She handed the rifle to her grandson, who laid it against one of the oaks, then threw her arm around Bonita and the boy.

"God, thank you," the older woman rasped through her tears. "Good Lord, bless you."

Isaiah's own damp eyes sought out Malibu and Sisquoc. He broke from the others to shake their hands in turn. "Thank you, too," he said. "How—how is Slash and his family?"

"They are well," Malibu replied. "Cavalry came to take them, Indians come and save—most unusual day."

"The shaman?"

"His enemies, Apache, take him back to Serrano tribe," Sisquoc said.

"Most unusual day," Malibu added.

"The men who started this?" Isaiah pressed. "What of them?"

"They are in jail at fort," Sisquoc replied. "I wish to be there in time to talk at trial. Then see them hang."

"Can I offer you food and drink before you go?" Bonita asked.

"They ate enough at the O'Malley place," Willa said. "We all did. Won't need food till I'm eighty-one."

"We go," Malibu said, looking around before urging his cavalry pony forward.

"Man of Colored own this place?" Sisquoc asked.

"He does," Isaiah replied.

Over his shoulder, Malibu said, "Most unusual day" as he rode out of the sunset.